Praise for
An Appetite for Murder

"I can't wait for the next entry in this charming series."

—*New York Times* bestselling author
Diane Mott Davidson

"For a true taste of paradise, don't miss *An Appetite for Murder*. Lucy Burdette's first Key West Food Critic Mystery combines a lush, tropical setting, a mysterious murder, and plenty of quirky characters. The victim may not be coming back for seconds, but readers certainly will!"

—Julie Hyzy, national bestselling author of the White House Chef mysteries and Manor House mysteries

KEY LIME PIE TO DIE FOR

As the last of the coffee burbled and sputtered into the pot, I hurried out onto the dock to retrieve Connie's copy of the *Key West Citizen*. I smoothed the paper on the café table in the kitchen and sat down for breakfast. Evinrude splayed out on the chair next to me, grooming his gray stripes into their morning order. I took a sip of coffee and almost spit it out when I saw Kristen's head shot looming from the box on the front page reserved for the crime report.

> *Kristen Faulkner, a longtime native of Key West, who had plans to open a restaurant on Easter Island and recently launched* Key Zest *magazine, was discovered dead in the apartment of a friend yesterday morning. Police have questioned several persons of interest in the suspected murder.*

My heart sank with a desperate clunk—suddenly the murder felt real, and my so-called involvement, very scary. Feeling queasy, I stopped reading and flipped over to the living section pages. My byline blared: "Key West Confidential: Key Lime Pie to Die For" by Hayley Snow. Could the timing of such a headline have been any worse?

AN APPETITE FOR MURDER

A Key West Food Critic Mystery

Lucy Burdette

OBSIDIAN
Published by New American Library, a division of
Penguin Group (USA) Inc., 375 Hudson Street,
New York, New York 10014, USA
Penguin Group (Canada), 90 Eglinton Avenue East, Suite 700, Toronto,
Ontario M4P 2Y3, Canada (a division of Pearson Penguin Canada Inc.)
Penguin Books Ltd., 80 Strand, London WC2R 0RL, England
Penguin Ireland, 25 St. Stephen's Green, Dublin 2,
Ireland (a division of Penguin Books Ltd.)
Penguin Group (Australia), 250 Camberwell Road, Camberwell, Victoria 3124,
Australia (a division of Pearson Australia Group Pty. Ltd.)
Penguin Books India Pvt. Ltd., 11 Community Centre, Panchsheel Park,
New Delhi - 110 017, India
Penguin Group (NZ), 67 Apollo Drive, Rosedale, Auckland 0632,
New Zealand (a division of Pearson New Zealand Ltd.)
Penguin Books (South Africa) (Pty.) Ltd., 24 Sturdee Avenue,
Rosebank, Johannesburg 2196, South Africa

Penguin Books Ltd., Registered Offices:
80 Strand, London WC2R 0RL, England

First published by Obsidian, an imprint of New American Library,
a division of Penguin Group (USA) Inc.

First Printing, January 2012
10 9 8 7 6 5 4 3 2

Printed in the United States of America

For Ang and Chris,
best friends a writer could have

ACKNOWLEDGMENTS

I offer my humble thanks to all the writers and readers who read drafts and drafts of this book and helped me polish every word: Christine Falcone, Angelo Pompano, Cindy Warm, Susan Cerulean, Hallie Ephron, Susan Hubbard, Mike Wiecek, Mary Buckham, and John Brady.

I'm grateful for the help of Martha Hubbard, chef at Louie's Backyard in Key West, Florida, who talked to me about real life in a kitchen, and for Steve Torrence and Bob Bean from the Key West Police Department for information about police procedure, and for Jonathan Shapiro for details about arrests from the defending lawyer's point of view. Any mistakes, misinterpretations, and exaggerations are entirely mine! And thanks to Lyn McHugh for listening to all my stories and making suggestions on cleaning. And to all my Guppy pals for ideas about tarot and book titles. Hank Phillippi Ryan deserves the credit for *Key Zest*.

The food writing conference at the Key West Literary Seminar came at just the right time—thanks to the universe and the organizers for that!

Thanks again to Paige Wheeler and the good folks at Folio Literary Agency for championing this book—and me. And to my editor, Sandy Harding, and the team at NAL for their excellent advice and enthusiastic support.

I thank my pals at Jungle Red Writers, Sisters in Crime, and Mystery Writers of America for their inspiration and friendship. And I'm so grateful for the booksellers and readers who make writing a joy. To my new friends in Key West—thanks for sharing paradise! Please know that all people and places in this book are either figments of my imagination or used fictitiously.

As always, nothing would happen without the love and support of my family, especially John.

"Because the goodness of the ingredients—the fine chocolate, the freshest lemons—seemed like a cover over something larger and darker, and the taste of what was underneath was beginning to push up from the bite."

—Aimec Bender

1

"A hot dog or a truffle. Good is good."
—James Beard

Lots of people think they'd love to eat for a living. Me? I'd kill for it.

Which makes total sense, coming from my family. FTD told my mother to say it with flowers, but she said it with food. Lost a pet? Your job? Your mind? Life always felt better with a serving of Mom's braised short ribs or red velvet cake in your belly. In my family, we ate when happy or sad, but especially, we ate when we were worried.

The brand-new *Key Zest* magazine in Key West, Florida, announced a month ago that they were hiring a food critic for their style section. Since my idea of heaven was eating at restaurants and talking about food, I'd do whatever it took to land the job. *Whatever*. Three review samples and a paragraph on my proposed style as their new food critic were due on Monday. Seven days and counting. So far I had produced nothing. The big goose egg. Call me Hayley Catherine "Procrastination" Snow.

To be fair to me, some of the blockage could be traced to the fact that Kristen Faulkner—my ex's new girlfriend and the woman whose cream sauce I'd most like to curdle—happened to be the co-owner of *Key Zest*. What if she judged the restaurants I chose impossibly lowbrow? What if she deleted my application packet the minute it hit her inbox? Or, worst of all, what if I landed the job and had to rub shoulders with her ice-queen highness every day?

My psychologist friend Eric had suggested ever so sweetly that it was time to quit thinking and start eating. Hence, I was hurrying along Olivia Street to meet him for dinner at one of my favorite restaurants on the island, Seven Fish. Of course, I'd left my roommate's houseboat late because I couldn't decide what to wear. I winnowed it down to two outfits and asked Evinrude, my gray tiger cat, to choose. Black jeans and a form-fitting white T-shirt with my shin-high, butt-kicking, red cowgirl boots? Or the cute flowered sundress with a cabled hoodie? From his perch on the desk, the cat twitched his tail and said nothing. But I bet Kristen would never go for "cute." I shimmied into the jeans, scrunched a teaspoon of hair product into my still-damp auburn curls, and set out at a fast clip.

Eric also pointed out not too long ago that I didn't seem to have the knack for figuring in the time it would take to get somewhere when I made plans. Did I think I would get airlifted from one place to another instead of walking or driving my scooter? I pointed out that if he wanted any friends left, he might want to save his psychoanalysis for his paying customers. But I doubted either of us was going to change.

Tonight was the kind of night that made people pine for Key West if they'd ever spent time here and left, and celebrate the good decision making that brought them if they'd stayed. The small, side-by-side conch-style homes I passed along Olivia Street weren't fancy, but a fringe of palm trees and pink bougainvillea wound with twinkling white lights made them look like fairy tale material. Add in weather just cool enough for a sweater, the gentle burbling of hidden fountains, and a couple of roosters pecking in the dust alongside the road, and it definitely felt like paradise. My slice of paradise. Light-years from a gray and dreary New Jersey November.

I broke into a trot as I approached the cemetery on the right, its listing, weathered stones protected by the iron bars of the surrounding fence. Despite the fascinating history of the tombs, which I'd heard as I rattled by on a conch tour train when I arrived three months ago, the place spooked me out. Town officials did their best to keep folks out of the cemetery at night, but still, our local paper, the *Key West Citizen*, reported regular incidents such as headstones being tipped over and encampments of homeless teenagers. Each fluttering shadow made my heart jump.

And then one shadow came to life. I let loose a screech loud enough to be heard all the way to Miami.

"Easy, miss," said a skinny man in a battered cowboy hat. "Could ya spare some change?"

I knew you weren't supposed to give money to bums,

especially ones that smelled like a day's worth of drinking, as this guy did. Editorials in the newspaper insisted that only perpetuated the problem. The cowboy moved closer, wheezing his boozy breath and smiling to reveal two missing incisors. My heart thrummed faster and I clutched the strap of my shoulder bag. There but for the grace of some capricious God could have been me.

"I haven't eaten since yesterday," he said.

Now I felt sick at the prospect of gorging myself at a nice restaurant while he, drunk or not, went hungry. I dug in my pocket and dropped a crumpled dollar bill and some loose change into his dirty palm, wishing I had more, but that's all there was. Then I waved off his mumbled thanks and rushed by.

Up ahead on the left-hand side of the street, a cluster of people holding wineglasses milled on the sidewalk in front of an unassuming glass and concrete block building—home of Seven Fish. Eric was already there, wearing his white Oxford shirt and nerd glasses—he would never be late worrying about how to dress because his outfit was always some version of the same thing. He carried two glasses of wine: one red, one white.

"It's a Spanish Albariño," he said, handing me the white and pecking me on the cheek. "They're just clearing our table now." He snuck a glance at his watch but managed not to mention my lateness. I got the point.

"Brilliant." I sipped, tasting overtones of apricot and peach. "Hope you're hungry, because we need to try a lot."

Which I didn't have to say because he knew the deal: He was in charge of making the reservations just in case someone might recognize me as a potential food critic (in my dreams) and I'd order for both of us so I could sample a range of their dishes. A dark-haired man swathed in a chest-to-knee white apron called out Eric's name. We followed him inside, past the four-seater bar to a room no bigger than my houseboat, and plainly furnished, without my roommate's tendency to tropical upholstery. He deposited us at a tiny table at the far end of the room. I took the seat facing the iron fish sculpture on the back wall so I wouldn't be distracted with people watching—or, even worse, absorb their opinions about the food.

Within minutes, the waiter came around and described the specials, including yellowtail in a mild curry sauce and sautéed grouper sushi rolls. I salivated with anticipation like a rat pressing a lever in a psychology experiment. "We're good to go," I said, and began to list the dishes I needed to try. "We'll start with the fish tacos, the grouper rolls, and a small Caesar salad with a crab cake on the side. For the main course, the gentleman will have the chicken with bananas and walnuts"—I grinned as Eric's face fell—"and I'll try your special curried yellowtail. And we'll have a meat loaf for the table."

"Anything else?" asked the waiter, deadpan.

"Two more glasses of wine. And no bread please." I smiled and handed him my menu. "Oh, what the heck, add the grilled mahi-mahi with roasted potatoes, too." He finished writing and swished off toward the kitchen.

Eric leaned forward to whisper, "He has to know something's up."

"We could be very, very hungry." I thought of the cowboy lurking near the cemetery.

Eric excused himself to hit the men's room. I whipped out my smartphone to check e-mail just in case one of the freelance articles I'd submitted on spec to the *Key West Citizen* had been accepted. The subject line of the third message down jolted me hard: "Food critic applications due Friday." The deadline for application packets had been moved up. Staff at *Key Zest* would only consider those that arrived in the office by five p.m. Friday. Signed by Kristen Faulkner.

Rat bugger.

My pulse hammered like an overloaded food processor. How could I possibly meet that deadline? Friday was only four days away. This was my first official restaurant visit. I'd counted on having the weekend to write and rewrite and rewrite again, and hope that the paragraph about my so-called style would make a miraculous appearance. Besides, every time I heard or saw Kristen Faulkner's name, I lost a little confidence.

Eric returned and I thrust the phone at him. "Maybe I should forget the whole thing. It's too much pressure. It's a message from the universe saying 'Just go home.' It's—"

"Ridiculous." He skimmed the message and then squeezed my hand. "Finish this one tonight and you have all week for the rest."

Eric's been an optimist for as long as I've known him—almost fifteen years since my mother first hired him to babysit me. Even during his awful college years, as he struggled with the realization that he was gay, we stayed friends. He was one of the reasons I had the guts to follow Chad Lutz—a guy I barely knew—to this island. Eric would always be there if things got rough. And they had.

I'd met Chad last summer in the "mystery and thriller" section of the New Jersey bookstore where I was stocking shelves. He was picking up the latest Mary Higgins Clark novel—signed by Ms. Clark herself—for his mother. He looked so adorable in his distressed brown leather jacket, flashing his dimples and talking about his mom: I fell for him instantly. And to seal the deal, my tarot card reader back home had predicted a big event in my love life only days earlier. So after some steamy, long-distance back and forth, I moved south to live with him in Key West. We had four sparkling weeks, and five that were a lot less shiny, and then twenty-one days ago, I'd found him in bed with Kristen Faulkner. (But who was counting?) I hadn't laid eyes on him since.

Two more glasses of wine and the first wave of appetizers arrived. I thanked the universe—and the waiter—for sending food to distract me from my deadline problem and yet one more swell of regret about losing Chad, and we dove in. The fish tacos were divine—no stale Old El Paso–style tortillas here—accompanied by shredded red cabbage and a spicy cilantro salsa. The grouper rolls were even better: a mélange of sweet, fresh fish, buttery avocado, and sauce-absorbing rice, wrapped in a crispy tissue of seaweed. We finished all of them before the Caesar salad was delivered, which I knew a real food critic would never do. A true professional would take a bite of this, a second nibble to confirm impressions, saving space and palate to try all of the dishes. Too late. This stuff was too good. And besides, eating calmed my nerves—and boy, did they need calming.

The server returned to remove our empty plates and then the main courses rolled in. I tasted each, jotting notes on the phone in my lap as I went. Three bites into the meat loaf, I had to unbutton my pants.

The waiter cleared the dishes and invited us to consider dessert. "We have strawberry whipped cream pie in a chocolate graham cracker crust. Or key lime cheesecake. Bananas flambé? That's on the light side." He grinned.

"Uncle," I groaned. "Just the check, please."

He delivered the bill and Eric paid with the cash I'd given him yesterday. As we stood to leave, the expression on Eric's face changed from happily sated to disgusted.

"Chad Lutz alert," he said through gritted teeth. "He's sitting at the bar. Just walk past him and don't say a word."

I gulped, sucked in my stomach, and rebuttoned my pants. There was no way out other than passing right by him. I could say nothing and avoid eye contact, but that would be just what he'd prefer. Was I going to make this comfortable for him? Not a freaking chance. Meek and mild had gotten me nowhere. "Is Kristen at the bar, too?" I asked Eric.

He nodded his head and grimaced. Yup. I snuck a look and saw Chad's sandy hair leaning into Kristen's, nearly white blond. Then I rolled my shoulders like a boxer facing the ring and barreled toward the exit.

"How're ya doing?" I asked Chad, clapping him on

his sculpted shoulder and squeezing. His muscles tightened under my fingers. "Long time no see."

"Hello, Hayley." He kept his gaze pinned on the mirror behind the bar, but he couldn't avoid me in its reflection. I was glad I'd worn the tight jeans and the red boots—he hated those boots. He thought they made me look like a tough from Trenton, which I interpreted as meaning sexy to the point of scary. Besides that, they added two inches to my five foot four. Even so, if Kristen stood up, I'd look like a shrimp in comparison. A slightly chunky crustacean, after the meal we'd just devoured.

"Hello, Kristen," I said, in a voice like molasses—treacly sweet with a little bite underneath. "This is my good friend Eric Altman." Kristen tucked a strand of glossy hair behind her ear, revealing the mother of all diamond earrings. Then she flashed a cool smile at Eric, but said nothing to me.

"Nice to see you," said Chad.

Eric poked me in the back—time to move on. But I wasn't quite ready.

"I saw the deadline for the food critic application has been moved up." I barely recognized my voice, squeaky and high. "Mine will definitely be in the *Key Zest* inbox by Friday."

Kristen still looked at Eric, that phony smile frozen on her face. "We have some excellent applicants," she said after a pause. "We're not encouraging amateurs without significant experience to waste their time."

Eric grabbed my hand and pulled me toward the door.

"Enjoy your meal," I warbled over my shoulder. "We recommend the crab cakes."

Which we didn't. They had a larger ratio of cake to crab than I preferred.

But I got a prick of guilty pleasure imagining Kristen ordering the *only* ho-hum item on the menu. Pathetic.

2

"All it really takes to be a restaurant critic is a good appetite."

—A. J. Liebling

My plans for writing up the first review had flown out the window after seeing Chad and Kristen in the restaurant. Instead I'd gone home with Eric and shared a third glass of wine with him and his partner, Bill. I needed the company to distract me from running the emotional script of the meeting over and over like a lousy sitcom—the helplessness, the outrage, the impotence. A million things I could have said to Kristen and I chose crab cakes?

But this morning I regretted the headache and the looming deadline. With my roommate, Connie, off to work early, I had no excuse for not pounding out the article. I poured a second cup of coffee and retreated to my tiny bedroom to work. Evinrude dozed on the bed, whiskers twitching and motor running.

As I settled at the desk, the cat quit purring and his ears stiffened to alert. I got up and peered out of the porthole. No one there.

Evinrude and I certainly hadn't planned to end up living on a houseboat in Key West, but my freshman-year college roommate, Connie, took us in when Chad left me in his dust, just like Dad left Mom. Except Chad had my stuff packed up and put out in the hall literally hours after I found him with Kristen—like I was the one who'd been caught cheating.

Sometimes living on a boat turned out not to be as idyllic as we'd imagined. Every sound carried on the water, from the sloshing of the Garrison Bight to random voices to the traffic on the causeway, ferrying tourists to their alcohol-infused oblivion in the tackiest bars on Duval Street.

Last night, my bed provided a front-row seat to the Renharts' squabbling on the next boat over. Money was tight and he hated the way she squandered it, and she insisted if he'd try the tiniest bit harder he might find a job that stood a chance of covering the bills. And so they spiraled off as he reminded her it was Key West, and the economy sucked and there were more people panting for every job opening than anyplace else on earth. Because everyone wanted to live in paradise—and wasn't it a damn shame that this was what paradise came down to—a shrieking wife on a stinking tub.

Then she cried because he'd gone too far—which drove him nuts, so the make-up sex ensued, the details of which no one outside the couple really wanted to hear. I had trouble looking them in the eye this morning when

I went out for the paper. And besides, all that reminded a girl who'd been recently dumped of exactly what she was missing.

I dragged my mind away from that personal sinkhole and back to my computer, staring at the blank screen that should have held the draft of my first review. Food criticism has had a tradition of showing the restaurant's setting, which made sense to me. People wanted to know what they were in for—how comfortable they'd feel spending their hard-earned bucks. I could start there.

After you've turned off Duval and stumbled four blocks down one-way, residential Olivia Street, you'll come upon knots of hungry would-be diners sipping wine on the sidewalk. You've reached your destination: Seven Fish Restaurant. But don't be put off by that unusual introduction—once the first bite of dinner melts in your mouth, you'll never mistake Seven Fish for a Duval Street tourist trap. Inside, the decor is bare-bones and the room is always packed and loud enough to make your eardrums vibrate (my kingdom for a few yards of noise-absorbing fabric on the ceiling), but those quibbles shouldn't keep you from a delightful meal.

I stopped writing, struck with a jolt of terror about describing the restaurant as "loud." This was one of my favorite places: Would they refuse to serve me the next time I came in? Would my review turn away customers and ruin their business?

Eric had reminded me sixteen thousand times that I

couldn't worry about these things if I wanted the job. So I scrolled through the notes I'd taken last night until I reached the appetizers—in my book, the best part of any meal. I began to salivate as I pictured the attributes of the sautéed grouper roll, and wrote all of them down.

My stomach rumbling, I got up and went to the galley kitchen to rustle up a snack. I could already spot the downside of food writing—I'd spend my days hovering in a constant state of starvation while describing what I'd eaten the night before. Possibly even be forced to join a gym or take up jogging in order to combat my expanding waistline. But I'd be willing to do all that and more to land this job.

A small plate of olive fougasse bread and garlicky cheese spread in hand, I returned to my desk to try to capture Seven Fish's main dishes in the twenty-five words I had left. How to deftly tackle my mixed feelings about ordering meat loaf or chicken (even *with* bananas and caramelized walnuts and even *if* they were outstanding) in a restaurant featuring "fish" in the name?

Evinrude startled again, caroming off the bed and onto my lap. And this time even I heard the hollow thud of footsteps coming down the dock. The clunking stopped and the houseboat rocked on its mooring. Someone had stepped off the wooden planks and onto the boat. Even a landlubber like me knew that climbing aboard someone's craft without permission was considered extremely poor maritime etiquette.

The intruder rapped sharply on the door. I rolled the indignant cat off my lap and edged into the living room. Outside the flimsy scratched plastic of the front door, located along the starboard side of the boat, a uniformed cop was poised to knock again. A tall man in a tweed blazer stood just behind him, my roommate's houseplants jutting up around him like a tropical jungle. I straightened my Seven Fish T-shirt over my cutoff sweatpants and crossed the room to crack open the door.

"Are you Miss Hayley Catherine Snow?" the cop asked.

I preferred "Ms." to "Miss," but this was not the time to make a correction. I nodded.

"I'm Officer Torrence and this is Detective Bransford. We'd like you to come down to the station."

"The police station?" I asked, my mouth dry and my knees wobbling. Police had this effect on me though I've never committed a criminal action. Except for that speeding forty-five in a twenty-five school zone ticket five years ago, and didn't everyone have one of those? "For what reason?"

The two men, Torrence, dark and heavyset, and what-was-his-name . . . Bransford, tall and broad-chested, exchanged glances. Bransford tipped his chin. Despite my rattled nerves, I noticed its pronounced and sexy cleft.

"We have some questions about the death of Kristen Faulkner."

3

Charles Barkley's weight loss secret: "If it tastes good, I spit it out."

After a short back-and-forth on the dock next to my houseboat, the cops agreed to let me change into jeans and a decent shirt, and I agreed to accept their offer of a ride the few blocks to the police station and then back home when we'd finished chatting. I spent my first five minutes ever in the backseat of a cop car trying not to think about who'd been there before me and why they'd been arrested. And what kind of DNA might have been left behind.

And then I wondered what the heck could have happened to Kristen. Surely they wouldn't need my opinion on a heart attack or a motor vehicle accident. Which left something worse . . . Oh, Lord, I might have said some snarky things about the fact that she stole my boyfriend, but I didn't hate her enough to wish her dead. Not by a long shot. I told myself there had to be a perfectly good reason the officers wanted to talk to me at the station, rather than at home on the boat.

Detective Bransford parked the car and strode toward the station, while Officer Torrence came around to my side of the cruiser to open the door like a well-trained valet. I hopped out, trying to suppress my jangling nerves, and followed him past an ugly tiled fountain that appeared to be out of commission and then past the public records office, which was designed like the pickup window in a takeout restaurant. Key West residents do as much as possible outdoors and the records department seemed to be no exception. Torrence held the main door open and ushered me inside the pink cement building.

Here the color scheme changed abruptly from soft pinks to a hideous greenish blue. Mental hospital blue, I couldn't help thinking. The same hue that had covered the walls of the hospital room where my mother took her breather after Dad moved out when I was ten. Not a good memory to have as I worked to keep myself calm.

We shuffled onto an elevator at the back of the building and rode to the second floor. Detective Bransford and another man were waiting in a small room down the right hall. With a lurch in my stomach, I recognized Chief Ron Barnes from his photos in the *Key West Citizen*. Why was he here?

A little late, it occurred to me that I could be in serious trouble.

"Miss Snow," said Detective Bransford without preamble, "how did you know Kristen Faulkner?"

I snuck a look at each impassive face, hoping for a little sympathy. They stared back, stone-carved and immovable. "I only met her twice in passing. I can't say I really *knew* her, if you know what I mean. But my boyfriend did. Rather too well, if you get my drift."

A puzzled look crept across Torrence's features.

"What I mean is, she was naked the first time I saw her. In bed with my boyfriend. Skewered."

I knew as soon as they were out of my mouth, those words sounded bad, like I was trying to throw Chad under the bus. It was just that the shock of that moment could still creep up and pound me like a meat mallet. I scrunched my face to keep from crying.

Torrence looked like he was trying not to laugh, but the other two were still frowning. I continued to babble.

"Other than that, she's the new co-owner of the style magazine where I'm applying for a job. The writing samples are due at the end of the week. But you can see how acquiring Kristen as my boss wouldn't exactly be an asset . . ." My words faded. Was it nerves making me yammer foolishly, or fear? Chad would have had my head for talking to these cops without a lawyer. If he cared—and let's face it, how much clearer could he have been that he didn't?

"So let me get this straight," said Detective Cleft Chin. "She had an affair with your boyfriend—"

"Stole him right out from under me," I said. "Next thing I knew, I had to find a room to rent or head home to New Jersey. That's why I'm living on my college roommate, Connie's, houseboat. She said I could work some shifts in her cleaning service in exchange for a place to live until I get back on my feet. My room's a little cramped—minuscule really—and she uses half my closet space for storing her supplies, so it always smells a little like bleach. But on the other hand, she let me bring Evinrude and not many landlords allow cats."

Detective Bransford massaged his forehead. "Was your roommate home with you this morning?"

"I can't say exactly when she left, but she was gone by the time I got up. She's a hustler—she takes any job she can get—the early bird and the worm and all that—"

The chief flashed a timeout signal and the detective nodded curtly. "Miss Snow, were you aware of anyone else who might have felt animosity toward Kristen Faulkner?"

Anyone *else*? "Honestly, I barely knew her."

"Any drug problems? Money problems? History of domestic abuse?"

I shook my head again, fingers pressed to my temples where a headache had begun to pound. "I have no idea."

"Miss Snow, where were you today between the hours of six and ten a.m.?" asked the detective.

"Right where you found me, Detective, on the houseboat. Just like I told you." My mouth went dry. "Wait a minute, what is this about?"

"It appears that Kristen Faulkner was murdered." That pronouncement came from the chief.

The way the questions had been coming, this shouldn't have been a surprise. Still, a sickening pit yawned in my stomach and for one brief moment I was speechless.

"When did you last see Miss Faulkner?" the chief asked.

"The bed incident," I whispered. "I never saw her after that." I felt the blood rush to my cheeks. "Wait, that's not right. My ex was out to dinner with her last night in the restaurant where I ate."

Bransford leaned a little closer. "Did you two talk?"

"Not really," I said. "I said hello and she blew me off. So I suggested they order the crab cakes."

The cops exchanged glances, as though they'd gotten hold of a real fruitcake, and the detective jotted a note on a pad on the desk.

"You've had no contact with her with regard to this magazine you mentioned?" he asked.

"None. So far the application process has been conducted by e-mail." I twisted my hands in my lap. "She did mention last night that they have some strong applicants."

For the next fifteen minutes, Bransford led me through my short history of Key West. I spilled the humiliating details of how I'd fallen for Chad in New Jersey, moved down here to be with him, and found myself homeless, jobless, and manless, all inside of three months.

Bransford scrawled a few more lines of notes and then looked up. "So would you say that Kristen Faulkner was responsible for all that?"

"In a way," I said. "But not really . . . I can't blame her for everything . . . My father is always telling me I should look before I leap."

"Did she know that you were involved with Mr. Lutz?"

"How could she not?" I asked. "My stuff was all over the apartment." My throat closed up and my eyes brimmed with tears. "Until he put it out on the sidewalk. Which didn't take long."

Bransford passed me a Kleenex. "Just to review, you say you were on the houseboat all morning?"

I nodded quickly and recovered my voice. "Connie, who owns the boat, wouldn't be able to verify it, but I swear it's the truth."

Chief Barnes broke in. "Won't it be easier for you to get this magazine job that you want so much with Miss Faulkner out of the way?"

My mouth dropped open as I took in what he was suggesting. "Oh my God . . . Listen, I disliked Kristen Faulkner right down to her plucked eyebrows, but I never would have killed her. Never. No matter how much I wanted to land that job." At this point, no amount of face scrunching could have stopped the tears. I blew my nose into the crumpled tissue. "Do I need a lawyer?"

The detective rose to his feet and hulked over me. "Miss Snow, you are not accused of anything. Yet. But we'll need to be in touch with you again soon. That means do *not* leave the island without contacting us first. Not even over the bridge to Stock Island. You can understand that we need you to make yourself readily available until we complete this investigation."

I didn't really understand what else I could contribute, but I gulped and nodded. The other men got up too, and I bolted from the room and scurried down the hallway, out into the bright sun.

"I'd just as soon walk home," I told Torrence, who followed me out. It was only a quarter of a mile, but he looked at me as if I'd said I'd be hiking back to Jersey. Finally, he dipped his head and I jogged out of the parking lot toward Roosevelt Boulevard.

"Free at last," I called dramatically as I ran, throwing my arms open to the sky. Which probably sounded a little silly if anyone was listening, but I'd felt like I couldn't *breathe* in that police station. Good God, Kristen had been *murdered*. And they were questioning *me*. So then I punched Chad's office number on my speed dial. He wouldn't take my call, but his assistant, Deena, would. And she knew every lawyer in Key West.

Unfortunately, Chad—who never answered his number if he could get someone else to do it for him—picked up.

"It's Hayley," I stammered. "Sorry for your loss." I was sorry. A little.

"I don't want to talk to you right now," he answered. "In fact, I don't want to hear from you again, ever. I can't believe—"

"I didn't call to talk to you," I said. "I called for Deena. The cops hauled me down to the police station to interrogate me about Kristen. They seem to think I might have killed her. I was going to ask Deena if I needed to hire a lawyer."

"I can't help you," said Chad, "and neither can she. As you can very well imagine, this is not a good time for me."

"It's not such a good time for me, either," I said, my desperation gathering momentum by the second. "Would there be any chance you would please, please call them and tell them I had nothing to do with Kristen dying?"

"I don't know that," said Chad in an ice-cold voice. "How would I know what you're capable of?"

My gut clenched as I realized he might have actually

fingered me. After I moved from New Jersey to be with him and two months of living together—his having to carry spiders outside because I couldn't bear the thought of murdering them when they might have a family—he believed I'd kill a real person? That made me feel helpless—and mad. I flashed on the belongings he'd failed to return, and that made me madder.

"Since I've got you on the line, could you at least give my stuff back? I've sent you four e-mails over the past two weeks and Deena swears your server is working just fine. You can stick the box out in the hall, as far as I'm concerned."

"I haven't kept anything of yours."

"Have a heart, Chad. You've got my books and my Japanese knives and my grandmother's recipe box—"

No answer from Chad, just the lonely void of a dead connection. Rat bugger.

I squeezed the END button. Almost home now, I dialed up Connie to see if she was free to help drown my sorrows while we thought of a plan. But my call went directly to voice mail. So as I made my way down the dock past Miss Gloria's little yellow boat and then the Renharts' boxy two-story, I called Eric, who on Mondays closed up his psychotherapy office at four thirty.

"Meet me at the Green Parrot? I'm buying."

He hesitated. "I'm beat. I had six patients scheduled and two extras had crises that couldn't wait. One of them involved decorating choices. White or beige?" He sounded annoyed and exhausted—he never talked about the details of his patients. The town was too small to risk spreading gossip. The coconut telegraph, he called it.

"That bluegrass band you like is doing a sound check," I said, thinking the promise of a mini musical set at happy hour would be more appealing than weeping. "That adorable guy you have the hots for will be playing the mandolin," I wheedled. "Besides, I really need to talk with you. Kristen Faulkner was found dead today and they think she was murdered. I think I'm a suspect," I finished, my words trailing off all weak and wobbly. "I need a voice of reason."

"I'll be there in twenty minutes," he said in his best calming shrink voice. "Don't blow a gasket."

"I hope you don't say things like that to your paying customers," I said, laughing through my sniffles of relief. "See you there." I dashed inside to slap on a little mascara and tell Evinrude where I was going, then trotted back down the dock to the parking lot. I hopped on my scooter, a secondhand silver KYMCO that allegedly gets ninety-eight miles to the gallon, and putt-putted out onto the road.

I motored up Truman (also known as the most southern and final leg of Route One) to Whitehead and two blocks right to the Parrot. "No sniveling since 1890" the sign outside read. Apropos for me today, for sure.

This bar, with its white frame, green trim, and wooden shutters pinned open, may have been named one of the top twenty-four bars in the United States by *Playboy*, but it still didn't look like much. The bar owners had gone for the kind of simple, homey decor that improved with spilled beer.

After ordering a couple of Sunset Ales, I grabbed a basket of popcorn—the only food available at the Parrot—

and headed to the Whitehead Street side of the room. I secured us space on the wide shelf by an open window, where we'd have a chance to hear each other without shouting over the music and the happy hour crowd. The mandolin player was flat-picking a cheerful duet of Rocky Top with the guy on banjo, which wasn't quite enough to keep the detective's last words from ping-ponging in my brain: Don't leave the island.

I checked out the room for familiar faces—not that I knew everybody after less than three months in residence, but the town was small enough that I had settled in quickly. And I'd gotten pretty good at figuring out who belonged and who didn't. A couple of women in batik dresses were clogging in front of the band. Definitely out-of-towners. On my right, four loud, sunburned men in even louder shirts argued about politics. Based on their volume alone, I suspected they'd been here most of the afternoon. Tourists. I sipped on my beer and tried to review the mess I was in.

There were two Key Wests—the enclave of million-dollar plus homes for the utterly wealthy who sweep in for Christmas and clear out by Easter, and the hard-scrabble everyman's island where people held down two jobs—or three—to pay for their housing, which might turn out to be a closet-sized rented room on a house-boat. I had plummeted from one Key West to the other in the space of a week. Despite my protests, the police chief and the detective had pegged it: Kristen Faulkner was pretty much responsible. But would they really consider that a motive for murder?

Feeling utterly anxious, I finished my beer faster than I should have and started on Eric's. I'd been too upset to ask about the details of how Kristen died, or whether there were other suspects. Not that the cops would have told me anything anyway. But wouldn't they have looked at Chad first rather than me? After all, he was the boyfriend. How did they even know to bring me to the station? I wished I hadn't been quite so honest about how much I disliked her.

I waved down a harried waitress to order another beer, and Eric arrived a few minutes later. The tightness in my head and chest released a little just at the sight of him. He hugged me and eyed the empty bottle on the ledge and the one half-empty in my hand.

"She's got you covered," I said, pointing to the waitress who approached with a frosted Sunset Ale on her tray. "I sure am glad to see you."

He took the fresh beer and clinked my bottle with his. "Now spill."

So I told him how I was working on my food critic assignment when the two cops came to the boat with the news about Kristen and then herded me to the station. "They wanted to know where I was this morning, but I don't have any way of proving I was alone on the boat."

"What actually happened to her?" Eric asked. "How did she die?"

"They said she was murdered," I said. "Maybe she really died of natural causes and they were trying to get a reaction out of me." I knew as I said them that those words were pure wishful thinking and sheer nonsense.

"Tell me everything you can remember," he said.

My stomach clenched tighter and tighter as I relived the details of the interview.

Eric pursed his lips into a worried frown. "They really told you not to leave the island?"

I nodded, blinking fast so I wouldn't cry. "And the more they asked about my relationship with Kristen and Chad, the more scared I got. So I called Deena to see if she thought I needed a lawyer, and unfortunately Chad answered. He was awful. Beastly." My sinuses swelled with a backup of misery. "I'll never get my things back."

"Lutz the Putz," said Eric, shaking his head. "I can't believe you called that jerk's office." He frowned and pushed his glasses up his nose. "And please don't tell me you're thinking about how to get back with him now that he doesn't have a girlfriend."

"Only for a minute—and not really. Especially not after he told me he didn't want to hear from me, ever."

"You can be sure a few weeks away and a tragedy will have done nothing to improve his character," said Eric. "In psychological terms, you're suffering from a repetition compulsion."

I raised my eyebrows and took a sip of beer.

"In other words, you have the unconscious urge to repeat a destructive pattern from your past. Unfortunately, you're destined to live it over and over again until you understand it."

"What pattern? I don't see it."

"That's because it's unconscious." We both laughed a little hysterically because sometimes the truth sounds a little funnier out loud than it really is. He leaned forward and tapped my knee.

"Obviously, I'm speaking as your friend, not your therapist," he said and glared at me until I nodded my agreement. "But why would you want a man who behaves just as coldly and critically as your father?"

I had to admit he was right. And creepier still, Chad even looked like my father: wide at the shoulders and narrow at the waist with a long, flattish face and sandy blond hair. I shrugged and let my chin sag toward my neck. "I don't. I shouldn't. I swear I'll think about it. But meanwhile . . ."

"But meanwhile, it wouldn't hurt you one bit to see a shrink."

"Who needs a shrink when I've got you for a pal and tarot at sunset?"

Eric sighed heavily as if my nuttiness were a great burden and squeezed his temples between his palms. "I'll ask around about a lawyer," he said. "You go about your regular business and try not to act guilty or get into trouble."

"Moi?" I laughed. "Ears open, mouth shut," I added, pointing to the respective body parts. "And thanks for coming out tonight." I set my beer on the window ledge and hugged him again.

"How're the reviews coming?" he asked.

I clutched my hands to my chest. "This sounds just awful to say, but what if they don't fill the job because of what happened to Kristen?"

"You don't have any control over that," he said.

"Right. You're right." I nodded briskly. "I've just

about got Seven Fish nailed. Maybe I'll run by Bad Boy Burrito on my way home and make some notes for the second one. Right after I have my cards read."

I needed a reading, badly.

And besides, I wanted to ask why Lorenzo, my favorite tarot guru, hadn't seen one bit of this coming.

4

"What is food to one man may be fierce poison to others."

—Lucretius

After leaving the bar, I drove my scooter the length of Whitehead Street toward Mallory Square to see if Lorenzo was working. Every night at sunset, except in the very worst weather, street performers marked off sections of the pier and set up shop to entertain tourists and part them from a few of their dollars. Along with the zaniness of Duval Street, the spectacle of the sun setting over Mallory Square tended to stick in the minds of visitors more than anything about Key West.

Lorenzo has been working the square for almost twenty years, wearing a star-studded turban, a deep blue cloak with a matching blue stone glued to his forehead, and a mustache waxed into loops. Sounded hokey, but even I felt more confident having my cards read by a guy who took the time to look and act professional.

I parked my scooter outside the Westin Hotel and trudged up the sidewalk past the four-times-larger-than-life Seward Johnson sculptures of dancing women that had been erected behind the Custom House Museum. As usual, a couple of giddy tourists were having their photos snapped as they lay under those enormous naked prancing ladies.

Farther up toward the water, Dominique the cat man was finishing his act by circling his audience and bellowing while a tortoiseshell feline clung to his chest. It was 5:39—the sun had already slipped below the horizon and the dusk was gathering. I hurried around the back of the aquarium to the main square. Aside from Dominique's perennially popular flying house cats show, the juggling fire-eater had gathered the biggest crowd. And Lorenzo was there without any customers, shuffling his cards and looking pensive. Probably wondering what kind of dinner was in his future.

I slid into the chair across from him and handed over a crumpled twenty-dollar bill. Some people go to therapy every week; I get my cards read. A tarot reader saved my mother's sanity when I was a kid— psychiatry, not so much. So consulting the cards felt natural. Mom has long since moved on to doing her own readings, but for me, Lorenzo's insights were like training wheels still welded to my psyche.

"Back again," Lorenzo said, smiling under that goofy mustache. "Another crisis?"

He has proven to be very big on that old saw "crisis equals opportunity," even in the short time I've known him. Like Eric, he has to be an optimist, taking money from his clients and then giving life direction, night after balmy night.

"The universe seems a little crazy right now," I said. "I'd like to get your opinion."

He had me sterilize my hands with a witch hazel spritzer and cut his deck of oversized, colorful cards, sticky with age and use. Then he laid out the first row, placing a metal lizard on top so they wouldn't blow away: the Chariot, reversed, the Five of Pentacles, and the Eight of Swords.

"Hmmm," he said, his brow creasing into the biggest worry lines I'd ever seen him wear. "You may be pulled in many directions . . . self-sabotage . . . a feeling of neediness? Seems like you're feeling a little out of control?"

"Tell me something I don't know," I said, leaning in closer to the cards. Mom has been encouraging me to study the ways of tarot myself instead of relying on Lorenzo. But at least this way, I controlled how often I visited him and how reliant I got on his card-reading expertise. And I didn't run the risk of incessantly revising my own fortune. Knees jiggling, I fished a tube of natural lip balm out of my pocket and slathered it on.

He slapped down another row of cards and peered across the table at me. "You know, of course, that death doesn't necessarily mean *death*."

"But that's the thing—there's been a murder. And it looks like I'm one of their best suspects." I started to hyperventilate. Telling Lorenzo made the whole thing seem even more real. And terrifying.

Lorenzo produced a pack of tissues from one of his voluminous sleeves and handed a few over.

"You're seeing something worse and you don't want to tell me," I suggested, trying to interpret the concern on his face.

"Good and bad are relative. Remember the cards are just guideposts," he said as I dabbed my nose. "It's how you handle what the universe throws your way that determines how your life turns out."

The lady waiting her turn to see Lorenzo rolled her eyes, jangled a couple inches' worth of gold bracelets on one thin wrist, and sighed noisily. I stood up. "I'll probably be back tomorrow," I told him, glaring at the woman as she slid into my spot.

"In the meantime, be careful," he said, adding a quick wink before turning his prim smile to the bracelet lady. "And keep your focus."

I took the shortcut out of Mallory Square, retrieved my scooter, and dropped it off its kickstand. What *was* my focus? My pal Eric would have liked that question a lot, and there wasn't much of Lorenzo's advice that he agreed with. My number one focus had to be my food critic pieces. Even I realized it would be tacky to call the desk at *Key Zest* and ask them if the boss's death would have any effect on the hiring. I felt guilty just having that thought. But I could continue to work on my writing so I'd be prepared by the deadline, in case the position remained open.

Number two: the murder. The cops hadn't confirmed that I was a suspect. On the other hand, Eric was clearly worried—and he didn't have my inherited tendency to jump to hysterical conclusions. Lorenzo had seemed bothered too. And what bothered Lorenzo bothered me.

Would it hurt to swing by Chad's apartment and see if there were any lights on? Or if any of the neighbors would talk to me about what happened? Besides my possible status as a suspect, the question of how Kristen died kept surfacing in the back of my mind. I pictured myself standing outside the courtyard gate and begging through the bars to be let in and get my questions answered. Forget it. I fired up the scooter and lurched into the postsunset celebration traffic toward Bad Boy Burrito.

Bad Boy was located in a storefront on Simonton Street, a couple blocks from the Atlantic Ocean. If you weren't looking carefully for it, you'd drive right by. But if I landed that *Key Zest* job, this was exactly the kind of place I hoped to cover on my beat. I'd want to let my readers know about the little restaurants and shops in town, not just the fancy places that only wealthy folks could afford. How could you not have a soft spot in your heart for an establishment that recommended jalapeño peppers on everything because of their high vitamin C content?

Bad Boy held two workers (at peak hours), a counter in the window with stools facing the street, one weathered wooden bench inside for waiting, and one bench outside on the sidewalk if you couldn't make it home without diving into your booty. I studied the blackboard menu, frozen between a Kobe beef burrito with the works and fresh fish tacos served in homemade corn tortillas with shredded cabbage, pico de gallo, verde sauce, and sour cream.

Feeling frozen brought to mind one of Chad's final

criticisms: "You couldn't make a decision if you were offered a seat on a lifeboat alongside the *Titanic*." Which stung hard since the decision I had been facing at that moment was whether or not to go home for Thanksgiving and how I could manage such a trip without hurting anyone's feelings. If I had dinner at my mother's house, how would I explain that choice to my father? Would he be satisfied if I explained that I preferred Mom's mashed potatoes and gravy to my stepmother's rice pilaf? Obviously not.

Chad was right: I was often afraid I would make a mistake I couldn't recover from. And I'd made a whopper recently—I'd moved in with him on the basis of sheer lust and dumb hope when I barely knew him, and look where that had gotten me. (This, of course, was one of the things I had screamed at Chad when he was moving my belongings out. Only I skipped the part about lust because why give him the satisfaction?)

On the other hand, if I didn't start making decisions and taking action, my life would continue to swirl the drain. *Glug, glug, glug*. I'd be headed back to New Jersey with my father's "I told you so" ringing in my ears before I even crossed the Mason-Dixon line.

So I squared my shoulders, stepped up, and ordered both the burrito and the tacos—to go. Then I added a fresh-squeezed limeade to help pass the time, and slumped on the bench to wait for the food. With all the excitement at the police station and my detours to the Green Parrot and Lorenzo, I hadn't had time for a proper lunch. Cheese and crackers did not, no way, constitute a meal. And besides, having danger read into my future had made me very hungry. Sliding my iPhone from my back pocket, I tapped in the opening bones of a possible review:

> *Fast food doesn't have to mean greasy, bland, or caloric. Some of the absolute most mouth-watering food in Key West gets carried out of Bad Boy Burrito in a paper sack.*

Then I snapped a few surreptitious photos of the glass counter loaded with limes, cabbage, and tomatoes, trying not to tip off the staff. Being the food critic for *Key Zest* would not bring the notoriety of that same job at the *New York Times*, but still, I would prefer to remain anonymous for as long as possible. Nothing would queer an honest review faster than special treatment from the restaurant chef. Or so I'd read.

Henrietta (Henri to her friends) Stentzel, one of the Bad Boy owners, called me up to the counter when my drink was ready. "Your order should be up shortly," she said with a smile, wiping her hands on a white full-body apron.

I'd met Henri when I had come in for lunch soon after I arrived in town and got pressed into filling in for a shift at the soup kitchen. She was a foodie who had owned and run a hip restaurant in Miami Beach until she burned out on the late-night hours and the constant search for competent, sober staff. Several months ago, she retired to make burritos in Key West. She had this theory about helping the homeless folks who flock to the island in the winter and spill over into the shoulder seasons: With a spin of the karmic dial, we too could have been living out of a filthy knapsack on the beach.

Chad, of course, didn't see things that way.

"These people are responsible for their own destinies, same as we are," he'd told me over a fabulous steak dinner and the best Bloody Mary I'd ever tasted at Michael's. "You're only enabling their lifestyle choices."

Looking back, *there* was a turning point I should have recognized.

At the counter in front of me, Henri busied herself wrapping a line of chicken burritos in tinfoil. I wondered, as I had the first time she'd mentioned her move from Miami Beach to Key West, whether she was truly satisfied with the change in her life path. It occurred to me that with her Miami and restaurant connections, she might have an inside track about Kristen's murder.

"Did you hear the awful news about Kristen Faulkner?" I asked.

"Unbelievable," said Henri, glancing up from her work. With the back of her wrist, she pushed a wisp of black hair off her forehead. "Not that she and I were close"—here she actually snorted—"but no one deserves to die eating something they love."

I felt a jolt to the gut. "So it was something she ate?"

Henri frowned as she tucked the sandwiches into a brown paper bag. "That's what I heard." Then she pinched her lips together and shook her head, like she wasn't going to say another word. "Hang on." She moved across the small kitchen space to the six-burner stove and stirred my beef, adding a handful of cilantro before flipping the steaming mass into a flour skin and dousing the whole pile with fresh salsa. She paused and glanced up, her brown eyes questioning. "Jalapeños on this?"

"Of course." I grinned.

"Say, listen," she said. "Are you by any chance going home by way of Higgs Beach?"

"I could."

She pointed to the sack of sandwiches she'd been working on earlier. "I packed up some leftovers for the guys who were in the soup kitchen yesterday. If you're not in a rush, could you drop them off? I'm running late here."

"No problem." I tucked the bag of food into my backpack and carried my loot to the outside bench, nearly swooning from the smell. I paused for a minute to think about Kristen, who would never again have the chance to eat something exquisite and tease out its meld of flavors. Feeling sad for that, I held her memory in what light I could summon, considering the circumstances. Then I bit into the first fish taco. Crunchy shell, crisp cabbage, flash-fried grouper, with just the right spicy zip. Heaven.

Once I'd gobbled that taco, I wiped my hands clean and returned everything to my backpack. I would save the burrito for later. Then I started up the scooter and drove the few blocks to Higgs Beach. The three guys Henri had described from the soup kitchen were drinking beverages from paper sacks at a concrete picnic table beside the bike path. One was the thin, walnut-brown cowboy who'd scared the daylights out of me at the cemetery the night before. A Coleman lantern spilled a pool of light over the playing cards on their table.

"Are you guys hungry?" I called, then steadied my scooter onto its kickstand. "Henri sent some goodies. Chicken burritos. They're still warm."

"Dude," said the cowboy. He stood, swept his hat off his head, and bowed. "You're a lifesaver."

The other two guys, a redhead with tangled hair, shaggy beard, and canvas shorts layered over his jeans, and a heavy man reeking of beer and wearing a Red Sox baseball cap, said nothing. Fifty yards farther, invisible in the darkness, the waves of the Atlantic Ocean hissed against the sand.

"Mah name is Tony," the cowboy said, gesturing to the empty spot at the concrete picnic table. "Reckon we could get you to join us?"

To be perfectly honest, the idea of eating with them here in the shadows made me the tiniest bit nervous. But would they think I thought I was too good to share a sandwich? Only Connie's kindness had kept me from similar circumstances. Though not really, I supposed, as I could always go home to New Jersey and mooch off my relatives. I dropped their food on the table, sat down, and pulled the second taco out of my backpack.

Tony unpacked and distributed the burritos to his friends and we began to eat. He swallowed his first mouthful and wiped his mustache on his sleeve. "Did we hear somethin' about y'all making a visit to the cop shop this afternoon?"

"Good gravy," I said. "How the heck did you know that?"

"Good gravy?" Tony chortled. "You sound like you stepped out of Mayberry."

"My grandmother used to say it," I explained stiffly.

He held up a grubby hand and grinned. "No offense. We were across from the station at Bayview Park this afternoon throwing a Frisbee for Poncho and hanging out." Tony pointed to the mottled dog that lay at the feet of the silent redhead. In this light, it was hard to say if his short fur was gray or just filthy. He bared his teeth without lifting his head. "Turtle here"—now he pointed to the redhead—"he noticed you pull up in the back of a black-and-white. What's up with that?"

Turtle's pale blue eyes flashed to my face for a minute, then back to his food.

"I don't know exactly," I said, and started to choke on the bite of fish going down my pipe. Tony pounded me on the back. I wiped my eyes and took a sip from my water bottle, wondering how much to say.

"You've probably heard about the murder, then."

Three sets of curious eyes confirmed that they had. If they knew about my visit to the police station, they probably knew a lot more too. *Give a little, get a little, Hayley,* I thought.

"The lady who died was my ex's new girlfriend. It was pretty much routine questioning—where was I between eight and five and so on."

"But how come they brought you to the station?" asked Tony. "Couldn't they ask you that stuff on your front porch?"

"The times I got taken to the station, they were pretty sure I done it. Whatever it was," said the man in the baseball cap with a mirthless laugh.

"I think they wanted me to tell the chief what I

knew." I stopped talking, my stomach churning. What *was* going on?

My cell phone buzzed with a text message. I fished it out of my back pocket—Connie's name flashed in a small box on the screen. I excused myself to read.

WHEN ARE WE EATING? NEED ME TO GET THINGS STARTED?

Her subtle way of saying: Where the heck is that home-cooked dinner you promised?

FORTY-FIVE MINUTES, I texted back. Then I packed up my food in a big hurry. "Sorry, guys. Gotta run."

5

"Time slows down in the kitchen, offering up an entire universe of small satisfactions."

—Ruth Reichl

I stopped at Fausto's Market on the way back to the houseboat and picked up a pound of shrimp, a length of andouille sausage, a sack of grits, and two packages of Whisker Lickin's for Evinrude. This morning, in a fit of extravagant gratitude for putting up me and the cat, I'd promised Connie that I'd make dinner for her and her boyfriend, Ray. Just because I'd spoiled my appetite with the fish tacos and talk about the police didn't mean they weren't hungry. And I could cut up the beef burrito into finger food to hold off the starving masses while I cooked the supper. Besides, cooking always helped me think.

I parked my scooter in the lot beside the Bight, slung the food-laden backpack over my shoulder, and hurried past the green Dumpsters and the tiny building housing the marina Laundromat to the dock. Two boats in along the wooden finger and more often than not one season ahead of the rest of the world, Miss Gloria had strung Christmas lights on her porch. They winked a cheerful welcome. She was watching the news in her living room, one eye on the dock. I waved and called hello through the screen.

"Your place looks fantastic," I told her.

She smiled modestly and ducked down to stroke her cat, a slim black tomcat named Sparky. "How's Evinrude settling in?"

"He'll never be a sailor," I said with a laugh, "but we're surviving." Then, since Miss Gloria hardly ever left her boat, it occurred to me to wonder if she'd be able to vouch for me with the police. I hopped over onto her porch, her boat rocking almost imperceptibly under the change in weight. "Did you happen to notice that I was here this morning working?"

"This morning?" she asked, looking puzzled. "I don't know. Were you? That nice young policeman came by, though. He's got such a strong chin."

"I know," I said glumly. Her touch of dee-mentia, as she called it, wasn't going to help me in this situation. "You two have a good night. And let me know if you need anything from the store tomorrow, okay?"

On the next boat over, the Renharts had decorated for Thanksgiving, their small front deck hosting a plastic turkey with a lighted sign around its neck that read "Eat More Ham." I waved hello to Mrs. Renhart, silhouetted by lights from her galley.

The lights were also blazing on Connie's houseboat, but only Evinrude greeted me, winding through my legs and offering a string of plaintive meows. A note on the counter explained that Connie and Ray had popped over to Finnegan's Wake for a beer and would be back by eight. She had signed the note "starving!"—underlined three times. Another note reported that my mother had called twice on Connie's landline since I didn't seem to be answering my cell. And a third note reported good news—the editor of the local newspaper called to let me know that my article "A Taste of Key Lime Pie in Key West" would be appearing in tomorrow's paper.

I read that last line two more times, vibrating with disbelief and then excitement. This would be my first official byline, sure to buff up my credentials for the food critic job. I cracked open a Key West Sunset Ale and toasted my change in fortune.

I started the water boiling for the grits, minced a pile of onions, garlic, and peppers and tossed them into a pan of crackling olive oil, and then grated a slab of sharp cheddar. While I sliced the sausage and shelled the shrimp, I gave myself a pep talk about calling home. I tried to keep things light with Mom. She'd had only that one official hospitalization, but she tended to feel things that happened to me almost more than I felt them. "Separation issues," Eric had suggested. Whatever you called it, she panicked faster than a house cat in a rainstorm when she sensed bad news. A feeling I could relate to.

To make things worse, I was lousy at keeping my cards close to my vest. I was much more likely to blurt out exactly what was on my mind than to keep a secret.

And there was a lot weighing on it right now: the tarot card reading, Kristen's murder, my trip to the police station, and Chad. Heck, even the homeless guys were worried about me. I jotted these things down on the back of the Fausto's receipt, wrote "Do Not Discuss" at the top in red ink, and dialed.

Mom answered on the first ring. "Hayley, what's wrong?" Obviously her antennae were already quivering near the red position on the maternal concern dial.

"And hi back to you, Mom," I said. "The only thing wrong here is I forgot to charge my phone last night."

"Connie didn't know where you were," she said accusingly. "She said you'd promised to make dinner and then you didn't show up."

"I'm cooking right this minute," I assured her, holding the phone over the frying pan so she could hear the comforting sound of vegetables sautéing themselves to satisfying limpness. "I'm making a cross between shrimp and grits and jambalaya."

"Sounds delicious," said Mom. "Tomatoes or no tomatoes? And how's it going with your writing?"

"No tomatoes," I said. "It's more of a creamy cheese sauce." Then I told her about my article getting published and how well I was doing on the critic assignment and finally eased her off the call to return to my cooking. Of all things, she understood the demands of a new recipe.

When it came to food, all roads led back to my mom, of course. I suspected my mother was secretly relieved to turn up pregnant her senior year in college—like her idol Hayley Mills, she showed a lot of career promise but flamed out early. My unexpected conception gave her a good excuse for settling down in suburbia rather than opting to attend law school or medical school as she'd told my father she planned. Instead of figuring out what she wanted to do with her life, she became a housewife and sank most of her talents and energy into raising me and cooking. She was the queen of local ingredients and fusion cuisine long before those trends ever got popular. She'd spend all day in the kitchen and then wait breathlessly for my dad and me to come to the table and make our pronouncements.

"The tarragon tries too hard," my father might say.

"Can we have hot dogs tomorrow?" That would be me.

In the end, the tarragon business wasn't a bad metaphor for the dynamic of my parents' marriage, before it went belly-up. My mother was the tarragon in the relationship and Dad was the snooty critic.

Once I got past the hot dog phase, I learned to love food. My dream was to go to the culinary institute in Paris, become a famous chef, and then write cookbooks. But my dad was writing the tuition checks: I was to attend college for an education, not a trade. And so I earned my degree in food science, the closest undergrad major to cooking I could find. With the unemployment rate at an all-time high after graduation, I took a job clerking in a local bookstore and wrote food feature proposals for the local paper, none of them published. Twenty-five years old and still drifting, as my father pointed out often.

Then, almost four months ago, I met Chad Lutz. After a whirlwind weekend of dating and another couple weeks of highly charged text messages and phone calls, I followed him to Key West, where he had a partnership in a small law firm—and I've been floundering like my mother ever since.

To be honest, I didn't think most people looked any further than what *they* thought they wanted from a relationship when they fell for a new lover. Shouldn't the Hayley Mills obsession have tipped my dad off? A grown woman who connected most strongly with a ditzy Disney actress from the sixties was going to be a little "different." As far as Chad and I went, there were lots of warning signals, if I'd only chosen to see them.

Connie clattered in the front door, with Ray bounding right behind her like a well trained whippet. She was small and sturdy with the shortest haircut I'd ever seen on a girl, while he was tall and gangly and wore his hair in a ponytail. *The long and the short of it.* She heard that all the time. We'd bonded instantly in our freshman year at Rutgers, but then her mother died and she'd dropped out to move to Key West and start a business.

"Smells divine in here."

"I'm so sorry I'm late," I said. "Wait until you hear about my day."

I loaded three plates with cheesy grits and layered the shrimp, sausage, and vegetables on top. We poured glasses of white wine and carried our plates upstairs to the deck, which had an amazing view just off Connie's bedroom. More anxious than hungry, I took a minute to sip my wine and breathe in the cool fall air. The full-timers in Key West waited for this weather all year long.

Stars were spackled across the sky and I could hear the strains of country music from a houseboat a few slips away. The spooky termite-ridden boat in the next row that was covered with a red tarp labeled "Poison!" receded into the shadows. And darkness hid the cruiser two doors down that was so full of trash that passersby could no longer see in the windows. Along with Miss Gloria, many of the residents had threaded their rooflines with little white lights in anticipation of the holidays. From this perspective, it really did look like paradise.

Connie and Ray dug into their dinners, and she looked up after her first bite. "This is fantastic! Fabulous! You should open a restaurant."

"No way," I said. "I'd rather just eat the food. And write about it."

She laughed. "Before I forget," she added, "are you still on for cleaning a few apartments tomorrow? Angie called in sick."

"Count me in."

"Where have you been all day?" she asked.

I loaded my fork up and then put it back down on my plate. "The cops came by and invited me to the station for a chat," I said in a hushed voice, not wishing to alert the rest of the neighbors about my business, just in case they hadn't already seen the whole thing unfold. I poked a shrimp farther into my mound of grits. "Kristen Faulkner seems to have gotten herself murdered."

Connie swallowed what she was chewing and sat up straight. "Kristen was *murdered*? What could you possibly have to say about that? And why would they even think to ask?"

"I'm not certain, but I have a bad feeling that Chad suggested they call on me." I described the short, painful conversation I'd had with my ex.

"He's a dick," said Ray. "Who do they think you are, Lorena Bobbitt?"

Connie giggled. "You're mixing your metaphors, buddy. Lorena didn't murder her ex's new girlfriend; she cut off his you-know-what and threw it into a field."

"Ouch," said Ray, shifting his plate to cover his lap. "What exactly happened to this girl Kristen?"

"The cops mostly asked me questions," I said, "but Henri at Bad Boy Burritos told me it was something she ate."

"Henri Stentzel? Didn't Kristen have something to do with Henri's restaurant in Miami folding?" asked Ray.

"Wow!" I hadn't heard that—and Henri certainly hadn't mentioned it—but it might explain the funny expression I'd seen on her face as she finished up my order. I didn't like to think anything bad of Henri—she struck me as a moral and dedicated businesswoman who insisted on the freshest ingredients, made a mean sandwich, and knew when to bail out of a rat race. But what if she hadn't *chosen* to leave her fancy restaurant and set up a funky burrito shop in Key West? What if she'd been forced out?

Connie was looking worried. "I hope you're not going to butt your nose into this," she said. "Let the police handle it. I'm sure they were just gathering information when they called you in."

"The homeless guys said if they were just collecting information, they would have interviewed me right here."

"I can phone my friend Matthew," Ray broke in. "He's the Web publisher for *Key Zest*. I'm sure he's got more information than you do."

I nodded eagerly. "Thanks."

He whipped out his cell phone and soon was deep in conversation. We only heard his side of it—"Incredible!" "You're kidding." "They think that?" He hung up, wiped his forehead with his napkin, and grimaced in my direction.

"They found her in Chad's apartment. Actually, Chad himself called it in."

"Oh my God," I said. "What if he killed her? And then panicked and pretended someone else did it? Like me?"

"There's more," said Ray. "She ate a poisoned pie. Key lime."

6

"It's easy to get the feeling that you know the language just because when you order a beer they don't bring you oysters."

—Paul Child

I stayed awake most of the night worrying. Would the cops read the *Key West Citizen* today? And if so, would one of them make it all the way through to the Living section? And if he did, would he make the connection between Kristen's poisoning and my newly touted expertise in key lime pies?

Though honestly, the lovemaking noises didn't help my sleeping either. First my housemates had a lively session; then the Renharts one boat over joined in—as if our boat's rocking and sloshing reminded them of the possibility of their own pleasure. I finally fell asleep around two and woke from the dead at six, exhausted, when Ray and Connie left the houseboat to drive to Miami for supplies.

A few weeks ago, when I snapped up the offer to move in with Connie, I didn't realize I'd be seeing quite so much of Ray. He has a position as a visiting resident artist at the Studios of Key West, though it seemed to me that he spent more time hanging out with Connie than practicing art. Not that I was complaining, but, just maybe, I harbored a smallish bunch of sour grapes. Ray and Connie had been together for eight months and still acted like they were madly in love. Chad and I flamed out in less than eight *weeks*. And Ray was nice to Connie in a way Chad never was to me—wildly supportive of everything she did. He even chipped in to help with her cleaning service when she was down a worker.

Whereas Chad had dumped me unceremoniously—packed up my things and put them out on the sidewalk in front of his apartment building where any passing stranger could have picked them over. And I was still missing some crucial stuff. Like my best chef's paring knife and the set of serrated steak knives I'd splurged on with my graduation money. And my cookbooks. But much worse than any of those was the box of my grandmother's handwritten recipe cards. My mother had passed them on to me a couple years ago, crying all the way through her ceremonious bestowal of the secret recipes. She hadn't wanted me to bring them to Key West, but I didn't have time to make copies. She would *die* if she knew they were missing.

I was pretty sure it was normal to feel angry and sad about the Chad business, but I scolded myself for feeling envious of Connie. I truly didn't wish her my kind of trouble—I only wished I could find happily ever after too. Eric's lecture in the Green Parrot about unconscious repetition of old patterns had me more concerned than I wanted to let on—even to myself.

I forced myself out of bed and into the kitchen. Connie had left a note on the counter with the addresses of the clients who expected their homes cleaned today, either by her or Angie. She asked me to choose three and leave the others for Lydia, who would work the second shift. I filled Evinrude's bowl with kibbles, popped a sticky bun into the toaster oven, and started a pot of coffee, grinding a cinnamon stick along with the beans for good measure.

Then I crossed the room to Connie's desk and leafed through the binder filled with laminated pages containing her clients' instructions. She prided herself on doing her job the way her customers wanted it done, varying the cleaning supplies, the frequency, and the approach according to their requests and peculiarities. I jotted down a few notes for the Hinand (clean and scrub the cat litter pan) and Kennedy households (sweep the lanai so the pool filter doesn't get clogged with debris from the golden rain tree; use second sink in the pantry for mopping floors, NOT the sink in the kitchen).

I couldn't help noticing that Chad Lutz's apartment was also on the schedule for today, though Connie would never have asked me to take it. She'd landed him as a client after I moved out and I very much doubted he would have hired her if he'd remembered our connection. The instructions he'd given her were longer and more detailed than most of her other customers; actually, I could have recited his cleaning quirks by rote. I knew enough to use expensive organic cleaners on everything but the toilets, which were to be double-scrubbed and then swished with Clorox. The list continued:

There should be no dust anywhere, including the tops of picture frames.

No smudges or fingerprints left on mirrors or doorframes.

No dust bunnies under beds or spiderwebs in ceiling corners.

Don't dust around objects; pick them up and clean under and around them; then return them to their original positions.

Hospital corners on sheets are preferred when making beds.

Aside from all that, Chad would probably have left a note in the kitchen for Connie, directing her to focus on the half bathroom that had contained my cat's litter box, even though Evinrude had vacated the premises weeks earlier.

Chad had regretted moving Evinrude and me into his place almost as soon as he'd extended the invitation. After our first week of cohabitation, he clipped out an article on kitchen cleanliness that had run in the *New York Times* and left it for me to read. A government food inspector had been interviewed and then come to the writer's home to rate her kitchen's hygiene. The inspector maintained that she would *never* eat in a home that had a cat in residence. Just imagining the cat's blithe transition from litter box to kitchen counter was enough to horrify her—and Chad as well. Good sex kept his cat contamination phobia in check for a couple more weeks; then the complaints began, marching from subtle to sledgehammer by the time I moved out.

And this got me wondering whether he'd been more welcoming to Kristen than he had to me. Had he really moved her in so quickly? And had she, for example, been given more closet space than the two feet I'd been allowed in his guest room? Would her papers and computer be spread across his second desk or would she have been required to load all her work into a briefcase stored under the guest bed, the way I had? Really, didn't it all boil down to why he'd found her more lovable than me?

Never mind. What could be more pitiful than comparing my love life to that of a dead woman? But the longer I looked at the list, the more upset I got about my missing stuff. He'd been downright mean to keep things that meant nothing to him and everything to me.

As the last of the coffee burbled and sputtered into the pot, I hurried out onto the dock to retrieve Connie's copy of the *Key West Citizen*. I smoothed the paper out on the café table in the kitchen and sat down for breakfast. Evinrude splayed out on the chair next to me, grooming his gray stripes into their morning order. I took a sip of coffee and almost spit it out when I saw Kristen's head shot looming from the box just inside the front page reserved for the crime report.

> *Kristen Faulkner, a longtime native of Key West, who had plans to open a restaurant on Easter Island and recently launched* Key Zest *magazine, was discovered dead in the apartment of a friend yesterday morning. Police have questioned several persons of interest in the suspected murder.*

My heart sank with a desperate clunk—suddenly the murder felt exquisitely real, and my so-called involvement, very scary. Feeling queasy, I stopped reading and flipped over to the living section pages and found my blaring byline: "Key West Confidential: Key Lime Pie to Die For" by Hayley Snow. Could the timing of such a headline have been any worse? I forced my thoughts away from key lime pie as murder weapon and skimmed the first paragraph to see how much the editor had cut.

> *Key lime pie may have been declared the official state pie by the Florida legislature, but there is no official state recipe for the confection. Nowhere is that more evident than in the restaurants of Key West. This reporter set off on a quest to taste her way across the island's pies, and then report on the sublime to the ridiculous.*

Then I'd gone on to discuss the pie as it was prepared in restaurants across town—the graham cracker crusts, the regular pie crusts, the lack of crust altogether. The pale yellow, the garish green, the use of key limes versus standard citrus, the unconventional addition of basil, the mile-high meringue topping, the whipped cream . . . If I hadn't been already eating breakfast, I would have made myself hungry. Even though I'd sworn when I finished researching and writing the piece that I'd never eat key lime pie again.

I washed up the breakfast dishes and then moved to my mini bedroom to sort through my clean laundry, which I hadn't yet put away in the built-in drawers. What was the point when I would almost surely be heading back to my mom's spare bedroom in New Jersey soon enough?

At the bottom of the pile, I found the shirt Connie asked all her workers to wear. Over the front pocket "Paradise Cleaning" looped in green script. "We clean so you don't have to" was written across the back of the shirt next to her logo, a figure in a hammock suspended between two cute little palm trees. I pulled it on, along with khaki cutoffs and red high-top sneakers, and kissed the cat.

"I won't be gone long," I assured him. He blinked his green eyes and curled up by my pillow. (Another horrifying realization for Chad: a cat sleeping near his precious face.)

I filled a square plastic carton with the supplies I'd need for the Hinand and Kennedy apartments. At the last second, I added extra rubber gloves and Chad's special cleaning liquids. If I finished the other two places quickly, I'd storm through Chad's apartment like a green tornado. This was my one and only chance to get my stuff without depending on him to cooperate. Connie would absolutely kill me if she knew I was thinking of bulling my way into his apartment. But I would clean, and clean to his exacting standards, while I was there. At least I'd be reducing her workload while snooping for the things that rightfully belonged to me. I hauled the carton down the dock to my scooter, bungee-corded it onto the backrest, and putt-putted across town.

With none of the owners home to distract me with chatting or snacks, I finished my first two assignments in record time. I loaded the cleaning stuff back into the crate and strode out to my scooter to tie it on. Did I have the nerve to do this? Yes. Was it a good idea? Maybe not. Starting up the bike, I headed over to Chad's. I paused across from the drive leading into the condo complex to pull on a Paradise Cleaning ball cap and my biggest sunglasses. If Leona—the nosy neighbor on the second floor who came out of her apartment almost every time the elevator dinged—recognized me, she'd be on the phone to Chad's office before I got the key turned in the lock.

I knew you shouldn't choose a boyfriend according to where he lived, but trust me when I say it was almost worth Chad's steady stream of low-level undercutting at the end of our relationship to live in his apartment—even for just two months. The condo complex sat at the very southern tip of the island, overlooking the harbor. His place sprawled over the upper-right-hand corner of a three-story whitewashed building that formerly served as the administration building for the U.S. Navy. He'd had the whole thing gutted and renovated before I ever laid eyes on it.

It wasn't just the view I lusted after—a head-on one-hundred-and-eighty-degree expanse of water with an occasional cruise ship for relief from all that Caribbean blue—or the Corinthian columns marching down his entrance hallway, or the soundproofed bedroom with its king bed dressed in earth-toned Egyptian linens, or the bathtub big enough for two with pulsing jets that hit just the right point on your lower back. Best of all was the most amazing futuristic kitchen I'd ever baked a cake in: three ovens, a six-burner stove, speckled granite counters, and every piece of cooking equipment I could have ever thought about using and some that never crossed my mind. Not that a pat of butter had ever hit a frying pan while Chad lived alone. He ate to live. And he didn't even like dessert. But I was in cook's heaven during my short stay.

I buzzed myself into the building, lugged the cleaning supplies to the elevator in the front hall, and whisked up to the third floor without encountering any neighbors. My heart pit-patting, I dug the ring of keys out of my back pocket, found Chad's, and eased the door open, listening. I heard nothing but the hum of his Thermador refrigerator, and outside the double-paned windows, the coarse buzz of a weed whacker from the front lawn. I stepped inside and closed the door softly behind me. My hands trembled as I crept down his hallway. I hadn't let myself wonder exactly where Kristen had died. Or whether remnants of the disaster might still be lingering.

I stopped and stared. The apartment was every bit as gorgeous as I remembered it. Chad's decorator had filled the place with shades of green once he'd convinced her he wasn't interested in the kitschy local style consisting of bright colors, lizards, palm trees, and roosters. (Though really, what was wrong with all that—he did live in Key West.)

Someone had swabbed down the counters of my dream kitchen inexpertly—they were still streaked with patches of greasy, black silt. Chad must have flipped out when he saw the police department's work. Not that solving Kristen's murder wasn't much more important than any mess they'd left behind, but he loved his empire. Although none of that would have been on his mind if he'd been the one to kill her. But he couldn't have. Could he? I rubbed the crop of goose bumps that had popped up on the length of my arms.

Setting the bucket on the floor near the double sinks, I poked my head into the living room, wondering again where the police had found her.

I desperately wanted to bolt, feeling one part voyeur, one part victim, and four parts creeped out of my gourd. But this would be the only chance to retrieve my stuff, because I surely wasn't coming back for a second look. So I returned to the kitchen and snapped on my rubber gloves. If Chad should return home—and he absolutely shouldn't; it was his day for back-to-back meetings—I could explain my innocence by pointing out the sparkling tile and spotless floors. After filling both of the stainless sinks in the kitchen with scalding water and

Green Clean-up, I began to wipe the black gunk off the counters.

Too antsy to contain my curiosity, I dropped the sponge and opened the refrigerator. It was almost empty except for three cartons of Greek yogurt (no fat) and a bottle of white wine. I realized I was holding my breath. What had I thought I'd find? An unfinished pie and utensils with poison clinging to them? Clues revealing Kristen's enemies? I needed to find my stuff, clean, and then get the heck out.

I tiptoed to the guest bedroom at the back of the apartment where I'd stored my things when I was there. There was nothing in the closet except for one of my steak knives, which lay on the floor beside a flattened stack of cardboard boxes. Brand new, super-sharp, and he had the nerve to use it like scissors. I picked it up and slid it into my back pocket.

My heartbeat quickened when I thought I heard a banging noise outside the front door. I froze and waited. Was it the maintenance man emptying the trash in the hallway closet? When I heard the elevator ding and the sounds fade away, I quickly searched all of the drawers and shelves, but found nothing else that belonged to me.

I went back through the kitchen and into the living room, past the two seating areas on the left, and into the master bedroom. The bedcovers had been pulled loosely over the pillows on Chad's side, and one pair of men's underwear lay just under the bed. I started to make the bed, but felt a little sick as the faint smell of a woman's flowery perfume wafted up from the pillow. Certainly not mine. Inside the master bathroom, I opened the closet doors—Chad's clothing was arranged by color and season. While I lived there, none of my stuff had been allowed to disrupt the order of his closet or even the bathroom counters. Of course I found no knife, no recipe cards, no more cutlery, no nothing. I felt frustrated and foolish.

Back in the living room, one shaft of light streamed through the front window, broken into jagged shadows by the coconut palm just outside. The sun lit up the tidy piles of paper on Chad's expansive and modern desk, burnishing the tiger maple to a soft bronze glow. This was the only place in the apartment he allowed clutter—and not much of it at that. Grabbing the feather duster from my crate, I brought it back to the desk and began to work, straightening the stack of papers, tucking a Cross pen into the top drawer, and lightly brushing the striations of the maple surface.

As I dusted, I riffled through the paperwork, which was filled with the kind of incomprehensible mumbo-jumbo that a divorce lawyer lives on. My heart hammered when I came across some handwritten notes about an upcoming settlement. Chad had strong handwriting, manly and brisk but with a hint of softness—just the characteristics I fell hard for on first meeting him in the bookstore. These notes hinted at a difficult divorce (as if any were easy)—he had pressed so hard writing the words "inform M's lawyer no settlement will be accepted that includes any part of the client's home, furniture, vehicles, or Irish setter dog" that the same words were indented on the paper underneath. During my brief tenure in this apartment, I'd gotten a little window into how ruthless Chad could be in negotiation. I was probably— no, certainly—better off out of the relationship. Thank God I didn't marry him and later suffer through a scalding and dispiriting divorce.

I heard a noise in the hallway and instinctively reached for the knife in my back pocket. As if a serrated steak knife would offer the least bit of protection.

The door to the apartment swung open.

"Drop your weapon and freeze where you are! Put your hands in the air!" called a fierce voice.

I let the feather duster clatter onto the desk, followed by the knife, and raised my hands above my head.

7

"When I made food, I made a tribe."
—Kim Severson

Officer Torrence crouched in a scary combat stance with his gun trained on me, looking even more substantial than he had yesterday at the station. Behind him was a stocky female cop, and just yards behind them hovered Chad. Leona, possibly the nosiest neighbor on the island, peered around his shoulder.

"Step into the center of the room with your hands on your head," said Torrence.

I shuffled forward, tears on my cheeks, knees wobbling. "I can explain everything. I work for Paradise Cleaning," I squeaked, and plunged my hand into my pocket to retrieve and show him Connie's ring of keys.

"Hands on your head!" barked the cop again.

I slapped my hand back to my skull. Chad winced in the background as my keys clanked onto his Italian limestone floor.

"She's lying," said Chad. "She's my ex-girlfriend. She could own the last bottle of Clorox on earth and I wouldn't have invited her to clean my toilets."

I could feel an unattractive line of mucus trailing down my upper lip. Even scared to death, I was bursting with a powerful and inappropriate urge to cackle—I was losing it. "The last bottle of Clorox on earth?" I lapsed into helpless giggles, crossing my legs so I wouldn't pee on the floor.

Torrence lowered his gun and blinked in sudden recognition. "Miss Mills? We're going to take you directly to the station to straighten this all out."

"It's Snow," I said. "Hayley Snow. But don't worry—a lot of people make that mistake." People over fifty who even remembered who Hayley Mills was, I thought but didn't say. I was in enough trouble without insinuating he was over the hill. "Can I bring my things with me? Connie will kill me if I lose her equipment." Connie was going to kill me anyway—and I couldn't blame her.

After a brief discussion with the cops, Chad declined to waste his time coming to the station. But he insisted that he wanted the book thrown at me. As we shuffled out into the hallway, he disappeared with a bang into his apartment. Leona pushed into the elevator for the ride to the ground floor, her big ears (which poked unattractively through her thin blond hair) soaking it all in. I said nothing, knowing every detail would be reported faithfully to the mah-jongg group that met by the pool tomorrow morning.

We adjourned to the police station, my cleaning supplies in the trunk, the police in the front seat of the cruiser and me in back again, secured behind the metal mesh. But this trip was no pseudofriendly invitation, like yesterday's had started out.

Connie was already pacing in the vestibule of the KWPD when I arrived with my double-barreled escort. Her face had turned a shade of red bordering on maroon and her eyes were a steely blue, not soft turquoise like they looked when she was happy. She was F-U-R-I-O-U-S, furious. With me.

Detective Bransford came around the corner and into the waiting area. "Thanks for coming down," he told Connie. "We'll be with you shortly."

The rest of us trooped upstairs to the room I'd visited the day before, where I was waved to the seat facing the wall clock on the near side of the table. Officer Torrence thumped the carton of supplies onto the floor and took the chair next to me. Bransford leaned against the wall, his tortoiseshell reading glasses perched on his nose and the sleeves of a white-and-blue pin-striped button-down shirt rolled up to the elbows. Underneath my anxiety and fright, and as ridiculous as it might have been, I couldn't help feeling a little quivery. Those feelings evaporated once I noticed the newspaper sticking out of his back pocket. I was too far away to read the type, but there was definitely a photo of a pie—the exact photo used to illustrate my article.

"Miss Snow, would you explain why you were trespassing in Mr. Lutz's apartment?" he asked.

Choosing the right words so I wouldn't be lying, I told him how it wasn't exactly trespassing, as I worked part-time for my friend and today was one of my shifts and Chad's apartment was the third one I'd cleaned today. I pointed to the box of supplies.

"That's the bottom line," I said. "But besides that, Chad kept some very important objects that were mine when we broke up, and I have to be honest, I did think I might find them while I was cleaning." I explained about the missing knives and the family heirloom recipes. "My mother begged me to copy them before leaving home," I added, "but I just hadn't gotten around to it. They mean so much to her—and to me—there was no reason why he should refuse to give them back. No reason at all." I tapped my fingers on the detective's desk for emphasis. Twice.

And then I told the smallest stretcher: how there'd been a misunderstanding over which apartments Connie wanted me to clean. Chad's place was definitely on today's schedule and since I knew exactly what his quirks were, I figured she would want me to do his too. I didn't think it would hurt to look around for my stuff while I was there cleaning.

"So you came to the apartment to remove some of his belongings."

"That's not fair!" I said, slapping my hand on the table. "It was my stuff and I'd asked him several times to return it." I straightened my shoulders and tried to look professional. "But the point is, I was doing a job for Connie."

"You must have been aware that this was a crime scene?"

"Look, this is Wednesday, the day he wanted his place cleaned. Obviously, if it had been marked off, I never would have gone in," I said. "But there was no signage, no yellow crime tape, nothing. Just some leftover fingerprint dust once I got inside. I would have thought Chad would be grateful that I was going to clean that mess up." Which wasn't true—I never expected Chad would be happy. I hoped he wouldn't find out.

The detective shook his head and asked one of the officers to bring Connie into the room. As she entered, I flashed her the most pitiful pleading look I could muster. She took the seat across from me.

"Miss Arp, Miss Snow says she was working for you and that's why she was in Mr. Lutz's apartment. Care to comment on that?"

She stared at me for the longest time and then nodded. "She's telling the truth. She does work for me and Chad Lutz was on today's schedule."

Phew.

The detective shifted his gaze back to me.

"Mr. Lutz said you were savaging the papers on his desk when—"

"I was dusting!" I threw my hands up in outrage—and Chad said *I* had a tendency to be histrionic—and then pointed to Officer Torrence. "Ask these guys. Didn't I have a feather duster in my hand when you burst in?"

The cop nodded. "She had the duster in one hand and the knife in the other."

Bransford stared at me again, then turned to thank Connie for coming in. "You're free to go." She picked up her carton of cleaning supplies and started for the door without looking at me.

"See you back at the ranch!" I called to her retreating form. She didn't answer.

The detective pulled the newspaper from his pocket, smoothed it out on the table, and tapped my byline. "Is there anything you'd like to tell us about this?"

"Just that it might be a long time before I have a craving for key lime pie?" I tried. No one smiled. "The timing was not fortuitous," I said. "But you can ask the editor at the paper. That piece was in the queue for almost a month—I sent it in even before Chad and I broke up. I wrote it on spec and there was no guarantee they were going to publish it, never mind when. But it's not like I wrote it last week and then got the bright idea to poison Chad's new girlfriend." I stopped to take a deep breath. "Why aren't you looking at him?"

He ignored my question. "I thought your editor was the deceased Kristen Faulkner."

"She was the co-owner of the magazine I hope to work for—a different entity from the local newspaper," I said stiffly.

He made me hash through another series of questions about my aspirations to become the food critic at Kristen's magazine and her aspirations to win my boyfriend. And I did my best to explain why these connections were unrelated to the murder.

"Where does your job stand in relation to Ms. Faulkner's death?"

"That's a darn good question. Look," I said, trying to

sound reasonable. "You've seen the security down at the Truman Annex. How would I even get into Chad's apartment to poison Kristen?"

Officer Torrence took a step forward and deposited Connie's key ring on the table, the same keys I'd dropped on the floor in Chad's place. "Exhibit one."

I should have thought of the keys before asking the damning question. I could only hope they'd believe I was too dumb to pull off a murder.

When I was finally dismissed, I found Connie had left for home without me. So I phoned Eric and asked if he could swing by to give me a ride back to the Truman Annex to collect my bike. It wouldn't have hurt me one bit to walk the twenty minutes across the island, but I needed the company.

When he pulled up in his Mustang convertible painted with scenes of sea life, I almost burst into tears—I was that relieved to see him. I slid into the passenger seat and began filling him in on the day's debacle. Sniffling all the way through, of course. I'd cried more over the past two days than I had in years. I didn't like it one bit. As we drove past Voltaire's bookstore on the corner of Eaton, my mother called.

"Hi, Mom," I said, trying to make my voice sound light and cheerful. "Eric and I were just headed out for a drink." I waved crossed fingers at Eric.

"You sound a little funny, Hayley," she said. "Are you coming down with a cold?"

This time my problems were too close to the surface to contain and I spilled out most of the story. Including the bit about the poisoned pie and my article, because what was the point of holding anything back now?

"Come home," Mom said. "I've got your room ready. I'll put fresh sheets on the bed tonight. And make some cookies. It's almost Thanksgiving anyway. Everyone's hiring holiday help. You can probably get your job back at the bookstore—just for the time being while you figure out the next step."

She'd always been big on my coming home while I identified the next direction my life should take. She'll be saying the same thing when she's ninety and I'm seventy and I'm mad at my husband because he forgot to take out the trash. If I ever snagged a husband. Prospects looked dim right now.

"I can't come home. I've been told not to leave the island," I said. Better to tell her that than try to explain what a complete loser I felt like at the moment. And how landing this food critic job and figuring out a way to stay in town was the only path I could see to resuscitate my battered self-esteem. And how I'd watched her struggle with her own self-confidence my entire life because she didn't have a focus outside of me and Dad. And food. "I'll talk to you tomorrow."

Eric double-parked alongside my scooter and shifted into neutral.

"I guess she's right," I told him. "There's not much point in hanging around here, really."

Eric just looked at me. "At what point did your mother give up on her life?" he asked finally. "Even younger than you, right?"

I started to protest. "Maybe she didn't give up. Maybe it was totally the right thing for her to become a housewife and mother. Not everyone can be a rock star. And to tell you the truth, she was a rock star as a parent." I blinked and squared my shoulders.

He gave me the inscrutable shrink look that means he believes I'm copping out.

"I know. I know. I have to figure out whether the universe is telling me to pack up and go home, or whether it's just the voice of my neurotic inner child, clamoring for a life path that's a little easier."

He busted out laughing. "That's not the way I would have put it, but you definitely got the concept."

My phone chirped again and the number from my father's office flashed onto the screen. I heaved a dramatic sigh and accepted the call.

"Hayley Catherine," he said. "Your mother informed me that you've been arrested."

"I wasn't arrested, Dad. There was a small misunderstanding and I was invited down to the police station to straighten things out." I screwed up my face and stuck my tongue out at Eric, who was rolling his eyes at my description.

"I agree with your mother this time," he continued. "It's time to come home and get a real job. You're wasting your talents and your education down there. Do you need money for a lawyer? Or a ticket home?"

I assured him that things were under control and that I'd seriously consider his input and, yes, let him know the instant I needed legal advice. Because his nightmare was having someone in his family choose an attorney based on an ad in the Yellow Pages and then end up in jail for half a lifetime after they were too dumb to use his connections. I hadn't bothered to tell him that no one my age would even think to search the Yellow Pages.

"What's up with that?" I asked Eric once I'd hung up. "Don't you find it odd that my mother would call my father and tell him all my problems when they've been divorced for years and maybe spoken five times in the interim?"

"They obviously still have a strong connection," he said. "More separation issues you could explore in therapy." He flashed a double eyebrow raise for emphasis.

I got out of the car and slammed the door. "Thanks for the lift."

Connie had already gone upstairs by the time I got home. But Ray's bicycle wasn't chained outside and the light was on in her room. Probably a good time for a heartfelt, double-knee-down, beg-for-mercy apology. I stumped up the stairs, Evinrude padding behind, and tapped on her door.

"Connie?" I tapped again when she didn't answer. "Can I come in for a sec?"

I took her "mmmrf" as a yes and opened the door. She was in bed reading a book I'd loaned her—*My Life in France* by Julia Child. I adored that book—Julia had fallen in love with Paris and French food the way I had with Key West. And it took her a long time to find the right man too, which gave me hope.

I sucked in a breath and smiled at Connie. "I'm so sorry about everything. I just want you to know that I would have cleaned that apartment so well you could have served supper to my stepmother on his floor. And that's saying something." I chuckled, longing for her to lose the disapproving expression and join me laughing. But she didn't.

"I appreciate that, but Chad already called and canceled my contract. And trust me, once the word gets out, that will be the end of any referrals from the Truman Annex."

I started to protest—no one would take his word for it, and she had plenty of references from around town—but Connie broke through.

"You should have heard his voice, Hayley. Stone cold. I worked my butt off during this trial period with him, dusting underneath every stupid artifact and spit-shining the tiles in all three bathrooms, and now it's all over." She ran her fingers through her hair, which stuck up like the stand of wheat grass I'd planted for the cat so he wouldn't miss going outside. "Counting that income, I was just about breaking even. And now?" She shrugged her shoulders and tried to hold in her tears. "I could lose the boat and everything I've worked for."

"I'm so sorry," I said. "With this whole breakup thing and now the murder—I'm just not thinking right."

"I appreciate that. But I don't think you understand how hard it is to make a living on this island. Up until a couple of months ago, before you came down, I was working nights tending bar and cleaning during the day. Most people can't afford to live here unless they do the same thing." She wiped her cheek with the sleeve of her flannel pajama top. "But I love it here, Hayley. This is my home. I don't want to have to start over somewhere else. My father isn't dying to take me in either; nor would I consider that an option." Another direct hit scored on my soft spot: I needed to grow up.

After more apologies and a stiff hug, I lugged Evinrude back downstairs and collapsed on my bed. Hard to see how things could get much worse. I'd ruined my best college friend's business and possibly our friendship along with it. I hadn't been thinking about anything but what I needed. Of course I knew how much she wanted Chad's business, and if I'd paid a little more attention, I'd have realized what my going there might cost her.

"Hayley?" Connie's voice floated down the stairs from her room, sounding worried. I bolted back up the stairs.

"What's wrong?

"Ray's friend Matthew, the one who publishes *Key Zest*? Ray happened to ask him how it was going with the food critic applications—he says your name is no longer on the list."

"Not on the list? But I definitely made the cut. They called last week to tell me."

Connie's eyes widened. "That's all I know. Sounds like you might want to stop over there tomorrow, straighten things out. If you're planning to stay on the island."

I couldn't tell if she was rooting for me to stay or leave. My phone was buzzing as I slumped back into my room. Not too many people I'd want to talk to, but I went over to look, just in case. Eric.

"Checking in to make sure you're okay."

"I've been better," I said. "I'm such a jerk. Connie's

so mad about the scene in Chad's apartment and I really can't blame her. And she just told me she heard my name's no longer on the application list for the food critic job at *Key Zest*." I lay down on my bed, curling around Evinrude's vibrating frame. "Wow, I can't even believe this. Maybe the universe is telling me it's time to get out. But I'd love to make lunch for you before I go. How about tomorrow?"

"Tomorrow's Kristen's funeral," he said.

"They won't be holding a pew for me."

"But I'm going," he said.

"You're going? Good Lord, why?"

"Her family's lived in Key West forever. I served on the board of trustees of the library with her mother for ten years. And . . ."

"And?"

"The rest is confidential. But you should come too."

"You're killing me," I said. "Why in the world would I do that?"

"Because if the cops think you're really involved with the murder, that's the last place they'd expect you to turn up."

"That's not true," I said. "The murderer always goes to the funeral. That's how they catch him."

Eric laughed. "Then consider that the other job applicants will all probably attend to pay their respects. Wanna be the only one who doesn't show? After you stop by the magazine office and straighten out the misunderstanding about your application, I'll meet you at the church."

"Sounds just awful," I groaned. "I hate funerals. And I'd feel like an imposter."

"And one more thing: Blue Heaven is catering the reception. Isn't that one of the places you wanted to review? I know your samples are due on Friday. Today's Wednesday. I'm just saying . . . I've known you since you were seven and you've never been a quitter."

"I'll think about it." I hung up, feeling nauseated at the thought of attending the funeral—what business did I have there? Didn't it make perfect sense to pack my bags and leave town? Or was I acting like a loser? I dropped off to sleep with those questions pinging in my brain.

And Lorenzo's words too: *Keep your focus.*

8

"Eat breakfast like a king, lunch like a prince, and dinner like a pauper."
—Adelle Davis

I woke up hungry—a good sign—and decided to take myself out to breakfast before I faced *Key Zest* or Kristen's funeral or any other hideous tasks. Mom always insisted this was the most important meal of the day. Except for my middle teenaged years when I'd argued with everything she suggested and subsisted on a gruel made of blender-whirred yogurt, berries, and wheat germ, I'd taken her advice to heart.

The problem: Where? There were so many breakfast choices in town; it was no easy decision. And this fact of course got me thinking about how Chad would use my enthusiastic appreciation of the plethora of local omelets as evidence of character weakness. I shut that thought down quickly and turned my attention to another potential article I could pitch to the paper: "The Early Bird Pays Off: Best Breakfasts in Key West."

I was definitely feeling feistier than yesterday—not willing to allow a computer error to torpedo my chances at a dream job. Nor to be held responsible for a murder I didn't commit. I swished on a little mascara and some blush, thinking I would stop at the *Key Zest* office after I ate and ask about the status of my application. I thumbed through last week's e-mail, found the one that had informed me I was on the short list, and printed it out.

After trying on half of the things jammed into my phone-booth-sized closet, I chose a sleeveless black swing dress that looked professional, would fit in at a funeral, and didn't need ironing—but also made the most of my curves. In the bathroom, I brushed my hair and for once the curls sprang out sweetly and framed my face as if I'd planned the whole thing. Like maybe I finally had that cute Hayley Mills thing going. Sometimes the best way to summon your nerve was to dress the part—or so my mother would say. So I added my black sequined high-top sneakers and headed out the door.

Miss Gloria was watering the potted plants on her deck, her black cat sunning on a faded canvas chair.

"Don't you look pretty!"

I nodded modestly. "Thanks. I'm going to a job interview, but first, breakfast."

She perked right up. For a skinny little lady whom I've never seen handling any edibles other than cat food, she loved to talk about eating. I liked to drop off little bags of groceries with items I knew she wouldn't buy for herself when I could. And I've offered to take her out to eat a few times, but so far she hasn't accepted.

"How about Pepe's?" she asked. "They have the most wonderful pancakes. And omelets. And Bloody Marys too." She flashed a mischievous smile.

"Early for that!" I said, strapping on my helmet and waving good-bye. Once on my scooter, I tucked the hem of my dress firmly under my thighs, dropped the bike off its kickstand, and started the engine. Pepe's it would be. I drove over the bridge with its grand view of Charter Boat Row, up Palm Avenue to Eaton and then right to Caroline. "'There's a woman gone crazy on Caroline Street,'" I hummed as I approached the restaurant. One of Jimmy Buffett's best. And appropriate for the day and the setting.

I settled at a table on the patio underneath a trellis twined with an enormous bougainvillea studded with pink blossoms. A small flock of brown birds twittered on the branches. One of the birds swooped down to the other chair at my table and sang at the top of his lungs, his little neck puffing with effort.

"Shoo, you!" said a waitress, flapping her order pad at the bird and then smiling at me. "What can I get for you?"

After ordering a mild green chili and Monterey Jack omelet, with a rasher of bacon (extra crispy), and an assortment of baked goods on the side, I took out my phone and began to rough out an introduction. Since I text as fast as the next guy can write, it seemed like the perfect cover for a food critic not wishing to draw attention to herself. I would look like just one more obsessed young person who couldn't part with her smartphone.

One of the great joys of vacation is breaking away from home-based habits. Instead of downing the same healthy but boring bran cereal and fruit, why not treat yourself to a full breakfast out? Luckily, Key West offers tons of choices. Pepe's, snuggled into a quiet section of Caroline Street, claims to be the oldest restaurant on the island—and frankly, the booths inside look it! This is not the setting for a diner who prefers upscale elegance, but it's chockablock with home-style food and local color. Make a beeline for the patio and enjoy people (and dog and bird) watching while you wait.

When my breakfast was delivered, I snapped a photo of the plate, and then put the phone away and dug in. At the table next to me, two men in wrinkled shorts and sandals discussed the vagaries of the real estate market and then segued to bonefishing. How could I not love this place? I no longer had the excuse of Chad to stay on the island, but by now I was hooked. Where else would I find this funny combination of locals ("conchs" they called themselves, pronounced with a *k* sound, not a *ch* as in Chad), rich people, homeless people, gays, cruise ship escapees on day passes, and people like me who love the weather, the water, the lack of pretense? Every day the local paper featured a "citizen of the day" who waxed on about the joys of living on this island. And the editor never ran out of prospects.

This was so not New Jersey. The thought of having to pack up my meager belongings and crawl home was utterly depressing. November in Berkeley Heights was a dreary, dreary proposition. The jaunty colors of autumn would have faded, leaving dim sun and plummeting temperatures. Even the birds would be leaving.

So once I'd finished my food and taken a few more notes about the fresh-squeezed OJ, the crusty wholegrain toast, and the omelet oozing cheese, I used that dread to force myself away from a third cup of coffee and on to the offices of *Key Zest*. The funeral wouldn't start until eleven, so surely someone would be working.

On my way from Caroline to Southard Street, I tried to figure out my approach. Direct would be best, I thought. I practiced: "Good morning, I've come to check on the status of my application for the food critic position."

But should I mention Kristen's death to the magazine staff? Maybe they were truly sad. Wouldn't it be callous not to bring it up? Though acting apologetic seemed like the wrong tack altogether since I hadn't murdered the woman. Expressing dismay and sorrow? Disingenuous. Surely everyone at the office would have heard about the brouhaha with Chad. Who would believe I thought anything but "she got what she deserved"? Hopefully they wouldn't know about my trips to the KWPD, but this being a small island, news flashed faster than crème fraîche went sour in the heat. The best I could do was approach the desk with an expression of subdued regret.

I parked behind Preferred Properties Real Estate and hiked up to the second floor. After running my fingers through my curls to fluff up the helmet hair, I tapped on the door and stepped inside. The *Key Zest* office looked as though someone had bought out the stock of Tommy Bahama products—all weathered wicker with faux tropical foliage upholstery and more fake foliage settled in the corners of the room and on the receptionist's desk. "Adrienne Kamen," the nameplate on her desktop said. Even she wore a silky yellow shirt studded with palm trees.

"Can I help you?" she asked without looking away from her computer. Like Evinrude, she seemed to be able to sense a change in the atmosphere without seeing it directly.

"I'm sorry to be a bother," I said, instantly kicking myself for sounding weak. "I'm Hayley Snow, one of the applicants for the food critic position? I was wondering if the deadline is still Friday?"

"Yes," she said, glancing up briefly, then dropping her gaze back to her screen and resuming a spurt of furious typing.

Another mental kick for asking a question that could be brushed aside like so many bread crumbs. "Is Wally Beile in?" I asked, hoping I'd pronounced the name right. Kristen's co-owner, who now held my future in his hands. I hadn't met him personally, but I had certainly seen his name on the masthead and his picture on the website. He looked one heck of a lot cheerier than Kristen ever had. "I'd just love one minute of his time."

She shrugged her thin shoulders and stepped away from her computer into a back room. I heard the rumbling of a man's voice and then her voice answering. She reappeared.

"Go ahead in. And by the way, I love your shoes."

"Thanks," I said, pointing one sequin-sneakered foot, grateful for any connection.

Wally turned out to be a thirtyish man with heavy black glasses and wiry brown hair—and the same yellow shirt as the receptionist. Cute, if you liked a nerdy style. He reminded me the tiniest bit of Eric, which was a good thing.

I pasted on my most authentic and regretful smile. "I'm so sorry about Kristen, er, Ms. Faulkner." Just what I'd told myself not to say.

"Thank you."

I wished I'd done some research on what their relationship had been like. Had he been one of Kristen's fans? Or was her passing a great, if unexpressed, relief? And then, too late, I realized I shouldn't tell him that I knew I'd been dropped from the list of applicants. What to say instead?

"I'm one of the applicants for your food critic job. I know this is a tough time to ask, but since the deadline is approaching and I was riding by anyway . . ."

My voice trailed off to a whisper and I could see I was losing him. A busy guy with too much to do and a dead coworker did not need a pathetic job applicant sucking up his time. Flashing on the empty bedroom in my mother's house and how much I would loathe returning to that life, I pumped myself back up.

"I love your magazine and I want this job more than anything. I just stopped by to say you'll have my articles in your in-box by Friday, as promised. Tomorrow, right? I knew that." I started backing toward the door.

He finally cracked a grin. "What's your name again?"

"Hayley," I said. "Hayley Snow. Hayley as in Mills. Snow, like the weather."

He smiled again and began to thumb through a stack of files on his desk; then, with a puzzled look on his face, swiveled around to his computer and tapped on the keys.

"Oddly enough, I have an e-mail in my spam folder from Kristen that came in last weekend stating that you had withdrawn your application."

"Oh gosh," I said, feeling that cheese omelet roil in my stomach. "That's so not true. It must be a misunderstanding." I leaned forward to try to get a look at his screen, and jerked back just as quickly so as not to appear pushy. "I made the first cut. At the beginning of last week, I got that news and was told my samples had to be in by Monday. And then, as I'm sure you know, the deadline was changed to Friday. Tomorrow." I dug around in my purse for the printout, feeling tears push their way past my sinuses—so not the right impression for a potential employer. "I am dead serious about wanting this job. Can I fill out a new packet? My articles are written—I have to go over them one more time to be sure there aren't any typos. But I'm so, so serious—"

He held his hands up and spoke in a soothing voice—the kind I'd used with my mother when she was winding herself up and almost ready to blast off. "Take a breath, Hayley, as in Mills. Why don't you have a seat and I'll look into this a little further. Do you need a glass of water? A Xanax, maybe?"

"I'm fine, really," I said, flashing a weak smile and

sinking into the wicker chair against the wall. I smoothed my black dress over my thighs, started to crack my knuckles, then clenched my hands in my lap. If this fell through, and Connie didn't want to employ me anymore—and let's face it, why would she with the mess I'd made?—it was hard to see how I could stay in town. Eric and Bill's place was too small for long-term guests, and besides, he was allergic to cats and he needed his space after all those hours of listening to his therapy customers. A neurotic, desperate roommate would not be an asset.

Wally scrolled through several more screens of e-mails. When he turned back to face me, his expression was carefully neutral. "Hayley. I should have remembered the name. But ever since we heard the news about the murder, it's been pure chaos here. I hardly remember my own name. But I think I understand exactly why your file disappeared."

"Oh my gosh," I said. "What happened?"

"Kristen and I had this discussion a while back. She said she couldn't work with you—there was a conflict of interest. Having to do with a man, I believe?"

I nodded sheepishly.

"She was an excellent businesswoman, except for a few blind spots. You being one of them."

"Were you her boss or the other way around?" I didn't mean to insult him, but why would he allow her to act so unprofessional?

"We were equally invested," he said sternly. "She was to work with Matthew, the publisher, on advertising and distribution, and I was the editor. I told her I couldn't allow her personal affairs to override our business decisions. Let the best applicant rise to the top. Period." He glanced back at the computer. "Then she went right ahead and deleted your file and told me you'd withdrawn."

"Wow." I wiped a few beads of sweat off my upper lip. "Any way I can get back in the queue?"

9

"It's important to begin a search on a full stomach."

—Henry Bromel

By the time I'd finished filling out the paperwork for the second time—thanks so much to Kristen for expunging my stuff from their records—I was almost late for the funeral. A half hour earlier, my new best friend Wally had changed into a button-down shirt and tie and left me with the thin-shouldered receptionist. Now, with the crush of vehicles, scooters, and bicycles on the street, I had to circle the block three times, finally easing into an alley six blocks from the church and sprinting over.

St. Paul's was a large, white stucco edifice right on the corner of Duval Street and Eaton. Though the doors were almost always open to the public, I'd yet to set foot in it. Since religion was one of my parents' battlegrounds, I felt anxious in churches under the best of circumstances. Raised by nonpracticing Quakers, my father detested what he called the pompous blah, blah, blah of organized religion. My mother came from a Presbyterian family (God's frozen people, per my father), and she insisted I attend Sunday services until I attained that pinnacle of teenage surliness where letting me sleep in reduced the number of hours we were fighting. In any case, questions of the great hereafter positively terrorized me, and that was one more good reason to frequent Lorenzo the fortune-teller. I found his definiteness reassuring: He seemed to have a better grip on the distant future than most religious leaders.

And funerals, of course, were the worst church services of all—the somberness of the ministers and the clear fact that even they don't exactly know where we're all headed crescendoed at a funeral. The questions I'd swept under the rug about what's next, if anything, couldn't help but knife to the surface of my consciousness.

I'd attended services for both of my grandmothers in the past five years, and those were brutal. I could only imagine that an unexpected funeral for a murdered young woman would raise even more horribly raw feelings. And besides all that, I didn't really belong here. I had barely known Kristen and what I did know, I didn't like. On the other hand, the pews were packed with mourners. Had Kristen been that popular, or was this evidence of her family's social standing on the island?

I grabbed a tissue from the box on a black lacquered table in the narthex just in case and pressed against the back wall, scanning the attendees for Eric. This was not the kind of event I wanted to face alone.

The crowd seemed divided into about half casually

dressed Key West types, and the rest more sophisticated sorts I guessed had driven down from Miami. Henrietta Stentzel and a couple of other local foodies were camped out in the second to last row, two of them wearing chef's clogs along with their funeral attire. Probably due at work right after the service. I shifted over a few feet to try to listen to them, but the organ pretty much drowned out their conversation. Then I noticed the three policemen at the far left of the sanctuary, including Bransford, the detective with the cleft chin. He caught my gaze for an instant, having clearly taken note of my entrance.

Just then a woman who looked a frightening amount like Kristen brushed by me, her hand clamped on the elbow of a white-haired lady in a black silk suit and old-fashioned pumps. These had to be Kristen's relatives—the likeness was too distinctive. The younger woman had Kristen's white-blond hair—the kind you simply couldn't get in a salon—and they both had long, thin noses and the same cold brown eyes. Even the perfume the young woman was wearing smelled like Kristen. The identical scent I'd noticed as I straightened Chad's bedclothes in the apartment yesterday. Something expensive, flowery, and—to me—nauseating.

The older woman shuffled up the aisle to the front pew, bent over like this service was more than she would be able to stand. I tried to tell myself maybe her posture wasn't a result of her emotional pain, but rather a minor case of dowager's hump. But tears sprang to my eyes anyway. I knew how my mother would be feeling if it were me in that coffin.

Eric and his partner, Bill, came up beside me. We exchanged hugs and filed into a pew across the aisle from the chefs. I craned my neck searching for Chad. How do you handle funeral etiquette with a relatively new lover's family? I very much doubted he'd have been invited to sit with them, but what did I know? More to the point, how would I handle Kristen's family? Staying as far away as possible seemed like the best plan. Show my respect, sample the food, all while acting subdued and innocent. And get the heck out.

Just before the service began, Chad slid into a seat several rows ahead of us, close enough that I couldn't help seeing how his starched white collar pressed into his skin. He'd had a haircut since yesterday. I tried to stop myself from imagining brushing my fingers along the soft stubble that faded into the nape of his neck. This kind of unwelcome leftover detail from our physical relationship had been filling my head for the past few weeks, like it or not. Especially when I was stressed, and that seemed like all the time lately. Probably I should be thinking less about what went wrong in the relationship and more about why I'd made such a lousy choice to begin with.

The organist launched into "All Things Bright and Beautiful" and the congregation stood and straggled through the hymn. The sniffling had already started as a man in a black robe took his place at the podium. "In John 16, verse 22, the Bible tells us: 'So you have pain now; but I will see you again, and your hearts will rejoice, and no one will take your joy from you.' "

He peered over his reading glasses to Kristen's family and I zoned out, pushing my attention to the contrast of the dark wood ceiling against the whitewashed walls. The stained-glass windows running the length of the pews had been swiveled open to catch a bit of breeze, but it still felt hot and sticky in the sanctuary. I squinted to read the text at the base of the window closest to me: "Donated by the Faulkner family." Of course.

Troubled hearts . . . God's love . . . lamb of God . . . The words floated toward me from the pulpit and my mind veered away again from the service and the dreaded closed coffin and back to the congregation.

Questions caromed through my brain. Why wasn't Kristen in an open coffin? Had the poison done something awful to her features? Was the person who killed Kristen in attendance? And why was she killed? How seriously did the police consider me a suspect? Ridiculous! They couldn't be serious. I couldn't wait for all this to be over.

Then the minister invited Kristen's sister to speak and my mind snapped back to attention. The blond woman I'd seen earlier mounted the steps, approached the podium, and angled the microphone closer to her lips.

"My name is Ava Faulkner. I'm Kristen's older sister." She drew a long breath and steadied her voice. "I've always heard that the oldest child is the most driven. But Kristen"—her lips curved into a rueful smile—"Kristen kicked my butt."

I chuckled nervously like most of the rest of the congregation. Who said "butt" during a eulogy? She was upset, that was all.

"It started in grade school," Ava continued. "Kristen brought home honors in first grade while I was in second. What kind of teacher even gives honors to first graders? Mrs. Randolph, that's who. She didn't seem to realize that she was setting us up for a lifetime of rivalry. Not that Daddy hadn't already done a damn good job of that." She flashed a mirthless smile.

"Kristen was just better at things than most people. She was an amazing businesswoman. She saw the potential for profit in places most people would never consider looking. And then she went after it."

Ava closed her eyes for a moment and pressed two pink-tipped fingers against her forehead. She blinked her eyes open.

"Some of you probably don't know that I dated Kristen's boyfriend briefly before her." Her gaze searched the audience until it landed on Chad. The back of his neck flushed red, red, red. The people sitting near him murmured and rustled.

"Don't worry—they were a much better match than he and I were. Guppies shouldn't swim with piranhas." She smiled. "But don't get the wrong idea. It's not that Kristen didn't see other people; it's that she saw her own goals so clearly.

"And this will always be our sorrow. Kristen had some amazing things to offer the world, but especially this adorable and provincial little community. Her magazine project was going to be brilliant. If she'd had the chance, she would have brought the style in this town to a new level. And her restaurant on Easter Island would have set a benchmark for fine cuisine. And you all know what she looked like—she was gorgeous. The world lost some *zest* when we lost Kristen.

"And whoever did this"—she glared over the pews—"to do it with key lime pie, the one dessert she could never resist. That was low."

I gulped and held myself very still, afraid to see whether anyone was looking at me. Eric took my right hand and squeezed gently. "Breathe," he whispered.

I bolted off the pew as the organist launched into the postlude, then snuck down the side aisle and out the back door, feeling desperate for a glass of *something*. Now I really wished I hadn't come at all. But damned if I was going to sit through all that and not get what I'd come for. I'd grab a drink, pay my respects, check out the food, and get the heck out. All while trying to appear normal.

The reception had been set up in the open-air courtyard connected to the church. Slinking around the people who'd begun to queue up to offer their condolences to Kristen's family, I made my way to the beverage and food tables. Sustenance first.

After snagging a glass of Prosecco, I filled a plate with nibbles—a mini choux pastry filled with crabmeat, an adorable miniature mushroom quiche, two shrimp cooked to just the right translucence and served with a caper-studded roulade sauce, and a small cup of spicy gumbo. I'd eaten at the Blue Heaven restaurant once last week and I had planned to make another visit before I finished writing my review, but life had gone haywire in the meantime. Luckily, this plateful gave me a chance to try a wide smattering of their offerings. Not that I was the least bit hungry after the breakfast at Pepe's, but I could sample enough to get the flavors and bang out the review.

Though the closer I looked, the less the food resembled what I would expect from Blue Heaven—it was fancy to the point of being fussy. I loaded a few more things on my plate, then retreated to a back wall and began to nibble. I swallowed a half spoonful of gumbo, which gave my mouth quite a spectacular jolt. I tasted again, slid my smartphone out of my purse, and tapped quickly:

Cajun gumbo takes many forms, but it almost always starts with the holy trinity of vegetables: onions, celery, and green peppers. Blue Heaven carries this balance off just right.

The reception was now mobbed with mourners who rushed the bar and flocked around the tables of hors d'oeuvres. One woman's voice floated above the din.

"I've never heard a eulogy quite like that."

"Ava knows how to pick her moments," a second voice said. "Made me think I'm lucky I don't have any siblings."

"I adore mine," said the first. "Do you think they'll still open the restaurant?"

"They've put a ton of money into the planning already. But if they don't get it going soon, I know for sure Robert isn't going to hang around town catering funeral receptions."

Now the voice sounded familiar. Henri Stentzel,

dressed in flowing black, her dark curls pulled into a ponytail. Her friend Porter, one of the regular sous-chefs at Seven Fish restaurant, was wearing the chef's clogs I'd noticed earlier.

"Working at a funeral reception?" she asked, grinning when she caught my eye.

"They say a food critic's job is never finished," said Henri. I choked down the crabmeat puff I'd bitten into and whirled around to see who might have been listening, certain I looked guilty.

"I'm not— I didn't—" The right words eluded me. First of all, I didn't have the job. And second, no one was supposed to know anything about my application. And third, was it blatantly disrespectful to be using the funeral food as fodder for my reviews? Definitely. Acutely embarrassed, a rush of heat burned my cheeks.

"We're only teasing," said Henri, patting me on the back. "I ran into Adrienne from *Key Zest* outside and she mentioned you were auditioning. Did you try the choux pastry? And seriously, how would you rate this spread if you were writing it up?"

Now I felt really ill. What else had Adrienne spilled to them?

"Don't pay any attention to her," Porter whispered.

Henri smiled. "Rumor has it that you've been questioned by the cops about Kristen's death. Is that right?"

I felt an even harder jolt to the gut and my breakfast omelet somersaulted and threatened to resurface along with the spicy gumbo.

"They're just fishing because they can't seem to find any suspects," I answered, exchanging my empty Prosecco glass for a second full flute from the tray of a passing waiter and trying to think how to deflect them away from my situation. "Wasn't that the saddest service? And what a big crowd!" My voice cracked and I took a slug of the drink.

The two women exchanged glances and Henri shrugged. "They say money buys friends. For a while. Oh look. There's Rhonda! Will you excuse me? And good luck with the job." She squeezed my arm and hurried off.

I narrowed my eyes, sipped the wine, and turned back to Porter. "She wasn't a big Kristen fan, was she?"

Porter smoothed her pale hair back into its braid. She narrowed her gray eyes and studied me for a moment. She started to say something, stopped, and then started again. "They had a long history. The restaurant business in south Florida is like a village. I won't say more, but Kristen made Henri look like the village idiot."

"But—"

"But much as any one of us in the food service business may have disliked her, we certainly wouldn't have killed her," she added briskly. "Any more than you would have. I'm just saying she made few friends up in Miami and she was working hard at killing the possibilities here."

"In what way?" I asked before she could turn away, thinking Eric would be proud of that open-ended question.

"You'll hear about it if you end up working for the *Zest*. And if you were wondering why this food doesn't taste like Blue Heaven, that's because it isn't. Kristen's sister fired them yesterday. This food has been prepared by the chef who was going to cook at the new restaurant on Easter Island."

The first I'd heard of this project was in Ava's eulogy. As far as I knew, that little island, a stone's throw from Mallory Square, had nothing on it but pine trees. It was surrounded by small sailboats whose owners couldn't afford an apartment or home in Key West. I knew, because I'd looked into a mooring myself. I only lacked the boat to tie to it. Besides that, I couldn't figure out how I'd handle the bathroom thing.

"Is that still going forward?" I asked.

Just then Chad appeared, a glass in his hand and a grim look on his face. I'd have hoped he might have softened a little from the ugliness of yesterday.

"Would you excuse us, Porter?" he asked. Porter made a face and quickly backed away.

"Why are you here?" he growled. "Haven't you done enough?"

"I'm sorry for their loss." I tipped my chin to indicate Kristen's family. Under the church roof's overhang, out of the sun, Ava helped her mother into a chair and then folded her fingers around a glass of wine.

"As if you cared one whit about them," he said. "You shouldn't be here."

"I'm not the one who was singled out as a jerk in the eulogy," I huffed, draining the second glass of Prosecco. "You take what you want until you're satisfied and then you just throw it away."

He sneered. "You're so naive, Hayley."

"And while we're on that subject, there was no reason

you had to fire Connie. She didn't send me over to clean your place—I did that on my own."

His newly shaved neck reddened again. "Hayley, I need to be able to rely on the people I employ, not worry about whether they'll give my apartment keys to people I don't trust."

"And I would never have even considered setting foot in your stinking apartment if you hadn't refused to give me my stuff. My grandmother's recipes are gone—can't you think for a minute how that feels? They were in *her handwriting*! And my best knife, and the serrated set I bought with my graduation money. Except for the one you were using to break down boxes. Why would you keep any of that stuff? You don't even cook!"

"I didn't keep it—it's in the Dumpster," he said.

As our voices rose, the people around us turned to look. Across the room, I noticed Detective Bransford staring at me. I realized right away that it wasn't the black swing dress, which fell a couple inches above my knees and made my legs look longer than they actually were, that caught his attention. Or the sparkly shoes or any Hayley Mills thing I had imagined earlier. It was me fighting with my ex at a funeral reception, possibly appearing guilty—and if not guilty, certainly out of control—to the trained eye.

Eric materialized from behind two gawking matrons in black suits, grabbed my arm, and offered a perfunctory smile to Chad. "I have someone you must meet, Hayley." He put my empty plate on a card table and dragged me away through the crowd of chatting mourners to the other side of the room.

"Who?" I asked.

"No one." He tapped my head with his knuckles and gave a tight smile. "I just rescued you from making an awful scene. And why waste one more minute talking to that blockhead?"

Eric's friend Bill approached us with an arm around a sobbing woman whom I vaguely recognized from somewhere.

"Meredith is having a tough time today," Bill whispered. "I told her you see a lot of grief and that it's perfectly normal to let your feelings out." He mouthed "help" in Eric's direction as the woman sobbed into his lapel.

"You must have been a dear friend of Kristen's," Eric said. "Come, I saw a bench in the hallway. Let's go have a chat. Hayley here was on her way out."

He glared at me and pointed to the door.

10

"Every pastry has the potential of making someone perfectly happy, of momentarily stripping them of adult worries and baggage."

—Gesine Bullock-Prado

I staggered away from the reception, my head thrumming with a jumble of feelings. I tackled the simplest problem: A food critic had to lay low in the local restaurant business. You simply couldn't give a fair review if the chef was sending out a parade of special taste sensations that ordinary diners don't ever experience. I hadn't given enough thought to how I would handle having friends in this business and how their feelings and their lives could be impacted by what I wrote. I flashed on the case of the chef who committed suicide after he lost his Michelin star. That event struck fear into the heart of even the coldest critic—I couldn't finish reading the article.

Maybe it was time to visit Lorenzo for another tarot card reading. His services weren't in my budget for more than once a week, but this had been an especially stressful string of days. I could use some external direction from an uninvolved party. No one was less involved than Lorenzo, who only weighed in if he had a twenty-dollar bill tucked into his pocket. Mallory Square was not exactly a direct route home, but not a major detour either. The Sunset Celebration participants should be just setting up, and I was willing to bet he'd agree to an early reading.

When I reached the main square, many of the performers had marked off rectangular spaces of territory with ropes laid out on the cement and were unloading the tools of their trade—knives and fire wands for the fire-eating juggler, musical instruments for the one-man band, and cages of restless felines for Dominique the cat man. A few tourists were lined up at the trolley bar in front of the Westin. Tony, the homeless cowboy I'd seen at Higgs Beach the other day, was lounging on the cement seawall, smoking cigarettes and drinking beer with several other men. I called out hello as I hurried by.

Fifty yards past them, Lorenzo was spreading a black cloth on his card table, his robe and hat folded neatly in a pile behind him. "Greetings," he said with a smile.

"I know I'm early. But could you squeeze me in for a quick one?" I sank into his chair without waiting for an answer and slapped my twenty on the table.

"For you, always," he said and offered me the witch

hazel spritzer and then the deck. I shuffled and cut the cards. He dealt them out and began to study the arrangement. And I tried to concentrate so I'd remember later exactly what he'd said. Sometimes the meaning of the reading didn't become clear until well after I'd left his table.

"You've experienced lots of struggle in the past." He straightened the corner of the Hermit card—a sad, old man carrying a lamp—and sighed. "Might you have regrets? But you must look inside yourself for answers. Your inner guide should lead you to the light." He ran a finger over his waxed mustache, smoothing it into a neat curve.

I ground my teeth, hoping he could come up with something that didn't sound like a syndicated horoscope in the *Key West Citizen*.

"Hmmm—the Emperor again. There's a strong man who's a pain in your life—perhaps he's keeping you from moving on? And with him comes a sense of recklessness. Has there been a divorce? Did he marry for money?"

He looked up to see if I was following. I nodded: Yes, Chad was a strong man. And yes he was a pain. And yes, yes, yes, there were nothing but divorces connected to him. He did divorce for a living—a very good living, at that. But as far as I knew, he'd never been married. And I didn't need a set of tarot cards to explain why.

"There is a child invited on a short trip. They should definitely go." Lorenzo lined up the edges of two of the cards and continued to study them. "You have an opportunity to go on a big trip—you should definitely go."

I sighed. Lorenzo didn't seem to be on his game tonight. Maybe he'd used up his psychic powers for the week. But this was not what I was spending my money for. Not a chance I'd be going on vacation anytime soon. I tapped my fingers on the table and waited, trying not to glare at him.

"There may be a small accident, but don't worry—nothing serious." He pointed to the Fool card. "There are new beginnings and surprises, but you must look before you leap."

Now I couldn't keep my exasperation from showing. "Isn't there anything about a murder?"

His eyes widened, but he composed himself quickly. "Ah. Not here. Though I did read about the incident in the paper. Was she a friend of yours?"

"Not mine. A friend of the man who's a pain." I pointed at the Emperor card.

He smiled as he turned over one last card, and then the smile faded. The brick tower, with flames bursting from its windows.

"There will be chaos. Do be careful. And remember what I said last time about keeping your focus."

I hurried off through the gaggles of tourists, goose bumps rising on my arms and legs, reviewing Lorenzo's words. The emperor—Chad—had behaved especially boorishly over the past few days. Which forced me to ask, for the thousandth time: What in the world had I seen in him? And why did I leave my home to live with him, when I barely knew him?

The second question was a little easier to answer: I

was looking for a way out of my life in New Jersey. Two point five years back in my mother's nest when I was a full-grown woman, not a fledgling, were two years too many. And, Chad or no Chad, the fact that Connie and Eric both lived in Key West made the move irresistible. His invitation had just given me the courage to fly.

The November chill was closing in as the sun dropped over the horizon. I felt worn down and a little jumpy as I reviewed the rest of my reading. Recklessness, a small accident, and chaos.

Eric disapproved of my fortune-teller addiction. He'd even explained to me why fortune-tellers' predictions appeared to come true: Easy mark visits charlatan. Charlatan predicts trouble in the form of a blue truck. Easy mark scans the horizon until that blue truck appears. Fortune-teller's powers confirmed.

"A hundred red vehicles might pass by, but you'd only see the blue one," he explained.

"And so what?" I remembered asking. But I was beginning to understand that Chad might have been the blue truck. And I should have let him drive on by.

I fired up my bike, settled my feet onto the footrest, and decided to make another quick stop before heading home. It was never a good idea to face an angry roommate empty-handed. Not that Connie was angry exactly; more like horribly disappointed. Which, in my mother's hands, had always felt like a bigger weapon than anger. As I considered which shops might be open, I remembered the hysterical girl who'd been comforted by Eric as I left the funeral. She worked at Cole's Peace. With any luck, she'd be there now and I could ask her some questions, killing two birds with one stone. From the looks of her distress, she must have known Kristen well. Maybe she'd have some insight into her possible enemies.

Cole's Peace Bakery was located almost at the end of Eaton Street just before it curved into Palm Avenue and roared past Connie's marina. As usual, Eaton was clogged with trucks belching diesel and old cars full of day workers heading off the island during our scaled-down version of rush hour. The stream of oncoming traffic finally broke and I veered across the road into the parking lot and left my scooter near a crooked and rusty bike rack.

I'd discovered Cole's Peace bread the first time Chad took me out to dinner at Sarabeth's, a branch of the original restaurant in New York City. I had devoured every crumb in the breadbasket and almost but not quite ruined my appetite for dinner. I've been a stalwart fan ever since.

The tiny artisanal bakery and sandwich shop was attached to the greatest restaurant supply store in the southeast. That could be an exaggeration, but I doubted it. Where else could I have found the cherry pitter my mother craved? Or the good grips corn stripper I planned to use every day in corn season? Or the wooden human head knife holder that I'd given to Chad as a funny housewarming gift? While I was there, I'd stop in and price replacement of the knives that Chad had refused to return. Not that I had the money to buy anything right now, or my own kitchen to put anything in, but someday . . .

I grabbed my backpack and yanked on the kitchen store's door. Closed. I hurried into Cole's. Reduced to swooning by the scent of baking bread, I chose two rectangular loaves—a hearty multigrain and a breakfast bread studded with chunks of orange mango. For good measure, I added a bag of salty bagel chips and one of their homemade cheese balls. How could Connie not soften when I came in with this loot?

"We're about to close up," said the woman behind the cash register. "Can I get you anything else?"

I pulled myself away from the other tempting delicacies in the cooler and brought my selections to the counter. This was definitely the same woman whom I'd left sobbing in Eric's arms just an hour earlier. Meredith, Bill had called her. The skin around her eyes had the puffy look of a serious cry. I deposited my stuff next to the cash register.

"Rough day," I said with a tentative smile.

Her eyebrows creased in surprise and then she looked leery.

"I saw you at the funeral," I explained quickly. "You're Meredith, right?"

She gave an almost imperceptible nod. "I take it you were there too."

"I'm sorry for your loss," I tried, hoping she'd tell me how she knew Kristen. If she turned out to be chatty, I'd ask more. Obviously. And if she asked me how I knew the victim, I'd have to rely on some vague explanation of how small the food world is in Key West.

"Thanks. That's twenty dollars and fourteen cents."

I'd have to be more direct. "I'm Hayley Snow," I said, putting my money on the counter and then reaching out to offer my hand. "Were you friends with Kristen?"

"We met in Miami years ago," she said with a tepid squeeze back.

Which honestly made it sound like it didn't matter too much to her one way or the other whether Kristen was dead. So now I wondered if death in the larger sense of the word had sent her into a Niagara Falls' worth of tears. Or was she possibly one of Eric's patients—the kind that gets so attached to him that a sighting of him in the real world reduces them to gelatin?

"Eric's a great guy," I tried next. "And an excellent psychologist. I'd go to him myself if we weren't old friends from way back." I barked a short laugh. "And don't think I haven't tried to talk him out of holding that line."

She smiled politely, as if she had no idea what I was blathering on about. And maybe she didn't. Maybe she wasn't his patient after all, but I'd certainly never find out from him. Probably not her either, the way this one-sided conversation was going. But it got me wandering down another blind thought alley: What was the confidential connection that had brought *Eric* to that funeral?

I tried one last tack. "It's spooky that they haven't solved the murder yet, don't you think?"

"It's only a matter of time," she said firmly. "What have you heard?"

"Not all that much," I admitted. "Can you think of

anyone from her Miami days who might have had it in for her?"

She shook her head. "These things are always about money. And right now, there's no bigger pot than Easter Island."

11

"I suppose there are people who can pass up free guacamole, but they're either allergic to avocado or too joyless to live."

—Frank Bruni

As I hiked down the dock with my packages, I spotted Connie and Ray lounging on our houseboat's top deck, drinking wine. Connie had switched on the white lights that outlined the roof of the boat and they glittered jauntily in the gathering dusk.

"I come bearing gifts!" I called up, my voice wobbling with the hopefulness of a wagging tail on a bad dog.

"Get yourself a glass of wine and come join us," said Connie. "Better bring a sweater."

Encouraged by her friendliness, I went into the galley, arranged the cheese ball and bagel chips on a pretty flowered plate, and poured myself a half glass of white wine. It was almost six o'clock after all, and my earlier

Prosecco buzz had definitely worn off. Not that I'd really enjoyed it anyway, between the stress of the funeral, the fight with Chad, and another disturbing reading from Lorenzo. I hiked up the spiraled stairs to the second floor, Evinrude trotting behind me. He liked happy hour as much as the next cat.

"What a day," I said as I came out of Connie's bedroom onto the deck. I slid the snacks onto a small table between my friends and collapsed into a beach chair across from them. The cat hopped onto my lap and I fed him a tiny taste of cheese. He purred with pleasure. I waved at the Renharts who were out on their top deck too, enjoying Budweiser from cans and Lay's potato chips from an oversized bag.

"Beautiful night," I called over to the next boat.

"Paradise," said Mr. Renhart, as he popped the top on a tall can of beer and dropped his hand onto his wife's thigh.

"I'm sorry I was hard on you last night," Connie said in a soft voice. "Somehow this will all work out." She leaned over and squeezed my wrist. "Did you go to Kristen's funeral?"

"Me and most of the citizens of Key West and Miami," I said, lowering my voice so I wouldn't blast my gossip to the neighbors. "I can't quite figure out why she was so popular."

"Her family's lived here forever," said Ray. "They own a ton of property, including Easter Island and half of Sunset Key."

Sunset Key is another small island just off the harbor, this one fully developed and inhabited by wealthy folks.

This here-but-not-here arrangement gives them the full benefit of the climate and allows an occasional escape into the town's funky party scene, without requiring a full commitment. Half of Sunset Key had to add up to big, big bucks.

"The clerk in Cole's Peace thinks Easter Island was behind the murder," I said. "I suppose it would be worth a ton too, if you had the money to develop it."

"Absolutely," Ray said. "And a lot of residents are not in favor of it."

"Oh!" I said, turning to face Ray. "I'd almost forgotten. I ran by *Key Zest* this morning and thank God I did. Kristen had erased me from the list of job applicants. She told Wally—the editor—that I'd withdrawn my application. So I really, really appreciate your tip."

"You're welcome," said Ray. "A shot from the grave."

"That's so mean-spirited," Connie said. "You'd think you stole her boyfriend, not the other way around."

"Which reminds me of something else. Kristen's sister, Ava, gave the most appalling eulogy. One of the many things she said was that Chad had hooked up with her briefly before he went out with Kristen."

"You've got to be kidding!" said Connie.

"How did he ever have time to fit her in? Where did Chad even meet her?" Ray asked. He spread a chunk of cheese ball onto a bagel crisp and leaned back into his chair. "Did he know her before he got together with you? I can't imagine moving that quickly." He grinned at Connie. "It takes me a while to warm up to a woman."

"It takes a while for you to figure out when a girl is

interested," she said, touching his knee where the skin and a few blond hairs showed through the hole in his jeans. Connie had lurked in his studio for weeks and had bought two paintings she could ill afford before he finally asked her out for coffee.

She laughed and turned her attention back to me. "You didn't know Chad that well either when you decided to move here."

I felt a warm rush of blood spread from my chest right up through the roots of my hair. I was not proud of jumping into Chad's life and his home so quickly.

"He moved even faster with Kristen," I said, choosing to ignore my impulsiveness and focus on him. "Of course I never asked him where he met her or how they had the chance to connect. I was too shocked and too busy screaming at him once I found them in bed."

I glanced over at the next houseboat, where the Renharts had moved to their bottom deck and were now grilling. Sausages, from the smell of it. My stomach rumbled. Maybe they were the big plump Italian kind that was hand-stuffed behind the meat counter at Fausto's Market. And maybe the Renharts had peppers roasting too. *Focus, Hayley*.

"Don't most affairs happen after the primary relationship's gone stale?" I asked. "If Chad and I went stale in under two months, that must be a record." My eyes welled up with tears even though I really wanted to be done crying over that rat.

Connie rubbed my shoulder and then fumbled in her pocket for a tissue and handed it to me. "I've dated guys for shorter times than that."

"But you didn't travel the length of the country to move in with them," I moaned. "I'm such an idiot."

"Don't you think he might have known *her* before he met *you*?" asked Ray.

"Of course he knew her. Everybody knows everybody in this town," Connie said.

"But what if you interrupted something," Ray said. "Or Kristen thought you came between them. That would explain a little better why she didn't like you."

"Despised me," I said glumly. "But he certainly never mentioned her."

"Of course he wouldn't talk to you about her. What was the funeral like?" Connie asked. "Was Chad there?"

So I described the scene at the reception—the big turnout of chefs and foodie types and how Henri Stentzel had reason to dislike Kristen too, according to Porter anyway. And how Chad had yelled at me with the cops watching. And then how Eric had rescued the poor sobbing female from Cole's Peace just before I left. "If I was in charge of the murder case, I'd see plenty of avenues to explore."

"Luckily, you're a food critic, not a detective," said Connie firmly. "So are your pieces ready to go off to *Key Zest*?"

I glugged the last inch of my wine and heaved myself out of the low-slung beach chair. This was my last chance to choose the reviews I would be sending over to Wally and polish them until they shined: Only a fool would squander it. "I'm headed to the computer right this minute."

After a quick stop in the kitchen to feed Evinrude

and pour myself a glass of sparkling water, I retreated to my cubicle and booted up the computer. While I was waiting, I made the bed, changed into sweats, and put away all the outfits I'd gone through this morning trying to find one that would span job interview to funeral.

With nothing else to distract me, I plunked down at the desk and mulled over my article choices. In the beginning, I'd thought it would make a stronger application packet to include two traditional restaurant reviews and one that was slightly offbeat. But both the brown-bag piece on Bad Boy Burrito and the breakfast article I'd sketched out this morning fell into the funky category. The Seven Fish and Blue Heaven reviews should be the anchors for my application. In fact, I'd already written a jazzy introduction to Blue Heaven, discussing the pleasures and concerns of sharing a meal with live chickens. Unfortunately, since Blue Heaven hadn't catered Kristen's reception, I was short on facts about their food.

That left me with one traditional restaurant review, one take-out restaurant with gourmet-quality Mexican food, and the scant beginning of an article on best breakfasts in Key West. And no time to research anything new. Kristen, I was certain, would have shredded an applicant like me in an instant. Would Wally be more tolerant?

I felt frozen, like I had a million times in college at eight or ten p.m. when a major paper was due the next day and I'd only just hit the library. "When in doubt, wait it out" used to be my motto. It hadn't worked well then and it wouldn't now either. I tried to visualize the instructions that the applicants had been issued at the beginning of the process: *Show us your style.*

In a mini blast of inspiration, I thought of rating my reviews with cute little palm trees instead of the same dull stars used in the Michelin Guides and at the *New York Times*. One palm tree for fair, two for good, three for excellent, and no trees at all if the place was truly a dog. I wrote this up in an opening paragraph, then sat back, mired in the same problem.

My mind shifted to the Chad and Kristen conundrum. And Ava's statement at the funeral reception that she too had hooked up with Chad. And it occurred to me that Deena—Chad's secretary—would certainly know what their relationship had been like before he met me. Whether she would spill any secrets was another question altogether. We'd gotten to be pretty friendly right after I moved to Key West. A few times I'd even ended up having drinks with Deena instead of Chad when he was working too hard to entertain me. I checked my watch. She was probably still at work—she often set aside Thursday nights to catch up on Chad's paperwork.

Suddenly it felt like I couldn't wait one more minute to find out what she knew about Chad and Kristen. And maybe she could explain too why Chad seemed so angry. About everything. I padded back out to the galley and poured another inch of wine into my glass—liquid courage. Then I dialed her work number.

"Deena," I said when she answered in her husky voice. "It's Hayley Snow. Sorry to bother you at work."

"No problem," she said, but not like she meant it. "I was just wrapping things up."

"I miss talking to you," I said. "That's one of the worst things about this stupid breakup."

"I know," she said. "Me too." Her voice warmed a little, which gave me the guts to forge forward.

"I don't mean to put you in an awkward position, but you know how painful these past few weeks have been. I'm trying to get some perspective." And then, before she could tell me she had nothing to say and that her first loyalty had to be to her employer, I asked her how long he'd known Kristen.

There was a hefty silence. "I wondered when you'd get around to asking," she said finally.

My heart plunged like an elevator on the fritz. "Get around to it?" I repeated in a dull voice. "Please tell me—it can't hurt anything now." Could it?

She didn't say anything, so I tried again. "Deena, please. You have to tell me. This isn't just a case of being nosy. The police think I killed Kristen."

She was still quiet. I could picture her thinking, tapping those long, red nails on her desk. How did she type with those talons anyway?

"Deena?"

"Kristen and Chad were pretty tight before he met you," she said. "But I'm not going to say anything more on the phone. His phone. Jesus, Chad would kill me if he knew I was talking to you. And I can't afford to lose this job."

"I'm sorry. I shouldn't have called you at work. I'll meet you anywhere—just name it."

"Tomorrow at the pier in front of the Truman Annex. I'll be walking Ginger at five."

I thanked her and hung up feeling utterly foolish. What a dupe I'd been. And a dope. I could just imagine the scene when Chad told Kristen that he'd gone north to visit his mother for a week and come back with a new girlfriend. No wonder Kristen couldn't stand my guts. No wonder she'd expunged me from the *Key Zest* computer.

I shuffled back out to the kitchen and made a cup of coffee. This news was going to require rethinking everything that had happened over the past two months. With a clear mind, if I could rustle one up.

I remembered the fool card that Lorenzo had dealt onto the card table. However he might have interpreted it, the meaning was clear to me.

12

"It is possible to imagine him having a small meal of minor critics for breakfast, as if they were kippers . . ."

—Dwight Garner

I lingered in bed longer than I should have the next morning, partly because of the minor post-Prosecco-and-white-wine headache, but mostly because the day looked exhausting and I'd only been awake ten minutes. The conversation with Deena had left me feeling stupid and heavy. And having teetered on the edge of playing the clown yesterday at the reception, I dreaded talking to Eric. Besides, I'd have to admit what he suspected all along about my move to Key West to be with Chad.

For a half hour, I stayed under the covers, listening to the sounds of morning at the marina. Someone at the end of the dock was hosing down his property, with KONK 101 AM blaring at top volume. Seagulls squalled, the Renharts' oversized wind chimes clanked, and I could smell the scent of the Laundromat's dryer wafting in from the parking lot.

Before I moved in, Connie had warned me that some folks find marina life to be the worst of both worlds: There is no pure experience of nature like you'd get on the open seas. And the place has all the lack of privacy and convenience that comes from living on a boat. In other words, some people might consider it an overpriced trailer park on the water. She loved this place though, and I was beginning to feel that way too.

I rolled over and reached for my phone. No new messages. I was dying to hear if Eric had picked up any more gossip after I left the church. And whether he'd come up with any bright new theories about Kristen's murder. But first, *Key Zest*. And before that, Evinrude, who'd started the morning by tickling my face with his whiskers and progressed to padding back and forth across my chest, meowing for breakfast.

I left a message on Eric's voice mail, extracted myself from the bedcovers, and trotted into the kitchen. Connie had left a half pot of dark roast coffee and a note wishing me luck with the application. I filled a big blue mug with steamed milk and coffee and splashed a taste of milk in a bowl for the cat. Busy crunching kibbles, he flicked his tail with satisfaction. I returned to my room and tapped out an introduction to my application.

Tolerance of differences among people seems to be higher than most places in our little patch of paradise, so why shouldn't this be true with food too? Yes, a hungry diner can find a multistarred dining experience in Key West, but she can also find mouth-watering takeout and breakfasts to die for. As the new food critic for Key Zest, *I will cover eating establishments from one end of the spectrum to the other. One human family—one interesting meal after another.*

And then I attached my three reviews to the e-mail, added a link to the key lime pie article in the *Citizen*, and pressed SEND. Now it was out of my hands.

I poured a second cup of coffee and brought it back to my desk, considering a shower. And then whether I should put a few applications in at restaurants on Duval Street where staff turned over so quickly that they always needed help. Depressing prospect, yes indeed, but at least I'd be doing *something*. A loud rap on our flimsy front door rattled the houseboat and Evinrude bolted off the desk and disappeared under the bed. I tossed on my bathrobe and hurried out to answer. With any luck, Eric would have stopped by for a visit.

Two Key West policemen were standing on the dock: Officer Torrence and another with Elvis-style sideburns whom I didn't recognize. I clutched the robe closed at my neckline, pushed the door open, and forced a smile. "Good morning. You have some news, I guess?"

"Miss Snow, I regret to say that we have been dispatched to bring you into the police station," said Officer Torrence. And not in a friendly voice.

"Again?" I said. "We have to stop meeting this way." No smiles. "I've pretty much told you guys everything I know." I wanted to sound lighter than I felt—the dread was gathering. They looked very serious. "Let me just grab a shower and I'll run over—"

"We need to bring you in now," said the officer with the sideburns, looking even grimmer than Torrence, if that were possible.

Once it became clear that now meant *now*, I threw on jeans and a sweatshirt and stumped down the dock between the two men. If anything could be worse than another trip to the station, it would be a trip to the station in rumpled pajamas with napping cats on them.

As we passed the neighbors' boat, Mrs. Renhart was hanging out her husband's clothes on a fold-up clothesline on their deck. Her weathered blue eyes widened in disbelief and I swore she pulled her cell phone right out of her pocket and dialed. This would be all over town by afternoon, but that was the least of my problems.

After a short ride in the back of the cruiser, I was escorted into the same conference room that I'd visited two times earlier. Detective Bransford joined the other cops and deposited a brown bag on the table in front of me. I could hope for doughnuts, but it had a long, flat shape unlike any pastry I'd ever seen and no tantalizing yeasty smell. In fact, the bag gave off a slightly rancid odor.

"Good morning, Detective," I said in a trembling voice. "Well, I hope it's a good morning for you. It's not going all that well for me so far."

He nodded gruffly, his dark eyes gleaming.

"Miss Snow, would you be so kind as to explain again your relationship with Miss Kristen Faulkner?"

"There wasn't much to it," I said. "I told you about

finding her with my boyfriend. And how she owns the magazine where I'm applying for a job. Owned, I should say. I don't know who's got her half now."

"So you applied for a job, but oddly enough, your résumé was deleted?"

I gawked and stared. How had they learned this? "Yes, it's true," I said, heaving a great sigh. "She deleted me on account of my relationship with Chad Lutz. I went over there yesterday and managed to get myself back on the list."

"Miss Snow, can you explain where you were exactly on Tuesday morning between six and ten a.m.?"

Of course he'd asked me the same question during our previous "conversations," just as all the TV cops I'd seen over the years asked repetitive questions of their subjects. I searched my memory for who I might have called that morning, and when I came up with no one, tried to puzzle out what the hell he had in that bag.

"Do you understand what I'm asking?" he repeated when I was silent for too long.

"I understand. And you guys must know that I had nothing to do with that murder. Don't you?" I took a deep, wobbly breath. "I even found out last night that Kristen and Chad were involved romantically before I ever came along and so doesn't it make sense that she'd want to kill me rather than the other way around? That's the way I'd be thinking if I was in your—"

"Miss Snow," the detective broke in. "I know you're nervous, but you need to pay attention. This is a very serious matter—a woman has been murdered. You have no alibi. You have motive. You are quite familiar with the weapon used to kill the victim. And you entered Mr. Lutz's apartment, where the victim was discovered, without his permission. In fact, we have a witness who places you at the condominium complex around the time of the murder."

I set my trembling lips into one firm line. "But that's not true! Your witness is lying. I was at home all morning, working. And I didn't kill her. I just didn't do it."

The cops exchanged unreadable glances; then Detective Bransford looked back at me.

"Can you identify this?" He snapped a white latex glove on, extracted an object wrapped in plastic from the brown bag, and set it on the table. I immediately recognized it as my own missing carving knife—or one just like it—the knife that could hack through a chicken carcass in one crushing downward blow. One of the knives I'd hoped to find in Chad's apartment. I peered a little closer. Underneath the plastic evidence bag, the knife appeared to be covered in green gunk, mixed with the black fingerprint dust that I'd seen everywhere when I started cleaning Chad's place.

"It's just like my knife," I admitted. "But Kristen wasn't stabbed. You said she was poisoned." Which, of course, they hadn't told me. Henri had. My eyes filled suddenly. "Oh my God, that's the poison pie isn't it? And you think because my knife was used to cut it . . ." I took a shuddering breath and tried to calm down and figure out the angles. "But that's ridiculous! She probably grabbed the knife out of the drawer and cut a piece herself."

The three policemen just stared at me.

The detective broke the silence. "We did find your

fingerprints on this knife, Miss Snow. Listen," he said, smiling warmly. "Probably you only meant for her to get sick—vomit a little and so on. Maybe an unpleasant night in the ER. Payback for what she put you through."

"But—"

"I'm just saying, to have her steal your boyfriend after you uprooted your life and moved a long distance to be with him. Isn't that what you told us the other day? And you don't have a job now or a place to live. I could imagine how a person in this situation might come a little unmoored. Unglued." He smiled again and offered a sympathetic nod.

And I realized that this was the point in every TV crime show that the poor beleaguered and innocent suspect lawyers up. I straightened my shoulders.

"I believe I would like to call a lawyer. But since I don't know any except for Chad Lutz who hates me and deals with divorce anyway, I would like to call my father and get his help." I slid my phone out of the back pocket of my jeans.

Detective Bransford leaned across the table, frowning, and held out his hand.

"I'll hold on to that until you leave. Officer Torrence will bring you a phone."

The veins in my temples were throbbing so hard I could barely remember my name, never mind a string of numbers that I didn't dial that often. I could have called Mom, but she had a tendency to flip out under pressure. So I closed my eyes and breathed until my father's cell number came to me, then accepted the phone and dialed.

After three rings, my stepmother picked up. I groaned aloud—an action I was certain would be mentioned in future family fights, but I couldn't worry about it. Right now, it seemed bad enough to have my own father thinking I was a loser—Allison lacked the blood connection that would soften my humiliation.

"Sorry, Allison," I said. "I thought I called Dad's cell."

"You did," she said. "He's in the shower. I saw the Key West exchange and since we haven't heard from you all week, I thought I should answer. He would be disappointed to have missed you. Anything I can let him know?"

How could I emphasize how crucial it was that he call me back without telling the whole truth? I couldn't.

"This may sound completely crazy, but please don't hang up. I'm about to go to jail and I only get one call. I need Dad to help me find a lawyer. Right away." I suppressed a sob—it sounded so awful—so melodramatic. "Wait a second. Let me figure out what number he should call."

"Hold on," said Allison. "I'm going to pull him out of the shower this minute. I'm going upstairs. Are you all right? Are they treating you okay? How in the world did this happen?"

As her sympathetic questions unrolled, I felt a whoosh of relief. "I'm fine—they're not beating me or anything." I made a small face for the benefit of the detective who had scared me half to death and was obviously listening to every word. "I just need a lawyer, that's all," I added, choosing not to address how I got into this mess.

"Just a minute," said Allison.

I could hear muffled conversation, as if she'd pressed the phone to her bosom while she talked to my father.

Then he came on the line. "Hayley, for the love of God, what is this about jail?"

Just the sound of his voice destroyed the rest of my fragile composure and I began to cry. I told him about Kristen being poisoned. "The police found my knife covered with poisoned lime custard—it's so green, now that I think of it, I believe the person who baked it used *food coloring*. Isn't that disgusting?"

"Stop talking this minute!" my father ordered. "Why in God's name are you discussing cooking? Do not say one more word to the cops. About anything. Give me the phone number there."

I got the number from one of the cops and repeated it to my father.

"Stay right where you are. I'll get back to you in no more than fifteen minutes."

He hung up. If I hadn't been feeling so completely distraught, I would have laughed. Where the heck did he think I'd be going?

I handed the phone back to Detective Bransford. "My father's finding me a lawyer. I guess I have nothing more to say until that's settled. Except I wonder if I might use the ladies' room."

He rolled his eyes and ushered me down the hall.

13

"Everyone needs a chocolate cake in her repertoire."

—Molly Wizenberg

A half hour later, Bransford returned to the interview room with my new lawyer. Attorney Richard Kane was a thickset man with bushy black hair and a burr of a mustache that looked as though it had been glued on. Glowering at the detective, he thrust his business card at me. They'd obviously done some talking before they got to the room.

"Is my client under arrest?" Kane's voice, loud and brusque, was a demand more than an inquiry.

Bransford frowned. "She ought to be in jail."

"But since she's not," said my lawyer, "I must assume you haven't read her her Miranda rights and she isn't under arrest. And I also assume you haven't been recording her illegally?" He pointed to the clock on the wall.

There was a *camera* in that?

"Of course we follow procedure, Mr. Kane," said Bransford, ice in his voice.

I felt like I was watching two bulls paw the pasture, tearing up the wildflowers and snorting. With me, the quivering red flag between them.

"So you're saying there isn't enough evidence to put her in jail?"

After a long stare-down, the detective stepped aside. "You're free to go," he told me, handing over my cell phone without meeting my eyes.

I followed Mr. Kane outside and across the parking lot to a large maroon-colored sedan with tan leather seats. The interior was about the size of my houseboat bedroom. "We'll talk in my office," he said as he started up the engine with a great blast of cold air and frenzied classical violin. We drove to his place on Fleming Street, a couple of blocks from the *Key Zest* office. He parked his boat of a car on the street in front of Living Dolls Adult Entertainment, shut off the screeching stringed instruments, and strode ahead of me to his office.

His secretary, a buxom redhead, sexy enough to have stopped over from Living Dolls, held out a handful of phone messages. He pointed me to the office at the back of the suite.

"Later!" he barked at the redhead as we hurtled by. "Coffee!"

"Your father paid my retainer," he explained once we were settled in cavernous leather easy chairs. "So let's begin. A, my job is to ensure that your rights are protected. And B, I shall examine the evidence against you so we can be prepared for any moves the police department might make. Do you understand what I'm saying?"

I nodded. "Though I don't know what evidence there could be."

It all sounded very serious and scary. I hadn't thought about a camera in the clock and who might have been watching me over the first two visits. Nor had I considered the possibility that I could just walk out of the station. As far as I was concerned, this lawyer was already on his way to earning my father's retainer. I should probably tell him everything. Even if there were things I might have ordinarily held back because I barely knew the guy, like the criminals did on TV. But I was no criminal. And I was way too nervous to sit there with my mouth shut and listen to him tell me more about how much trouble I was in.

"As I explained to the policemen, Kristen had more motive to want me murdered than the other way around. Apparently she slept with him first. Then I came along, and then he went back to her. The whole thing makes me sick."

He cut me off. "Explain this business about a knife."

"Yes, they have my knife and it looks like it's plastered with poison. But Kristen wasn't stabbed to death, so what difference does it make whether my cutlery was used to cut the pie?" My hands and lips were shaking and I could feel little gobs of spit gathering in the corners of my mouth. "Do you think they'll give the knife back?" As soon as the question left my mouth, I realized how silly it sounded. My mind just wasn't working.

Mr. Kane leaned forward from his chair and tapped the legal pad on the coffee table between us with an expensive-looking pen. "Miss Snow, I understand this is a stressful time—"

"Oh, please call me Hayley. All this Miss Snow business is frightening me half to death."

He grimaced, the mustache undulating like a wooly caterpillar prepared for a cold winter. "Hayley. It's important that you listen to me, because if you were to be charged with a felony, this would change your life."

"You really think I'm going to be charged?" My mouth felt dry as a fever. Even while the detective had listed the reasons I might have for poisoning Kristen, I never thought they'd actually pin the murder on me. Or maybe I knew deep down it could happen, but didn't want to face it.

"No, certainly not," he said, preening a little as if he wanted me to be sure I understood the importance of his influence. "Not yet. And I'm taking that to mean that the evidence against you must be sketchy. Probably circumstantial and weakly circumstantial at best. Those cops were hoping you'd crumble, confess, and save everyone a lot of trouble. So let's go back to the beginning, shall we? Tell me everything you know about this murder. Including," he said in a lower voice, "whether you killed her." He leaned forward to scribble something on the pad, and I strained to read it upside down.

Did she do it?

Which I couldn't believe my own lawyer would write. "Of course I didn't kill her!" I nearly howled. "I told you that already."

"Yes, you told *me* that. But then why do you suppose they suspect you of committing the murder?"

"I'm sure my fingerprints are all over Chad's apartment. But for crying out loud, I lived there for nine weeks. Wouldn't they expect to find them? Of course that knife is going to have my fingerprints on it. I'm the only one who cooked or cleaned up or emptied the dishwasher. Before I moved in, Chad only ordered out or ate out. He doesn't care about food.

"And stuff like hair and skin flakes and all the things you see on *CSI*—they'll probably bring that up next. No matter how good a job the housecleaning service does—and Connie is the tops on this island—something's bound to be left behind. So what do we do now?" I asked. "I swear I never touched the girl. Or fed her any poison. I've never even made a key lime pie. To be honest, I'm totally freaked out by the idea of meringue."

"Ms. Snow—Hayley," he broke in. "Settle down. Let's go over the conversations you've had with the police, all the details." A timid knock interrupted us.

"Come in!" he shouted. The redhead entered with two white porcelain mugs and set them on the table in front of us. He grunted his thanks without looking at her or asking me whether I took cream and sugar and waved at me to continue.

So I told him about my first visit to the station—how it had been all chummy and *you must understand how much we appreciate your assistance*, and then how things had gone sharply downhill.

"We hit kind of a bumpy spot in our relationship when they trapped me in Chad's apartment armed with a feather duster." I couldn't help snickering. "Me, I mean. The cops had regular guns and whatever else those dudes carry on their belts."

His smile faded. "Trapped you in Chad's apartment? Explain." I watched him write *breaking and entering* on the legal pad and a belated beading of sweat broke out on my upper lip.

Then I told him about going over to look for my things, including the recipes. I stole a glance at his face—impassive. "And after I looked around, I was going to clean the place and get the heck out. But one of the neighbors ratted me out and called the cops." I wished I hadn't used the words "ratted me out"—it made me sound guilty. "I went there as my friend Connie's employee," I added in a firm voice.

"And it never occurred to you to think how suspicious that might look, sneaking into the apartment where the murder took place?" Still not a friendly cell flickering on the guy's face.

"Honestly? It sounds ridiculous when you put things that way, but no, I didn't think along those lines." I pressed my fingertips along my cheekbones, willing myself to hold it together in front of him.

"So here's the thing." He jerked his thumb at the door, as though the police were waiting right outside to take me in. He took a slurp of his coffee. "The cops are operating on a hunch—the hunch being that you must have had a reason to want this young woman dead."

"I understand that, but it isn't true. Well, not exactly. I mean, she did steal my boyfriend and try to kill my job prospects. But all that said, I'm not a violent person. I would never have wished her dead, never mind actually do her in."

Another pained expression flooded his face and he scribbled on the yellow pad again. *Motive, yes. Unpremeditated?*

"Their case depends on collecting enough evidence to prove that hunch to be true," he said. "That means tracking all the leads they can turn up, looking for witnesses that either prove or disprove your presence at the time of the murder. We need to be working at the same time to prove the opposite—that you couldn't possibly have been involved."

"Okay." I bobbed my head. "How can I help?"

"I'm going back to the department later today to press Bransford hard about how close they are to having enough evidence to arrest you. Meanwhile, you should make a list of all the people I need to talk to about your relationship with the deceased and your whereabouts on the day of the murder. Any questions on that?"

"No questions," I said. "Well, other than, if the evidence is so flimsy, why me?"

He slid his fancy pen back into his pocket and crossed the room to get a pencil from the desk drawer. Back in front of me, he ripped off the top sheet containing his notes and slapped the pencil next to the pad.

"Everything you remember."

14

"The most remarkable thing about my mother is that for thirty years she served the family nothing but leftovers. The original meal has never been found."

—Calvin Trillin

After I'd made my list and explained that I'd been in Connie's houseboat by myself the morning of the murder, working on my articles, and that I had no one to verify my alibi, even my expensive lawyer didn't seem to believe this reprieve was any more than temporary. I waved off his offer of a ride and walked home, starving by the time I approached our dock.

Right now I could have used a little something from my mother's comfort-food repertoire. Since she wasn't available, making a nice lunch and luring Eric over to share it was the next best thing. I rummaged through the refrigerator and found some white eggplants that I'd bought at the farmer's market last week. I sliced and salted them and, leaving them to drain in a colander in the sink, headed out to score some mozzarella.

I almost left my helmet home so I could whip up the Atlantic Beach side of the island with the wind tousling my hair and the sun warming my face. But notwithstanding moving to Key West with Chad when I barely knew him, I've never been much on taking risks. So I strapped the helmet on and drove up the usual way. I parked the scooter on the upper end of Duval Street with its gorgeous rug shop and art galleries and charming bars where the cruise ship tourists often don't go, and dashed into Franco's Deli for a large ball of fresh cheese. For the lunch I was envisioning, the rubbery white glob passed off as mozzarella by processed food manufacturers would not do at all.

Franco's was bustling with lunch customers waiting to order their Italian heroes. Steam wafted from the trays displayed on the counter—lasagna, stuffed shells, and meatballs in Sunday red sauce. I got in line and dialed Eric while waiting. When I'd first arrived in Key West, we designed a system for alerting him to when I really, really, really needed to talk, as opposed to when I'd sure like to or when I felt a little lonely and could use a chat. The latter two cases he did not consider emergency situations.

"Quick lunch, my house, half an hour?" I asked when he answered. "This is a three-rooster alert. I was just released from the police station and had to ask my father to hire a lawyer." I had dropped my voice so the other customers wouldn't hear everything, but I picked up the volume again to describe the lunch I had in mind. "I'm picturing a towering stack of fried eggplant, fresh tomato, and Franco's mozzarella woven in between the slices, topped by a nest of arugula drizzled with balsamic vinegar."

"I'm drooling," he said. "Make it forty-five minutes?"

I hung up and used the last few minutes of my wait time to take a few pictures of the food in the display case and the folks in white aprons behind the counter constructing sandwiches. Only then did my panicky thoughts overtake my mind. The last few hours felt surreal—how could I have gotten into so much serious trouble for hardly doing anything wrong? I didn't know pop squat about this lawyer, and certainly my father didn't know him personally either. What if he decided I was guilty and insisted on making a plea bargain instead of proving my innocence? Remembering that he'd jotted "unpremeditated" on his pad made me especially nervous. That would be good news if a criminal had actually committed a murder, but I hadn't. I could end up spending the best years of my life in jail instead of writing about food in paradise.

I bought my ball of cheese and sped back to the houseboat. Once home, I washed and dried the weeping eggplant slices, dipped them in egg and flour, and dropped them into a pan of hot oil. While they fried, I sliced tomatoes and mozzarella, and whipped up a vinaigrette with mustard, olive oil, and balsamic vinegar. By the time Eric arrived, the towers of eggplant were fully constructed.

"Come on in," I called. "The masterpiece awaits."

"You are amazing," he said, and folded me into a hug. "Which reminds me—any word from *Key Zest*?"

"Not yet, but I only sent the application in this morning."

We carried our plates and glasses of Orangina on ice upstairs to the deck off of Connie's bedroom and settled into beach chairs. Eric glanced at his watch. "Tell me more about the big emergency. I don't have much time, so better make it the short version."

I described my third trip to the police department and how the lawyer had whisked me out after determining that the cops didn't have enough evidence to arrest me. "The detective claimed I had a good reason to kill Kristen and no one to vouch that I was here on the boat that morning."

Oh, such an exquisite relief to transfer the building anxiety from me to him. I sawed off a piece of eggplant, added a bite of the salad, nibbled, and swallowed. The eggplant was soft inside, crispy out, and set off perfectly by the sharp tang of the arugula and the dressing.

Then I described the dramatic unmasking of my knife.

Eric stopped chewing and stared. "Where the hell did the knife come from?"

"Chad's apartment, I presume. I'm sure they collected it as evidence once they found Kristen murdered."

"But why wait until today to wave it in front of you?"

"Maybe they ran out of leads. Or other suspects." I could picture them abandoning other leads, more flimsy even than those that pointed to me, and narrowing their focus to the ex-girlfriend. Me. There was probably a lot of pressure from Kristen's family to solve the case. I stopped eating too and laid my fork on my plate.

"What's your lawyer's name?"

"Richard Kane."

Eric gulped and turned a little pale.

"What? What's wrong with him?"

"This eggplant is amazing," he said, a little too brightly. "Did you do anything special to it before you fried it? And what kind of oil—"

"Look," I said. "Never mind the darn recipe. Obviously, you know something private. As usual. But in this case, you have to tell me."

"I'm sorry. I can't," Eric said.

"Shoot," I growled. "Doesn't it seem to you that we ought to be doing a little research and not leaving my entire defense up to a lawyer I've never laid eyes on before he burst into the KWPD this morning?"

Eric patted his lips with his napkin. "Yes. You absolutely have to think about protecting yourself. And gathering information that might help him defend you. He suggested that himself, didn't he?"

I told him about the very short list I'd made to help the lawyer establish my alibi: one half-demented old lady with whom I'd bonded over cats. And I described how someone at the Truman Annex had ratted me out as being on the premises the morning Kristen was killed—or so the detective claimed.

"Can they lie about something like that?" I asked.

"Of course it happens," he said, pushing his glasses up the bridge of his nose. "Everyone lies in this business—the police, the lawyers, the criminals. Even folks who didn't do anything wrong panic and lie." He threw a funny look my way and then speared the last bit of mozzarella on his plate and dragged it through the pool of vinaigrette. "All cops say things that aren't exactly accurate to increase the pressure in hopes that their suspect will crack and tell them something new."

"I'm definitely close to cracking," I said with a weak laugh. "As for something new, I don't have it. Should I go over and canvass Chad's neighbors? Obviously Leona had no qualms about turning me in on Wednesday, but I know some of them liked me. I was courteous and friendly while I lived there. And I followed all the rules. Of which there are many."

Eric grinned. "I'd hate to encourage you to make more trouble." He glanced at his watch and stood up from the beach chair. "I need to get back to the office. I'll call you later and we'll brainstorm, okay? The lunch was fantastic."

"I'll clean up; you go." I hugged him.

"Ask Connie's boyfriend, Ray, about your lawyer," he called over his shoulder as he clumped downstairs.

Ask Ray? Why would Ray know anything? I carried everything to the kitchen, gave Evinrude a tiny piece of cheese, and started washing the pile of dishes in the sink. What had Eric heard about my lawyer and why couldn't he tell me? There were a couple of possibilities: First, he was one of Eric's patients. Unlikely. Kane had shown no signs of the self-reflection needed in therapy. Two, he'd slept with one of Eric's patients—or was married to one. Or three, Eric had dated him. That bit of lousy judgment might cause Eric to blanch, but it wouldn't be a professional secret that he couldn't share.

As I stowed away the dishes, the questions kept coming. What was the conflict about the restaurant on Easter Island? Was it big enough to murder someone over? The woman at Cole's Peace had pointed directly there. What had been Kristen's relationship with Wally at the magazine? What really went on with Chad and Kristen—and Ava—before I blundered onto the scene? Why had he left her for me? And then bounced back? And what had actually happened with the chef at Henri's Miami Beach restaurant?

The more I could find out about Kristen, the better chance I'd have of identifying her killer. And hadn't Miss Gloria mentioned talking to the cops just the other day? Now I wondered if she was referring to a second visit.

I sat at the kitchen table and started a list on my laptop.

At the end, I wrote: Who could have baked the poison key lime pie?

Everyone and anyone, that's who. There were a million purveyors of pie in our town, and probably plenty of amateur cooks who were proud of their recipes as well. But not all of them would stoop to that bilious green color that I'd seen on the knife in the police department. Especially not a professional chef with a reputation riding on their production. Then I remembered reading the recipe for a Weight Watchers pie that consisted of sugar-free lime Jell-O, lime yogurt, and low-fat Cool Whip.

What could be more disgusting? And green?

15

"Envy dulls the appetite."

—Christine Muhlke

At twenty to five, I motored down Southard Street to meet Chad's secretary, Deena, at the pier. A half dozen dogs and their owners were already strolling along the water, which lapped against the concrete barriers ten feet above the Navy Mole harbor. Others were wrestling and playing with Frisbees and balls on the triangular grassy space in front of the Mills Place condominiums. The grass petered out to just a tail at Harbor Place, Chad's condo complex. If I kept walking, I'd end up a stone's throw from the Harbor Place pool and gardens. Only this time I'd be on the far side of the chain-link fence that separated property owners from riffraff.

Off in the distance, I recognized Deena, dressed in tight white jeans and black heels, walking a medium-sized yellow mutt. Even dressed for dog-walking, she looked gorgeous: her black hair curling past her shoulders over a sparkly gold lace top; her face perfectly made-up. I went over to give Ginger a pat and Deena a hug, which she returned without her customary warmth.

"Thanks for talking to me," I said. It would have been polite to make some small talk, ask about the office and whether there was anything new in her love life. But I didn't have it in me and she didn't seem interested. I added: "I don't expect you to take my side on anything. I'm just trying to get to the bottom of this. I'm a whisker away from being arrested for Kristen's murder."

"You can't be serious," said Deena with a frown. "That's ridiculous."

"You're telling me," I said.

Deena threw a tennis ball and the dog scampered off to chase it down. The dog brought the ball back and dropped it in front of Deena's feet, panting.

"Good girl." She offered her a tiny dog biscuit and threw the ball again.

"So you were saying that Kristen and Chad were seeing each other before he met me? I have to say that floors me. I guess I wasn't paying attention to anything but hormones."

She tucked her arm around my waist and squeezed. "I'm sorry about all this. I know it's hard to absorb. But honestly, it was more than casual dating, Hayley. I was waiting for an engagement announcement—which is saying something if Chad's involved."

"An *engagement* announcement?" I pulled away from her, trying to make sense of this latest bit of shocking news.

She accepted the slobbery ball from Ginger a second

time and repeated the treat and throw routine. She had a better arm than I would have predicted for such a feminine-looking woman—the ball went long and straight.

"You thought they would be getting married? Married," I repeated dully. "Chad and Kristen."

"Yes. I mean, he seemed more serious about her than any of the other girls he'd gone out with before. And I've seen a lot of them come through in the ten years I've worked for him." She flashed a rueful smile and gathered her hair into a ponytail with a gold scrunchie. "You know yourself he makes a very good impression."

I sighed. "I can't understand why I never heard about this. It's so embarrassing. My friend Eric knows everything that happens in this town and he never said a peep. If he'd known, surely he would have warned me."

But would he have warned me? What if the information he'd heard had been told to him in a confidential session, like whatever he seemed to know about my lawyer? He certainly hadn't encouraged me to fly down and move in with Chad. How many times had he urged me to take my time and get to know Chad before I took such a major step? This whole line of thinking left me feeling light-headed and a little queasy.

"If it makes you feel any better, they didn't make their connection obvious," said Deena. "They went to dinner once in a while and attended a few benefits as a couple last winter in the high season, but she didn't move in with him. And you know how he is about public displays of affection." She raised her eyebrows and wiggled them.

"Too well," I admitted with a weak chuckle. "He seemed different down here than he did in New Jersey. Less affectionate. More constrained. It sure makes sense now."

"When he came back from visiting his mom and informed me that any calls from you were to be put through immediately—that was a shocker," Deena said, rubbing her dog's ears and tossing the ball again. "And I was completely blown away when he said you were moving in. Everyone was surprised when you moved down—probably no one more than Chad himself. I don't mean anything bad by this, but after you and I talked a few times, I couldn't imagine you two were much of a match. You're so sweet and he—" Her words trailed off.

"He was so . . . ?"

"Not." She laughed. "Oh, Hayley, stop. There's no point in torturing yourself with the whys and wherefores. Kristen was never going to be as much fun as you are. You lightened Chad up—most likely that's why he fell for you. There he was, away from the pressures of the office, and you looked as though you could be part of a different life. He probably didn't believe that you'd actually come. Or think through whether you'd fit in."

She took a tissue from her tiny black-and-gold-checked purse and wiped the dog goo off her fingers. "I doubt he even thought about whether he'd be happy with such a big change in his life—I suspect he and Kristen had had a spat before he went up to visit his mother. But in the end, he's driven and ambitious. Period. Did he ever talk to you about the case he was working on over the last couple months?"

I shook my head. Seemed there had been a lot he didn't mention.

"He represented the husband—you know he prefers male clients. He says he can't stand hysterical, angry women, unless they're in court ranting about the settlements he's won against them. That, he kind of enjoys." She pulled the scrunchie off and shook out her hair. "Anyway, he wiped his client's ex-wife out. Took everything, including the dog. She couldn't afford a big-shot lawyer and she paid for it. See, Kristen could relate to something like that. She understood winning. You, on the other hand, would only feel sorry for his opponent."

"So you're pretty definite that I broke them up, not the other way around?"

She frowned, gripped my shoulders, and gave me a little shake, looking me dead in the eyes. "He dumped her for you. And then he dumped you for her. Now, is that the kind of man you want to go moping around town for?"

"Not really," I said. "I'm trying hard not to mope." I managed a small smile. "Did you know that Chad had a relationship with Kristen's sister before he started going out with Kristen?"

"That's a new one on me," she said. "Not that he tells me everything. But it's hard not to hear more than I want to, sitting right outside his office."

Then I asked the question I'd wanted to ask right from the beginning. "Why do *you* stay with him?"

She rubbed the fingers on her right hand together. "For this island, the pay is outstanding. He relies on me—and he knows it, so he treats me like a queen. He couldn't bear having me hired away. You saw a little of how ugly divorces can be. I'm pretty good at heading off the hateful exes and would-be exes."

I nodded. I'd heard her side of a couple of these conversations, and she was a master at managing chaos and deflecting it away from Chad.

She flashed a crooked smile and patted her dog. "You're better off without him."

"Rat bugger," I said.

After Deena left with her panting dog in tow, I continued down to the end of the pier where a group of men were talking, some with fishing lines bobbing in the water. And one dressed like Elvis. From the other side of the fence, when I'd been relaxing by the condominium pool, I'd often seen them in the morning and again at sunset, but I'd never gotten close enough to chat. Not that I would have anyway—they tended to clump together, looking somewhat ominous and often loaded.

"Miss Hayley!" called a familiar twangy voice. Tony emerged from the group, wearing his battered cowboy hat and jeans with more holes than denim. "Whazzup?"

"Same old, same old." I waved and started to turn back toward town.

"You stayin' out of trouble? Anything new in the murder case?"

"Not that they're telling me." Or that I would necessarily tell him. He'd been sympathetic and all, but . . .

But then it occurred to me that one of these fishermen, with their clear view of Chad's condo, might have caught a glimpse of the murderer delivering the pie last

Tuesday. They weren't likely to talk to me about it, but they might tell Tony.

"Actually, I could use your help. It seems that someone at this complex"—I pointed to the whitewashed condominium building—"told the cops they'd seen me here the morning that Kristen Faulkner was murdered. It's not true, but the problem is, I have no way to prove it."

"Bummer," said Tony. He lit a cigarette and blew out a cloud of smoke. Then he pointed at me and grinned. "You need another witness—someone who isn't making crap up."

"I sure do."

"Wait here. Lemme ask around."

"Thank you so much. It was Tuesday morning. It was raining, if that helps," I called after him as he shambled back to his buddies.

I lowered myself to the cool cement and sat with my legs hanging off the edge, not wishing to get any closer to Chad's building. All I needed was him out on his balcony with a pair of binoculars, jumping to the conclusion that I was stalking him.

The multistory cruise ship docked at the far side of the Navy Mole sounded three blasts on its horn and pulled away from its mooring, the cruisers crowded out on the decks to see Key West off. I felt a sharp surge of yearning for that kind of simplicity—my life dictated by a pleasant even if touristy vacation itinerary.

I was struggling to digest Deena's news. I believed everything she'd told me—why would she lie? But if Chad was seriously involved with Kristen, why in the world had he hooked up with me? Was he so panicked at the thought of getting engaged that he'd chosen to blow the relationship to bits? Jumping off the cliff with me certainly derailed his prospects for marriage. He knew how to be direct with his clients, but maybe talking about his deep inner feelings with a girlfriend was not a skill he'd mastered.

Tony ambled back over and squatted down beside me. He smelled a little of the beach and cigarettes and old beer and a little of something fried—maybe the lunch that had been served at the soup kitchen this morning.

"None of these dudes was fishing Tuesday. But I'll letcha know if I hear anything, okay?"

"Sure, thanks for trying," I said, disappointed.

I scrambled to my feet and headed across the pier toward my scooter, trying to push my mind away each time it pinged back to Chad. Revving up the bike's engine, I pulled on my helmet and started up Southard. Once past the Truman Annex gatehouse, I turned left down the little road behind the post office and right onto Fleming, thinking about dinner and filling Eric and Connie in on the latest. Dusk was rolling into darkness and it felt chilly, like more rain was coming. I wished I'd worn my fleece and some heavier socks. My teeth were chattering by the time I reached the marina and settled the bike on its kickstand in the parking lot.

Our finger of the dock seemed unusually dark. Had we had a power outage? Even Miss Gloria's houseboat was blacked out. Odd that she didn't have her Christmas lights on—she must have gone out this afternoon, I thought as I passed her place. Maybe one of her kids was visiting and had taken her out to supper. Did she have kids? I didn't remember her ever mentioning her family.

Halfway up the walk to our boat, I noticed a heap on the planks, as though someone had dropped a sack of something right in the middle of the dock where anyone could trip over it. Annoyed, I picked up my pace. When I moved in, Connie had stressed how important it was to the community that everyone pitch in to keep the place clean. Shipshape, she called it. *Don't worry about whether you dropped it or not. Just pick it up.*

Only five feet away, I realized the heap was Miss Gloria, left in a pile like yesterday's garbage. My heart began to hammer and my hands felt slippery with sweat. I ran up to her, yanking the phone from my pocket, and punched 911. "It's Hayley Snow. At the Tarpon Pier Marina. Something's wrong with my neighbor." I crouched down next to her, smoothing a strand of white hair from her forehead.

"What kind of trouble is she having?" asked the operator.

I described Miss Gloria's pallid face and then—oh my God—the bloody gash visible through the fine white hair covering the top of her skull.

"Is she breathing?" the dispatcher asked. "Does she have a pulse?"

I held my hand in front of her lips. "I can't tell," I moaned. "She's so frail."

"Keep her warm and don't move her. We'll send someone right over."

I hung up and screamed for help.

16

Part of the secret of success in life is to eat what you like and let the food fight it out inside.

—Mark Twain

Mr. Renhart emerged from the cabin of his boat wearing torn jeans and a tan T-shirt that read "Habitat for Insanity: Fantasyfest 2011!"

"Jesus, Hayley, what's all the screeching about?"

"It's Miss Gloria—she's hurt. Can you bring me a blanket?" I crouched beside her, ready to take him on if he insisted we move her somewhere else. I'd overheard enough of his arguments with his wife to know that he always believed he was right.

But he ducked back inside and then sprinted over carrying a brown wool army blanket that smelled of must and fish. Wrinkling my nose, I took it from him and tucked it around Miss Gloria's limp little form. Oh dear Lord, what if she died?

"She must have fallen," said Mr. Renhart. "She's too old to be living in a place like this all by herself. Wouldn't you think her kids would care enough to move her into a home?"

"She didn't fall," I said, tamping down the urge to snap his head off. "How the heck do you think she'd get a gash on the top of her head from falling? Unless she was leaping or somersaulting. What are the chances of that?"

Probably she *had* fallen. But I hated to think of her being forced to move away from the marina she loved. And it wasn't fair to lash out at him, but the more minutes went by without seeing the rise and fall of her chest, the more hysterical I felt.

"Did you just get home? Did you hear anything?" My questions came out wobbly and shrill. "What if someone hit her?" I stood up and peered into the darkness, listening for someone running. "What if they're still around?"

"Don't you think I would have come out if I'd heard something?" he asked, his voice defensive. "I'm working the night shift this week, so I sleep all day. This is the first I've been outside."

We both perked up as the wail of an emergency vehicle's siren drew near. Then whirling red lights cut through the darkness and an ambulance pulled into the parking lot followed by a police car, its red and blue lights flashing. Two paramedics and two cops burst out of the vehicles and trotted down the dock toward us. I stood up, waving, and pointed to Miss Gloria. "Right here."

"What happened?" asked Officer Torrence. I cringed as a look of recognition crossed his face.

"I was on my way home and I noticed this heap. And it turned out to be Miss Gloria. She's our neighbor. This is exactly how I found her," I said. "Is she going to be okay?"

"Step aside and let us take a look." I backed away and two paramedics, a burly, bald man and a thin guy with a ponytail, knelt down and began to examine her. They conferred in low voices and the big guy trotted back to the ambulance and unloaded a gurney from the back.

"Name and address?" asked Torrence.

"Her name is Miss Gloria. She lives in that first little boat on this finger." I pointed to her cheerful yellow home.

"Gloria what?" asked Torrence.

"Do you know her last name?" I glanced at Mr. Renhart. He shook his head.

"We can get that from the dockmaster on the way out," said Torrence to the other cop, a young guy with a white-blond brush cut. "Does she have a history of falls?"

"I don't think so. I'm fairly new here, but she's always seemed sturdy enough to me. Is she breathing?" I asked the men working on her.

"Barely," said the paramedic with the ponytail, as he slid an oxygen mask over her head. He jostled it into place over her nose and mouth and pulled the elastic snug. Then he fastened a collar around her neck, and the two men loaded her onto the stretcher. "We're going to get her to the hospital. Next of kin?"

I shrugged helplessly. "She never mentioned any family. Should I come along?"

"Not necessary. Not unless you're related. Right now you'd only be in the way. You can call or visit later and find out how she's doing."

They transferred her from the dock to the gurney and bumped her away to the ambulance.

"I'll need your names and contact information," said Officer Torrence.

"Joshua Renhart."

"Hayley Snow," I added, thinking how odd it was that I'd never heard Mr. Renhart's first name.

Torrence turned to the young man with the crew cut—Officer Batten—and muttered in a low voice that I barely caught: "Faulkner murder. POI." To me he said: "Do you have a key to her place?"

I shook my head. "She's almost always home. There was never a reason. As I said, we're acquaintances. New friends. I haven't lived here very long."

After the policemen had finished pelting Mr. Renhart and me with more questions we couldn't answer about Miss Gloria, they left to look over her houseboat. I continued the last yards down the dock to Connie's place, feeling worried and sad.

Our boat was just as dark as Miss Gloria's had been. I remembered that Connie and Ray had dinner plans this evening and wouldn't be home until late. It wasn't until I stepped onto the deck that I could see well enough to realize that something was wrong here, too. Connie's houseplants had been kicked over and the door to the boat was swinging open.

I froze for a moment. Should I go in? What if the intruder was still on board? But Evinrude was in there somewhere. Terrified. And my computer and all of Connie's things. Sprinting the length of the wooden walkway toward the road, I waved madly at the cruiser, which was still idling in the parking lot. Panting, I rapped on the passenger-side window and motioned for the cop to lower his window.

"Someone broke into my houseboat!"

The two officers scrambled out of the car, juggling flashlights and guns, and followed me up the finger. Officer Torrence barked into his radio as we jogged.

"Stand back, Miss Snow," said Officer Batten once we reached Connie's boat. "You stay on the dock." Then he yelled "Police!" into the open door. "Come out with your hands up."

Nothing happened. Pointing their guns into the boat, they exchanged glances, and charged in.

I waited, pacing, nearly sick with worry. The lights went on in my bedroom, and then upstairs in Connie's room, and the two men emerged from her doorway onto the top deck. They shone flashlights in every corner and went back inside.

Officer Torrence pushed open the front door. "No one's in here now," he told me. "But we're going to look around a little more, so you stay put."

"Did you find a gray cat?" I asked the cop. "Gray stripes all over except for one white paw."

"Not so far," he said. "Let us finish and then you can have a look."

A second police car screeched into the parking lot and two more cops thudded up the walkway.

"Need some help here?" one of them asked. "Dispatcher said you'd called for backup."

"We've got it," said Officer Torrence. "Looks like attempted burglary, pure and simple." He rubbed his chin and grimaced. "Though you could start checking in with the other residents—see if anyone saw anything. The old lady who lives in the yellow boat was just taken to the hospital. Possible assault."

The two new cops headed toward the Renharts' boat. I sat on the edge of the dock, my feet dangling above the water, feeling helpless and distraught. The thought that I'd been pushing away sprang into my mind: Miss Gloria hadn't fallen at all. She'd been attacked by the same person who'd ransacked our boat. Too antsy to sit, I got up again and jumped back onto the deck of the houseboat. Maybe I could rescue some of Connie's plants. Somehow, like the other troubles that had accumulated over the last few days, this too was beginning to feel like my fault.

The biggest houseplant, a Norfolk Island pine that Connie had decked out in tiny white lights and fish-shaped ornaments made of glass, appeared to be a goner. Its blue ceramic pot was shattered, the trunk had been snapped off at the base, and bits of broken glass were scattered across the deck. The lights still sparkled on the decapitated tree. I managed to stuff the pineapple tree that Connie had been nurturing for two years back into its container and righted three of her orchids, which would probably not survive the shock of having their roots exposed to the night air.

Then I noticed something bobbing in the water beside the boat—Evinrude? I would just die. Grabbing the large net that we used for picking up trash, I fished for the object. It dove underwater and surfaced a foot to the right. With a sigh of relief, I pulled out Connie's oversized spider plant. Another total loss, but at least it wasn't the cat.

Officer Torrence appeared at the front door and frowned when he saw that I was straightening up. "Don't touch anything else," he warned. With gloved hands, he fiddled with the door's latch. "This appears to be broken."

"It's been like that since I moved in a couple weeks ago," I said. "We leave it unlocked," I added sheepishly. "Everyone looks out for everyone down here."

"Obviously, not everyone," he said, eying the mess of plants and pot shards on our deck and then jerking his thumb in the direction of Miss Gloria's boat. "You need to get this fixed. Key West may look like a small, friendly town, but plenty of troublemakers wash in with the tides."

"Any sign of the cat?" I asked.

"No." He turned and went back in. My eyes filled with tears. I'd never forgive myself if Evinrude was gone. Yet one more argument I'd had with my mother: She didn't think it was fair to drag a pet on my ill-considered adventure. But I didn't think I could live through that much change without him.

Torrence came back to the door and invited me in. "Take a look around and see if anything's missing," he said.

I ran directly to my bedroom and crouched down on all fours to look under the bed. "Kitty, kitty," I called in my most reassuring falsetto. No cat. I returned to the galley, grabbed the half-eaten package of Whisker Lick-in's from the counter, and shook it. Like me, Evinrude always turned out with enthusiasm for a snack between meals.

"Kitty, kitty." But he still didn't show.

Then the wreckage inside the boat came into focus. Our cupboards were flung open, drawers were hanging askew, and stuff was tossed out everywhere.

"Oh my God," I said, turning slowly to take it all in. "Who did this? What did they want?"

"It has the feel of someone looking for drugs," said the younger cop, eyes narrow and lips pinched. "And like maybe your little neighbor got in their way."

"They won't find any here," I said, my panic swelling. And guilt along with it, though I kept reminding myself I hadn't done anything wrong. "Except for a prescription for antibiotics that I didn't quite finish. I know that's incorrect—you're supposed to take all the pills, but I felt so much better and they were upsetting my stomach so I quit. And my mother gave me a few sleeping pills from her stash when I moved down here. Just in case things got rough in the transition." I could tell from the stunned looks on the policemen's faces that I was babbling nervous nonsense.

Officer Torrence shook his head. "Marijuana? Speed? Coke? Anything like that?"

"Of course not!" I said.

"You can speak for your roommate too?" Torrence pointed up the spiral staircase to Connie's room.

"Speak for me about what?" Connie asked, as she came onto the boat. "What in the world happened to my plants—" She gasped and blanched as she took in the mess and the cops. "Oh my God, what happened?"

"This is Connie Arp," I told them. "She lives here too. She's the owner." I grabbed a broom and dustpan and began to sweep up the broken glass in front of the sink. Anything to avoid looking at the tears that had started down her cheeks.

"Your home was ransacked. We were telling Miss Snow," said Torrence, "that the break-in looks drug-related. You say there weren't any drugs here, so any idea what they were after?"

Connie sank into one of the kitchen chairs and pinched the bridge of her nose with two fingers. "I can't believe this. On top of everything else this week . . ."

"Miss Gloria was attacked too," I hurried to tell her, hoping to head off hashing through my latest visit to the police station. I told her how I'd mistaken her limp body for a sack of trash. "And Evinrude is gone." I leaned on the counter and started to cry, feeling nauseated and weak.

"Is anything else missing? Money? Jewelry?" asked Officer Torrence. "Take a look while we're still here."

Connie started upstairs to her bedroom and I pulled myself together and went into mine. First I rustled through my small stash of jewelry in the closet. Mom's gold chain, my grandmother's pearls, and the sapphire earrings were still there. Then I turned to the desk. In my worry about the cat, I had not noticed that the surface that had held my laptop was now bare.

17

"You can let it go in the privacy of your office, you can weep in the walk-in, but at the bench, you must pick up your knife and finish boning out those chickens."
— Gabrielle Hamilton

I rushed back into the kitchen. "My laptop's gone!"

Connie came back down the spiral stairs and reported nothing missing from her room.

The police took down the information I gave them about my missing computer. "You need to get that lock fixed," said Torrence again, pointing at the front door. "And get some locks on the windows too. You can't be too careful. Call us if you have any other problems. We'll be in touch if the computer shows up. It's possible that it will be pawned." The way he said it, he didn't hold out much hope that I'd see it again.

"What the heck?" said Connie, once they'd tromped down the dock.

"I'm so sorry," I whispered. "I'll help you clean everything up."

We spent the next two hours straightening up the boat. The worst of the destruction was confined to the downstairs. Connie's room had definitely been searched, but mine was trashed.

Every fifteen minutes, I took a break and walked from one end of the dock to the other, calling for Evinrude. I even took a few trips out through the parking lot to Palm Avenue, looking for flattened masses on the pavement. He could never make it across this busy street alive. Not that he'd want to run away, but in his fear, he might blindly bolt. Searching for me. And home, of course. And lately, home was hard to find. A flicker of despair iced my heart.

"No luck?" Connie asked when I returned.

I sighed and sank into the wicker loveseat beside her. "No," I said, tapping my fist on the seat's arm. "I'm going to try checking on Miss Gloria again."

I dialed the number for information at the hospital and asked to be transferred to her room. On one of my trips searching for the cat, I'd stopped at the dockmaster's office and located Miss Gloria's last name on the list of mailboxes. Peterson. A name that common would make it hard to search for her relatives, if she had any. I had no idea how long she'd even lived in Key West or where she'd come from before settling on the island.

"We have no information on a Gloria Peterson," the clerk replied.

"What does that mean?" I asked. "I know the EMTs

were bringing her to your hospital. I saw them load her into the ambulance myself."

"She may still be in the emergency room," said the clerk. "Processing patients takes time. Or if it was a very serious injury, they might have airlifted her to the Miami trauma hospital."

I reported that news to Connie. "I wonder if we should check on Sparky?" Miss Gloria's sleek black cat.

"Would she want us breaking in?" Connie asked.

"We won't—we'll go in if her door's open. She'd definitely want someone to take care of him. Who else would think of it—Mr. Renhart?" I smiled, trying to picture him worrying about a neighbor's pet. Although he'd come through stronger than I might have expected in the case of Miss Gloria.

Connie rustled through the junk in one of the kitchen drawers until she came up with a flashlight. "Did the cops look at her boat? I wonder if it was tossed too? Should we take a weapon?"

"They said they were going to check it out," I said, then added: "You have a weapon?"

Connie laughed. "I have steak knives and my father's antique putter."

"Stand back or we'll sink the putt!" I said.

We left our boat and started down the dock. A heavy cover of clouds had rolled in, obscuring the moon. And a chilly breeze had picked up, whistling from the west. The water of the Bight slapped against our row of houseboats. At home in New Jersey, I would have predicted snow.

"It's spooky out here," I whispered, and then pointed. "This is where I found her."

"A little old lady is attacked in broad daylight. Why?" Connie asked. "You think the guys who trashed our boat also clocked Miss Gloria?"

"The timing works, but again, why?" I asked as I hopped onto the bow of Miss Gloria's boat. "What were they looking for? Did she see something happening?"

I tried the door: unlocked. Inside, a squeaky mewing greeted us. Sparky materialized out of the dark and began to wind himself around my legs. I bent down to scratch behind his ears and stroked his spine to the base of his tail. "Poor kitty, I bet you're hungry." I flicked on the galley light, found his food in a plastic container in the cabinet under the sink, and filled his bowl. But he stayed close to me, mewing piteously and ignoring his dinner.

"He's lonely, isn't he?" Connie asked. "He knows something's wrong. Let's bring him home until we figure out what's going on with Miss Gloria."

If we figure it out, I thought but didn't say, as I scooped up the cat and tucked him under my sweater. We retraced our steps up the finger, now slick with rain. Once back in our boat, I retreated to my room, settled the purring black animal onto the bed, and used Connie's computer to check my e-mail. First in the queue was a note of congratulations from Wally Beile at *Key Zest*, addressed to me and a woman named Sally.

Dear Hayley and Sally,

Congratulations! You've made it through our final cut for the food critic position at the magazine.

The competition has been amazing. To that end, we invite you two to write and submit one final review. The file will be due in my in-box by five p.m. tomorrow. It goes without saying that this should be your finest work!

After an initial burst of euphoria, a slow knot of terror began gathering in my midsection. How could I possibly manage this with everything else in my life falling apart?

A second e-mail was from Eric, asking how the conversation had gone with Deena. I texted him back: NEIGHBOR ASSAULTED, HOUSEBOAT TRASHED, EVINRUDE MISSING.

He phoned me immediately. "I'm coming over."

I didn't argue—I wanted him there.

"Eric's coming over," I called out to Connie in the living room once I'd hung up.

"Ray is too. And he's bringing a pizza." She came to my bedroom door and grinned. "Can we whip something up for dessert?"

"Of course." I closed up her laptop and crossed the living room to the galley. Molasses cookies. I could bake them in my sleep. I turned the oven on to 350 degrees. Then, grabbing a stick and a half of butter from the freezer, I nuked it until soft and began to beat it with sugar, molasses, and an egg.

"Ray thinks our break-in could be related to Kristen's murder," Connie said, as she collapsed in the goosenecked rocker by the window. "Because what's the common denominator?"

"Unfortunately, it's me, right?" I added the dry ingredients to the wet, dropped spoonfuls of the batter onto a cookie sheet, and slid the pan into the oven. "I bet you're sorry you ever invited me to live here."

"It's not your fault, Hayley," she said, not sounding entirely convinced.

By the time the cookies were out of the oven, both Ray and Eric had arrived.

"It's raining like hell," Ray said, shaking himself off like a wet dog. "Supposed to be a lousy day tomorrow too."

I could only think of Evinrude, huddled out in the cold and wet under someone's car or on their boat deck or . . . Feeling myself growing panicky, I forced my mind back to my friends.

"Did the police say anything about Kristen's murder while they were here?" Ray asked after devouring his third slice of pizza.

"Nothing was said, but I know the guy I've seen twice this week recognized me," I said. "I heard him mutter to his partner that I was a person of interest in the Faulkner case. Other than that, they didn't discuss it—certainly not with me."

"But if you're a real suspect," Eric said, dunking a molasses cookie into a glass of milk, "they aren't going to tell you anything. Did you figure out what's missing here?"

"As far as we can tell," Connie said, "even though they left a big mess, only Hayley's computer was taken."

"And that was no prize," I added. "A five-year old Mac that was on its last legs."

"So maybe they were looking for content rather than hardware," Ray said. "What were you working on?"

I finished chewing and swallowing the cookie I was eating, because it would have been rude to spit it out. But it went down like a mouthful of sawdust. "A list of everything I know about Kristen and the murder. Just like you and I talked about doing." I stared at Eric. "But how would someone know I was making the list? And why would they care?"

"They would care if they were on it—or if you were getting too close," Eric said. "And if they figured you would turn your notes over to the police." He reached across the table to squeeze my hand. "We'll figure this thing out."

Connie fetched a legal pad and a pen with the Paradise Cleaning logo on it and we re-created the list of notes that I'd been drafting earlier in the day. They included: Henri Stentzel, Chad's relationships before me, the proposed restaurant on Easter Island, the key lime pie itself, and possible alibis for me the day of the murder. Including Miss Gloria.

"Obviously, Miss Gloria can't help because she's unconscious in the hospital," I said. "Some hospital, somewhere."

"Which is probably not coincidental," Connie added, and scribbled two stars next to our neighbor's name.

I groaned. I had imagined that my friend had been attacked because she tried to stop someone from boarding our boat—which was bad enough. I hadn't pictured her being put out of commission because of what she might know about Kristen's murder.

Connie typed "Easter Island restaurant proposal" into her computer's search bar and scrolled through the list—two blog posts weighing in against the proposal, an article in the *Citizen* about the history of Easter Island, several fixed-price menus for Easter dinner.

Connie clicked several links and finally reached the second page. "Here's a YouTube video taken at the hearing about rezoning Easter Island for commercial purposes," she said, and placed the computer on the coffee table so we all could watch it.

The video, which appeared to have been captured on the phone of someone in the audience, jumped into action just as the man at the podium called for comments from the public. We could see the heads of the people sitting in front of the photographer and a grainy podium in the distance.

Eric squinted at the screen. "I think that's the chairman of the city council running the meeting."

A small man with a neat mustache shot up out of his seat, obscuring the screen for a moment. "Let's face it—the rich people in this town have us by the short hairs. And our city council is more concerned with increasing revenues than any shoddy pretense of maintaining a decent quality of life on this island. The proposed development will cost the citizens of Key West for services such as electricity, water, and fire and police departments. And what will we get in exchange? A restaurant where most of us can't afford to eat."

He looked like he wasn't planning to cede the floor anytime soon, but the city council chair broke in from the podium to ask for other comments. He pointed to a man on the other side of the room, and the video swooped left.

"We voted not to change the zoning on this piece of property five years ago," said the second man. "Why is this issue back on the docket? What is the point of rehashing something that's already been decided?"

"Money!" a woman hollered in a muffled voice. The video swung around to the back of the room to focus on her. "The Faulkners have enough to buy the whole town off. Or at least our so-called public servants on the city commission."

"Order," yelled the chair, barely audible above the comments now being shouted from the audience. He banged the podium with a gavel. The video ended abruptly and we played it through a second time.

"That looks an awful lot like Wally Beile," I said, leaning closer to the screen and pointing to the back of the head of the man who had asked why the vote was being revisited. "Kristen's co-owner at *Key Zest.*"

"So Wally was against Kristen's restaurant?" Eric asked.

I held my hands out. "No idea. Though they sure didn't agree on everything else. She purged me from the list of food critic applicants and he stuck me right back on it. In fact, I nearly forgot—I made the cut! I'm one of the top two candidates. He wants us to submit a final review tomorrow."

"Hayley, that's wonderful," said Connie. The guys chimed in with their congratulations.

"What restaurant are you going to write about?" Ray asked.

"I have no idea. The idea of choosing turns me to jelly. What if I pick Louie's Backyard and he's looking for something really casual like B.O.'s Fish Wagon?"

"Don't overthink it," said Eric. "Just make a decision and go with it. They obviously like what you're doing, or you wouldn't have made it this far."

Miss Gloria's black cat pranced into the room and rubbed on Eric's ankle. "Who's this?" he asked, reaching down to stroke her.

"Miss Gloria's Sparky," said Connie.

"Any news about Evinrude?"

I choked out a no and went outside to call for him yet one more time. The sympathy on their faces would only make me start crying.

When I returned, Connie was explaining how we'd found the cat on Miss Gloria's houseboat and taken him in until our neighbor came home. "Back to the list that was on your computer," she said. "Anything else we should add?" She tapped the legal pad with her pen.

"Related to the Easter Island restaurant," I said, "is the business about the chef Kristen lured away and whether his leaving caused Henri's place to fail. If it did, she must have been really pissed at Kristen. But other than interrogating Henri, I don't see much that can be done there."

Eric got up to leave, kneading my shoulders while I packed a small plastic bag of cookies for him to share with Bill.

"Why don't you run home with me?" he asked. "Then you can borrow my car to get around town tomorrow.

It's supposed to be horrible weather and I'm not going out. You know how to drive a stick, right?"

He overrode my weak objections and we dashed out into the rain. On the way across town, I filled him in on what Deena had told me about Chad's love life. Which I'd been too embarrassed to mention in front of Connie and Ray.

"You were right about this one. How dumb could I have been, not to pick up on the fact that he already had a serious girlfriend?"

He laughed and patted my knee. "We all take our turns being fools for love. Obviously he showed you what he wanted you to see. He's a champion at compartmentalizing. And he's a divorce lawyer—he only sees relationships unraveling. That would make it hard to be an optimist when it comes to marriage."

"According to Deena, he prides himself on not allowing his clients to negotiate. I don't think any good divorces come out of that office. If there is such a thing."

"Oh, there is," Eric said. "Some of my patients are way better off having moved on from a bad match." He turned onto Petronia Street in the Bahama Village section of town and drove past several thriving restaurants and shops, followed by a block of rundown concrete homes. Then he pulled over in front of the pale green conch house he shared with Bill.

"Thanks for everything," I said as he got out. "You're the best friend I could imagine. I'm so lucky you're here."

By the time I arrived back at the marina, the rain was pouring buckets so I gave up searching for Evinrude. No way he'd come out in this kind of weather—dark, wet, and cold—even if he heard me calling. I thumbed through my e-mail one last time and found a new message from my lawyer, Richard Kane.

Had I had any luck on producing witnesses who could support my alibi?

Not yet. And I'd also forgotten to ask Ray what was wrong with my lawyer.

I popped one of my mother's emergency sleeping pills and went to bed with Sparky tucked into the space between my chin and my chest.

18

"Hunger knows no friend but its feeder."
—Aristophanes

When the black cat walked across my chest in the morning, I was groggy enough to think at first he was Evinrude. My heart ached, tallying yesterday's losses: Miss Gloria, Connie's plants, my computer, and worst of all, my cat. Through the sheet of steady rain that pattered against my porthole, the sky looked cold and gunmetal gray. I pulled on sweats and thick socks, fed the cat, and started a pot of coffee.

After a quick breakfast of blueberries and granola from the Sugar Apple Natural Foods store (not quite as good as mine, but who'd had time to cook?), I got dressed to go out. Connie loaned me a voluminous yellow slicker with matching rain pants and I set off on my first mission. My thin maroon-colored rain jacket would be no match for this weather. I planned to hit every houseboat in the marina this side of Palm Avenue, asking three questions. Had they seen my cat? Were they at home the previous Tuesday morning? And had they seen any strangers at our marina yesterday afternoon?

No one answered my knock at the boat two slips down. The windows were so crammed with trash that the interior was virtually obscured. I'd never seen a live person there—either it had been abandoned or was inhabited by a night crawler.

Then I tapped on the Renharts' door. The missus answered, her blond hair pulled back into a limp ponytail. She wore a T-shirt that read: "Don't bother knockin' if our boat is rockin'." There was an image I'd just as soon not get stuck in my mind.

"Come in out of the rain and have a cup of coffee," Mrs. Renhart insisted. She poured me a cup of dark roast that tasted so bitter I had to wonder whether the pot had been made yesterday and sat on the warmer overnight.

"Joshua told me all about Miss Gloria's mishap," she said in a whisper. "He's just gone to bed, or I'm sure he'd want to hear the latest.

"It's such a shame about her falling," she added. "A marina is really no place for the elderly." She lit up a cigarette and blew out a fog of smoke. "Honey, what in the world were you doing with the police the other day?"

I sidestepped that question by telling her about our break-in, assuring her that the police felt it was related to the attack on our neighbor. Which wasn't a sure thing at all, but I wanted to get off the Renharts' worn-record-groove belief that Miss Gloria had fallen. And I hoped that mentioning the possibility of a stranger in the neighborhood would jog her memory. No luck—she hadn't gotten off her shift until eleven. I thanked her for the coffee, refused a slice of Publix coffee cake, and moved on.

After leaving the Renharts, I canvassed the green and white boat that looked like it had been airlifted from a trailer park, the boxy turquoise boat with faux gingerbread trim, and a brown house the size of a small apartment complex with faded siding and a full-sized bike rack. None of the residents had seen a cat or a cat burglar. Mrs. Dubisson, my last hope, began to cry when I told her about Miss Gloria.

"The police asked all about this yesterday," she told me. "We moved in around the same time. I'm going to say it was about fifteen years ago. Her son has never liked her living here, but she's a spunky lady and she told him he could do what he wanted with her once she was an old woman and her mind was gone. Or her body." She resumed sniffling. I found a clean-looking tissue in the pocket of Connie's raincoat and handed it to her.

"Do you remember her son's name?" I asked.

"Teddy," she said, wiping her eyes with my Kleenex. "I promised him that I'd check on her every day and I have. I'd just stopped by to see her yesterday afternoon before all that commotion. She was fine—that's what I told the police officer. But then I got so upset I couldn't talk anymore and he had to help me go lie down."

All my early-warning systems went to alert. Maybe she'd seen something more that she hadn't remembered to tell the cops.

"And did you happen to notice anyone unfamiliar at our end of the finger?"

She wrinkled her forehead in concentration. "There was a man with a backpack in the parking lot. Looked like one of the homeless guys you see over at the park. But he took off when he spotted me. I don't think he came as far as Miss Gloria's boat. But on the other hand, I don't know if he was coming or going."

"What was he wearing?" I asked.

She shook her head. "I was in a hurry. It felt like it was going to rain any minute and Judge Judy was coming on the TV at four. I'm sorry. That's all I noticed." She looked like she would cry again. "It was important, wasn't it?"

Back home, I collapsed on the wicker love seat in front of Connie's computer and checked my e-mail. Two messages from Mom, requesting a call sometime today. And the link I'd sent myself last night to the city council meeting on YouTube. I clicked on the link and watched it through a third time, this time noticing the smallest snippet of an interaction at the back of the room, almost offscreen. Between Kristen Faulkner and Henri Stentzel. I couldn't make out the words over the crackling noises on the video, but neither one of them looked happy. I very much wanted to be able to eliminate Henri from the pool of murder suspects, but Eric's voice echoed in the back of my mind.

"What if she did it, Hayley? Are you willing to go to jail for her?" I imagined him asking.

I dialed the phone number for Seven Fish Restaurant

and asked to speak to Henri's chef friend, Porter. She came on the line, shouting to be heard over the banging of pots and pans in the background.

"Yes?"

"Porter, it's Hayley Snow. We met at Kristen Faulkner's funeral the other day."

"Yeah, Hayley, hi. What can I do for you?"

"This will sound odd, but it's important. Were you at the hearing about the Easter Island restaurant a couple of months ago?"

"No, I wasn't."

"Reason I'm asking," I added quickly before she could hang up, "is I saw a video of the event where Henri Stentzel was arguing with Kristen. Any idea what that was about?"

"You don't give up, do you? Listen, Henri didn't kill Kristen, if that's what you're sniffing around at."

"I appreciate what a good friend you are," I said, "but you have to understand that I didn't kill her either."

I heard the *whoosh* of a cigarette lighter and I could imagine Porter inhaling a blessed hit of nicotine.

"If you want the facts on what went wrong between them and Henri won't tell you, talk to Doug. He took over as head chef at her restaurant. He still works there, as far as I know. He was there for the whole mess—I only have second- and third-hand gossip. It's Saturday. I'm sure he's working. Hola's in Miami Beach. Speaking of that, have to go. Every table is booked tonight, including the seats at the bar, and I'm already behind."

I thanked her and got off the phone, no further along than when I'd started. My stomach rumbled, and I realized with a start that I hadn't given any more thought to the food critic piece due in Wally's office by five p.m.

So I called my mother, figuring I could allay her fears and suspicions and get some help with a decision in one fell swoop. After the initial dodge and weave, performed with fingers and toes crossed—yes, I was fine, no more problems with the police, et cetera, et cetera—I told her about the request for one last review.

"It has to be lunch," I said, "because that's all the time I have left. Fancy, casual, expensive, cheap—I have no idea what they're looking for."

"Have you checked out the pieces their last critic wrote?" she asked.

"There was no last critic, remember? It's a brand-new position in a brand-new magazine." I groaned. "It's too much pressure to come up with a dazzling review in less than twelve hours. Six hours and fourteen minutes, to be exact."

"Obviously, they loved what you've done so far, sweetie. Do you have time to run up and consult with Lorenzo?"

"I have to go this one alone, Mom," I said. "Lorenzo's not on duty until five, and that's when the piece is due. And it's raining here—I doubt he'll show up anyway. Besides, he about scared me to death when I saw him yesterday."

"What did he say?"

"He turned over the Tower card. And told me to watch out for the chaos. But you could see on his face that he was worried."

"Oh, I hate getting the Tower," she said. "When I get

that card, I know to keep things simple for a while. No fancy recipes, no specialty shops, no quail eggs in jellied goose liver." She laughed. "What are you in the mood for eating? There's no point in trying to force a meal down that doesn't match your mood."

"Comfort food," I said. "Something fried, not broiled or steamed. A burger. Fries. Fish and chips." I laughed. "You're a genius, Mom. I'm going to B.O.'s Fish Wagon as soon as we hang up."

19

"When I asked how he was holding up, he just grinned—a cook likes to cook and he was, pardon the metaphor, on fire."

—Julia Reed

It wasn't the best day for lunch at B.O.'s, an eating establishment with no real walls and no heat either. The front of the restaurant consisted of a narrow counter with stools that faced the street. The left wall was actually not a wall at all, but a rusted-out, vintage pickup truck with a manikin at the wheel. Above the truck, tropical foliage and strings of lobster buoys filled in the space. Inside, exposed beams were plastered with old license plates, more buoys, and signs to keep visitors entertained while they waited for their food. Concrete floors and listing wooden tables and benches completed the decor.

Today the rain and humidity brought out a descant of the usual Key West restaurant odors—beer, fried fish, hamburger grease. At least the line at the ordering counter was short—only me. I perused the specials that had been scratched out with Magic Marker on wooden boards propped around the counter, and selected a representative variety: fried grouper with black beans and rice, grilled scallops with fried onions and a side salad, and a burger, medium, all the way. At the last minute, I added an order of conch fritters, which I didn't care about but my future readers might.

"Wow," said the big man behind the counter after he'd scribbled my order on a small pad. "I hope you're expecting company."

When I smiled without comment, he handed me an industrial-sized plastic glass of water and took my cash. I shoved three dollar bills into the glass tip jar and he squeezed a squawking rubber pig to celebrate. Then he clipped my order to a short clothesline over the sandwich counter and the chef set to work.

I carried my glass of water laced with lime to a table at the back and shrugged off my raincoat. A skinny old cat was curled up on a newspaper on the bench beside me. I pushed away thoughts of Evinrude and slid my phone out of my jeans pocket to look over the notes I'd jotted from a previous visit.

B.O.'s Fish Wagon, named after owner Buck Owens, is a must-try for visitors yearning for a taste of quintessential Key West. Go on a warm day and don't look too closely at the dirt floors and rough wooden tables and you'll find yourself picnicking in comfort-food heaven. B.O.'s calls its burger Mother's Finest, and I have to agree. Order it grilled medium with the works—and prepare for a four-napkin feast. The grouper, when available—

My food was delivered, so I saved what I was writing and put the phone away.

"Are you waiting for someone?" the server asked, looking a little worried. Probably thinking "bulimia."

"All set. Thanks." I gave a friendly but dismissive salute. Then I started on the burger, cooked pink and loaded with mustard, mayo, grilled onions, pickles, lettuce, and tomato. After three bites, I pulled myself away from the perfect burger and began to rotate through the other dishes—an edge of crispy grouper, a bite of sweet scallop—imagining how I would describe each with words that would make Wally Beile sink to his knees in culinary celebration. When I couldn't squeeze in one more bite, I packed the leftovers in to-go containers in case I ran into Tony or one of the other homeless guys. Then I shoveled my paper plates into the plastic trash barrel and dashed through the rain to Eric's car.

At home, I settled in to finish the review on Connie's computer, which was, frankly, older than Julia Child herself. When my Gmail account wouldn't open and hers refused to accept an attachment, I printed out a copy. I would drive it to the office, which I was sure would be open. They were too new and hungry to take the whole weekend off. A little friendly face time with the staff couldn't hurt. And if there was a way to work it in naturally, maybe I could feel out Wally about the disagreements he'd had with his deceased partner. I considered stopping at Cole's Peace Bakery for an assortment of scones, but decided a food bribe from a poisoning suspect wasn't such a hot idea.

Tucking the review into a manila envelope and then safely under Connie's yellow slicker, I hurried out to Eric's car and headed up Southard Street, the windshield wipers flapping briskly. I parked behind the *Key Zest* office, skipped over the gathering puddles, and vaulted up the stairs to the office. The same girl in the same palm-tree-studded shirt I'd seen earlier in the week manned the front desk. I peeled off the dripping yellow raincoat and hung it on a peg on the wall.

I shouldn't assume she remembered who I was. "Adrienne, I'm Hayley Snow. We met the other day. I was so excited about making the cut for the food critic position that I decided to deliver my last selection in person."

Fresh out of folksy B.O's Fish Wagon, I flashed a big old country-style grin, plunked the envelope on her desk, and waited for any sign of encouragement.

"Yes, I remember." She extracted my page from its protective cover, glanced over it, fluffed up her highlighted hair, and finally smiled. Then she leaned toward me to whisper: "I'm not allowed to say this officially, but I loved your little palm tree rating thing."

Her voice skipped back to its normal register. "Of course, Sally—she's the other contender—she's done restaurant criticism before, so naturally her writing is more polished," she continued. "And she reviewed the big three in town, so it's hard to compare with takeout. Or breakfast at Pepe's. Or heaven forbid, B.O.'s." She tucked my review back into the envelope. "But no offense—

chacun à son goût, as they say in Paris." She shrugged her shoulders, the palm-tree silk shirt rustling. "Anyway, lots of luck."

"Thanks," I said, my stomach plummeting. I wondered which "big three" my rival had targeted—probably Louie's Backyard. Maybe Michael's Steakhouse? Azur? Pisces? Places I couldn't have afforded to set foot in. Nor could a lot of the folks who visited this town. I squeezed my hands into fists and tried to push down my disappointment. Might as well at least try to fish for some information, since a job offer was looking bleak.

"How are things going without Kristen? This must be an awfully difficult transition." I cringed inside at my awkward segue, but how do you slide gracefully from food criticism to murder?

She blinked heavily mascaraed eyelashes to contain the tears that suddenly filled her eyes. "I've never known anyone who died," she said. "Certainly never anyone . . . you know . . ." She carved a tear from her cheek with one long fingernail. "I keep thinking about her biting into that pie. And then taking another bite, and another, until she got sick. She loved all her sweets. But key lime pie especially. I swear I don't know how she stayed so thin."

"I didn't know her that well," I said apologetically.

A worried look crossed her face like a scudding cloud.

"But please know that I had nothing to do with that pie. Nothing." Did she believe me? "Of course my ex-boyfriend did, but that's another story. I mean, he knew her well, not that he had something to do with the pie," I hurried to add.

She wound her hair around one fist and squinted, tapping a lacquered nail on the desk. "Kristen and I were not separated at birth either, if you get my drift. Wally's a hundred times easier to deal with as a boss."

"How did they get along?" I asked.

"Not good. He may look young and hip, but he's old-school," she said. "She didn't think there was a thing wrong with advertisers paying to have their restaurant or their store or their spa or whatever reviewed."

"That's not a review," I said. "That's advertising."

"That's what Wally said. He wanted all of our articles to be unsolicited so there wouldn't be any bias."

"Hard to argue with that."

"Oh, but she did. 'Isn't every piece of writing filtered through the writer's mind?'" She let go of her hair and shook it out. "Oh my gosh, she said that a thousand times if she said it once. She thought as long as the food critic went out in disguise, like Ruth Reichl used to for the *New York Times*, there wouldn't be a bias problem. It was not at all clear who was going to win that argument," Adrienne added. "But only one of them was going to be left standing. And I would not have put money on Wally."

I drew my lower lip over the upper and nodded, trying to look empathetic. "Do you think they'll go forward with the Easter Island restaurant? The one Kristen was working on?"

"I have no idea," she said. "The change in zoning was

going to be such an ugly fight. I can't imagine who else but Kristen would have the guts to take it on."

Just then the door burst open and Wally dashed in from the hall, shaking off delicately like a damp cat. He looped his worn yellow raincoat onto the peg next to mine.

I sprang to my feet, sure I looked guilty of pumping confidential information from his staff. And Adrienne looked equally guilty about spilling office secrets to me.

"Hayley came by with her last review," the secretary explained. "It's very cute." She winked at me and waggled her fingers: Go for it.

I cringed, certain that "cute" was not what they were going for at *Key Zest*. I stammered through my spiel about how I was so excited to be in the running that I brought the piece over myself. Admitting that I had complicated computer problems and didn't trust my e-mail would not be reassuring to a prospective boss.

"I know you're busy. I didn't mean to take up—"

"Come in," he said as he started across the room to his office. "I only have a minute." I trailed behind him, thanking him profusely for considering me and apologizing for any trouble and trying to keep from yammering myself right out of a job.

Honestly, to see him seated at his computer, wearing his tropical shirt and black glasses, it was hard to imagine this man baking a poisoned pie and delivering it to his co-worker. Wouldn't it have been much easier to hash things out with her? Or, if the relationship was truly in tatters, quit and start another kind of magazine? Murder was an awfully big step.

"We like what you've done so far," he said as I handed over the fish wagon review. "It's going to be a hard decision and we appreciate your producing another review without much notice. On a Saturday. We're a small office, so each of our staff has to be ready to pitch in until an issue is completed. Frankly, we've had enough drama in the past three months for a lifetime."

I managed to resist telling him I'd never finished a paper on time in my entire academic history. It wasn't that I didn't care—I cared too much and that tied me in knots.

"I am definitely a team player," I squeaked. "I love working with people. And animals. Not that that pertains to this job, but I'm just saying . . ." I could see his eyes darting to his computer screen, probably desperate to tackle his inbox.

"Good. If you don't have any questions, we'll be in touch."

As I bolted out of the office and down the stairs, feeling like a bumbling fool, my phone rang. ATTORNEY RICHARD KANE came up on the screen, title and all. My hands started to sweat just like Pavlov would have predicted. I dashed through the rain, flung myself into Eric's car, and managed to peep out hello.

"Miss Snow, this is your attorney calling. Richard Kane. Unfortunately, so far we have not found any witnesses that could verify your whereabouts on the morning the murder took place. A dead end."

All the fried food I'd sampled at B.O's threatened to surface. "You're giving up? I swear I was right there on the boat all morning. Surely someone—"

"Naturally my man will continue looking, but I did

wonder if you'd remembered any facts that we haven't already covered. Any phone calls you made that morning? A trip to the dry cleaners or the gym perhaps?"

"I didn't go anywhere. I was working. I called my friend Eric about four times, because he was talking me through my article. But I can't see how that will help. I was on my cell phone so I could have made those calls from anywhere. And besides, who's going to believe an alibi from one of my closest friends? For God's sake, Eric used to babysit me when I was a kid. He's known me forever."

There was a long silence that left me wondering whether he'd hung up.

"There have been some other developments you should probably know about," I said. "My neighbor who lives a couple doors down was attacked last night. And our boat was ransacked and robbed—my computer was taken."

"Was your neighbor a busybody? Would she be likely to accost a stranger and instigate a conflagration?" he asked.

Did he purposely try to sound pompous and offensive, even to his own clients?

"She's a sweet little lady who loves life on the marina," I said stiffly. "If she spotted a stranger on our finger, she might go over to introduce herself. That's all." Then I remembered what Mrs. Dubisson had said about seeing a homeless person with a backpack, and with some misgivings, I reported that conversation.

"We always look at the homeless first," he said. "It's a simple fact of life in this town."

"That's a little unfair, don't you think? Assuming they're criminals because they don't have a place to live?"

"In my experience—and I've been in practice for many years on this island—homelessness equals addiction. The crimes you're describing at your marina are the sine qua non of an alcoholic or a crack addict. Smash, grab, and then dump the goods with the pawnbroker—God help whoever might get in their way. And then, bingo, they have booze for a night or a week or whatever. Though a five-year-old computer wouldn't bring much. Maybe one night's high." He gave a self-congratulatory laugh, as if he knew it all.

Whatever else might have been wrong with my new lawyer, he was a first-class bigot. Certainly not a supporter of the Key West motto: "One Human Family."

"Are the cops looking at any other suspects?" I asked.

"Not that they've mentioned. You are in the unfortunate position of having a decent motive and no alibi. And you're a cook with more than a passing knowledge of key lime pie."

"I'm not really a cook; I'm a writer."

"The police won't be dissecting your job history," said Kane. "They're looking for a killer."

He severed the call, leaving me feeling helpless and slightly frantic. It sounded as though he was starting to believe that I was guilty. And not looking very hard for information that would knock me off the list of suspects. I tapped my fingers on the steering wheel, trying to think of a plan. At least I could find out where my father got this bozo's name.

I called my father's home number. Allison answered.

"Your dad's gone out jogging. How are things working out with the new attorney?"

"That's exactly why I'm calling," I said. "Did he come highly recommended? Because not only does he have a miserable personality; he doesn't seem to believe that I'm innocent."

"A disadvantage in a defense lawyer," said Allison. "Though I don't suppose it's absolutely necessary. In any case, I'm not sure who your father called for the reference—it all happened so fast. You should definitely find someone else if he's not taking care of you. Can Chad be helpful?"

"Not at all," I said. "He's not speaking to me at the moment."

"I'm sorry. He seemed like a nice enough guy when we met him. I really did like him."

The four of us had had coffee the night before Chad flew home from his visit to New Jersey. Chad had charmed both Allison and my dad with his lighthearted stories about practicing law in Key West, like the custody fight over the thirty-pound parrot who cursed at visitors. In retrospect, I realized how unusual it was for him to agree to meet my parents. Not to mention conducting himself with such warmth. The guy I thought I followed to Key West turned out to be a very different man once I got there.

Allison broke through my thoughts. "I wonder if he finally picked up on your desperation and that scared him and made him retreat."

"My desperation?" This was not an attractive description, and I had to admit I was floored to hear it from Allison.

"I mean about getting away from home, getting out in the world. No offense, honey, but probably everyone except your dad noticed."

"Sheesh," I said. "Next time you notice something that big, let me know, okay?"

"Will do," she said. "Tell me more about what happened to the poor woman who was murdered. What kind of poison was used?"

"Only a chemist," I said with a laugh, "would ask that question. It was a pie, which was a disgusting green color." I described my knife at the police station, covered in green goop. "Obviously, it was fast-acting, because she was dead in a matter of hours. That's all I know."

"So you don't know what her symptoms were or the time line—"

"Oh Lord, no." A wave of malaise washed over me.

"The cook couldn't have used something bitter," she said, "or the victim would have stopped eating after one mouthful—maybe even spit it out. Something with no taste would work best. Let me think about that and I'll call you back."

"The cook!" I said. "I've been assuming that the person who baked the pie was the one who added the poison. But maybe the murderer added it after the fact."

"Like the Tylenol fiasco," she said.

After a few more minutes' chatting, I hung up, feeling the slightest bit better—my stepmother and I were bonding over poisons. But on the downside, my lawyer seemed to be basing my defense on the hope that the cops would eke out a confession from a homeless person. Motive, lack of alibi, and a passion for food and cooking—that's what I had going against me. Even with that damning trio and the alleged sighting of me near Chad's condo the morning of the murder, I still had trouble grasping why I made such an appealing suspect. How often did a dumped lover actually kill the new girlfriend?

My thoughts circled back to the way I'd felt after finding Chad with Kristen. Yes, I'd been outraged for a few hours. But after that first shock, I was more embarrassed and disappointed than anything. Not murderous. But someone was furious enough with Kristen to actually kill her. I couldn't help thinking of Henri Stentzel and how angry she'd looked at the meeting about Easter Island. And how odd her first reaction to Kristen's death had been.

I took out my phone and tapped in the Bad Boy Burrito Web site. They were closed on Sundays and Tuesdays, the day the pie had been delivered. So she couldn't have had her work as an alibi.

I glanced at my watch—quarter to two.

If I went home to change into something comfortable and then drove like crazy, I could get to Henri's former restaurant in Miami Beach and interview the new chef before the dinner rush started. Henri's friend Porter had told me that if I arrived by five, I could probably talk to Doug. Eric wouldn't appreciate the extra miles on his car, but he'd understand once I explained that in order to get myself off the hook, I had to find someone else with a motive. A real motive. My fancy lawyer wouldn't approve of the outing either, but what was he doing for me?

And Detective Bransford had definitely told me not to leave town, and that was days ago, when I was just another well-behaved citizen. But right now it felt like the only person totally in my corner was me. I put the key in the ignition and fired it up.

20

"To a hungry stomach, any drive can seem like forever."

—John Linn

Since I'd flown the friendly skies to Key West when I moved down in early October, the drive up the Florida Keys to Miami sounded adventurous and even romantic. But, in fact, with the rain steady, the windshield wipers sluggish, and the traffic heavy, it was the longest one hundred and twenty miles I'd ever driven. At some points along the way, the Atlantic Ocean and the Gulf pressed in so close to the road from both sides, it was hard to imagine that people staked their property and their lives on such a fragile connection to the mainland. Through the wheezy blasts of the Mustang's heater, I could smell the bloated fishy odor of a very low tide.

Finally I reached the narrowest stretch of island past Key Largo, the Atlantic Ocean visible ten feet to the right and the Gulf of Mexico ten feet to the left. Then the two-lane road lined with bright turquoise Jersey barriers spilled into the town of Homestead, where I picked up the highway and civilization. With the help of Eric's GPS, I pulled into the parking lot of Hola on Miami Beach at twenty after five.

Inside, the restaurant looked perfectly nice, though maybe a little worn around the edges. I imagined that the frayed carpet and slightly faded upholstery would be less noticeable in the candlelight. The staff, dressed in black trousers and crisp white shirts, were busy setting up the tables, filling salt and pepper shakers, and folding napkins into sharp quarters for each place setting, in preparation for the Saturday-night onslaught. After a few minutes, the maître d', an officious man with black hair combed and shellacked like rows of young corn, noticed me at the host's stand and hurried across the room. He took a moment to look me over, from red sneakers to blue jeans to the long-sleeved Cat Man of Key West T-shirt.

"Sorry, we don't open until six. And we are fully booked until nine thirty. May I help you make a reservation for another night or recommend a place to get a drink?" he asked.

Thinking, I was sure, that I might prefer to come back on an evening when I was better dressed.

"Actually, I'm hoping to have a word with Doug Rodriguez," I said, flashing a phony smile. "I'm writing an article on Florida's rising chefs and it's going to press tomorrow and my editor tells me I have room to feature one more. Henri Stentzel—the former owner here—she said it would be a criminal oversight if I didn't speak to Hola's chef. Please." I extracted a small notepad and pen from my back pocket and tapped the pen on the podium for emphasis. "Ten minutes."

"He's preparing dinner," the officious man said.

I rustled a twenty-dollar bill out of my wallet and laid it on the reservations book.

"Henri said that?" he asked, sliding the bill into his pocket.

I nodded my head vigorously and forced another hokey smile. "Really, I'll hardly take any of his time."

He wheeled away and came back shortly. "He says he can talk to you for a few minutes while he works."

"Thank you so much!" I followed him down a narrow hallway, past the restrooms and their lingering scent of industrial cleanser, and through a swinging door into the clang and bustle of the kitchen. I sniffed the air, picking up the fragrant odors of sautéed onions, cilantro, and long-simmered beef.

"Over there," said the cornrowed receptionist, pointing across the room to the man at the stove.

Dodging past two women in white coats chopping piles of onion and garlic and a pastry chef painting layers of phyllo with butter, I approached the chef, who wore a white jacket that had probably started the shift pristine, chef's pants dotted with dancing chili peppers and a few random splotches of sauce, and a tall, pleated white hat. His face had the pitted pizza look of untreated adolescent acne. He was sautéing something in a skillet.

"My gosh, it smells incredible in here!"

He gave me a brisk nod and adjusted the angle of his toque. "What magazine did you say you were writing for? Eduardo didn't catch the name."

"I didn't tell him. But I'm Hayley Snow and I'll be working for the new style magazine, *Key Zest*. What are you preparing tonight?"

He jiggled the frying pan—sliced plantains?—and frowned. "*Key Zest*? I haven't heard of that."

Rather than dig myself deeper into a pit of lies, I told him who I really was and spilled everything out, starting with how I'd driven three-plus hours in the rain and ending with Kristen's murder and my status as a suspect.

"I'm so sorry I fibbed to get in here, but I'm kind of desperate," I said. "Actually, not kind of—I am desperate."

He picked up the frying pan and tossed the vegetables with an expert flick of the wrist. "So you're not a journalist?"

"I am a journalist, but more or less freelance. I'm so sorry," I added again, "but I never thought I'd get in to talk to you if I told the truth."

"You wouldn't have," he said and turned the flame off under his pan. "Leave some of those onions in bigger chunks," he called to a woman chopping at the counter nearby. He wiped his hands on a towel, lifted the lid of an enormous pot on the back burner, and stirred the contents. A cloud of fragrant steam escaped. My stomach gurgled.

"Listen," I said, "it's not only that I'm in trouble. Henri's a suspect too. And you are probably the only person who would understand the possible connection between Kristen's death and Hola's former chef. And if I could figure that out and pass it along, the cops can quit wasting their time and track the real murderer down. I'm sure you knew Henri," I said. "Porter said she hired you—that she hand-picked the entire kitchen staff."

He knocked his spoon against the side of the pot, laid it on the counter, and frowned. After a minute, he looked back up at me and said: "We were shocked when we heard Kristen had been murdered." He tipped his head to include the rest of the kitchen staff. "What do you need to know?"

I asked him about what had really happened between Kristen and Henri and what the story was with the previous chef's departure. "Was it the money that drew him away? Was Kristen able to offer him more celebrity than what he might have found here? Or what?" I didn't want to insult him by suggesting this slightly shabby restaurant didn't look like a chef-maker, especially when his food looked and smelled delicious.

"Let's sit for a minute," he said, and led me to a small table at the back of the kitchen. "You know that Henri and Robert—that's the chef—were seeing each other, right?"

"I had no idea."

Doug rapped his fist on the checkered tablecloth. "She had ten years on him and she was his boss, but still they fit together pretty well. Robert's always been fiery, but Henri knew how to handle him. Even the times he got raving drunk and quit in the middle of the dinner rush—and it happened more than once—she was able to talk him into coming back before much damage was done. I think, in his heart, he knew how much he owed her, too."

"So if they were a good fit personally and she helped him professionally, why did he leave?" I asked.

He sighed, took a red handkerchief from his pocket, and mopped his face. "Working in a kitchen is brutal work. It's hot, a lot of pressure, long hours. We all blow off steam at the end of the night by going to bars in other restaurants—the ones that stay open later. The third shift, we call it. Some of us used to wake up in the morning just hoping we weren't in jail." He flashed a crooked smile. "Henri, being the owner, usually had to stay late to close up this place." He gestured to the door leading to the dining room. "Used to be her place anyway. We started hanging at Kristen's restaurant, the Blue Giraffe. She'd often be at the bar. And then, well"—he shrugged—"sparks started to fly between her and Robert."

"Sparks?"

"Like raw meat hitting hot oil. You could literally smell the attraction between them. We all saw it coming, but who had the balls to warn Henri? So one night Henri finished up here in time to join us for a glass of wine. Only Robert wasn't at the Blue Giraffe. He'd gone home with Kristen."

"Was this before or after Kristen offered him the job on Easter Island?"

He shook his head. "Honestly, I doubt she'd have been that interested in Robert the man if he hadn't been such a brilliant cook. She wanted Robert the chef. And she was going to use whatever she had to lure him over. But after that night, Henri gave him an ultimatum. And Robert never could resist a challenge. So he left with

Kristen for Key West. And the stuffing seemed to leak out of Henri. Soon after, she put the place up for sale and moved on herself."

"I can't even imagine how embarrassing that must have been, to have the whole staff witness him defecting." I could imagine it really—I'd been through something very similar. At least I hadn't been humiliated in front of a dozen employees. "Would you say she was angry?" I asked. "Or more sad?"

"Angry at Kristen, sad about Robert. Very angry," he added. "I was pissed off too—we all were. We thought we were cresting a wave—that this restaurant was going to open doors to our future. We'd heard rumors that the food critic at the *Miami Herald* had us in his sights."

"But you're the head chef now, right? Couldn't that still happen for you?"

"Yeah, sure." He shook his head in disgust and stuffed the handkerchief back in his pocket. "But the damage was done with Robert's name off the masthead and then Henri selling the place. No one wants to spotlight a restaurant in terrible flux." He lowered his voice and looked around. "And you might have noticed that the new owner isn't so particular about keeping the place up. Or sometimes even buying the best ingredients. Though I fight for that." He sighed. "Your dinner is only as good as what goes into it."

I thanked him for talking to me and wished him luck. Then I couldn't help it—I asked him about tonight's dinner specials. He grinned for the first time since I'd come in.

"The special tonight is *Costilla de carne*, braised short

ribs served on a chili and cumin puree. On the side, a medley of sweet corn and poblano peppers. And those fried plantains."

By the end of his description, I was drooling like a dog in front of his supper dish.

"Would you like to try it?"

"I'd love to." He got up from the table and returned with a glass of merlot and a plate of his stew. He turned to go back to work, but then paused a couple steps away. "Call me if you find out what happened to Kristen." I nodded. "Or if you have any more questions. Bon appétit."

"Thanks for everything," I said.

The meat absolutely melted off the bone and the corn accompaniment was fresh and bright. And the clanking of pots, clattering of knives, sizzling of meat, and cheerful banter of the sous-chefs were better than any background music I could have chosen.

When I'd sopped up every drop with the last quarter of a buttery corn meal biscuit, I wiped my mouth and returned to the stove to thank him.

"I'm almost a food critic," I said. "I'll find out if I got the job this week. But if I reviewed your restaurant, I'd be raving."

I didn't say that if he was this good, his top chef, Robert, must have been amazing. Kristen wouldn't have gone after someone average for the restaurant she planned to open. He had to be great.

And maybe not only in the kitchen either.

21

"The tricky part about being omnivores is that we are always in danger of poisoning ourselves."

—Jeffrey Steingarten

The rain had picked up again by the time I got back to Eric's car. I rustled through his CDs and selected Rosanne Cash singing her famous father's list of essential country tunes.

"I'm growing tired of the big-city lights," Rosanne began. Me too—enough of Miami. After almost two months in Key West, I liked the feeling of coziness and containment on the island and I loved being always near the water.

I drove south on the highway and back to Route One, rolling Doug's rant over in my mind. It had never occurred to me that the thing Henri and Kristen had in common was a man. I knew they had shared a male chef, of course. But the man part hadn't registered. I thought about Doug's description of Kristen's relationship with Robert—like raw flesh crackling in hot oil. Didn't sound like something you could sustain over the long-term. Or would want to.

And I wondered why Henri would choose to move to Key West, where she knew her ex-lover had settled in with Kristen. Although he hadn't really settled in with Kristen because Kristen was seeing Chad for the second time around. The time line for all this drama was extremely confusing—a fast game of musical beds that I hadn't even realized I was playing.

I made good time right up until I hit the turquoise-lined two-lane bridge leading over the water to Key Largo. Then the rain began to pour down in torrents and the darkness closed in on me like a too-warm blanket. I had to drive slowly, peering yards ahead to stay on the road. The emergence of Shell World or an occasional boat yard or even a gentleman's club brought a little light and relief from the long, stressful ride. My shoulders tightened to cords and a headache pulsed across the back of my neck and coursed up to my temples. I considered stopping at the Winn Dixie in Tavernier to use their facilities and buy some aspirin, but convinced myself I could make it home fine if I pushed on nice and steady.

As I drove through Islamorada and onto Tea Table Key, a car with super-bright lights pulled up behind me. I cocked my hand above my left eye to shield the glare from the side-view mirror. In the rearview, I could barely make out grinning grillwork and halogen lamps riding my bumper way too close for comfort in this lousy weather. I slowed down so the driver could easily pass. But the other car slowed right down with me. A game of chicken I had no interest in playing. I pressed on the accelerator. Maybe if I upped my speed I could shake them off. The sedan clung to my tail.

For the next ten miles, I tried everything—faster, slower, weaving from my lane to the opposing and back again—praying that a cop would be waiting in the bushes and pull one or both of us over. But not another soul was out in this teeming rain. My heart was pounding out of my chest. My hands sweated so heavily I could hardly hang on to the wheel. And my phone was buried in my purse, on the passenger side floor. I didn't dare reach for it or take my eyes off the road.

As I drove over the Saddle Bunch Bridge, the car following me banged into the rear bumper of Eric's car.

"Stop it!" I screamed, careening toward the concrete barrier. Just before crashing, I yanked the wheel, swerved back onto the road, and mashed on the gas. Eric's engine roared in response.

The black sedan raced up behind me and slammed the bumper again. Who could this be?

I hydroplaned across the oncoming lane, and scraped along the left-side barrier, fighting for control. But the Mustang spun, jumped the concrete barricade, and flipped over the palmetto bushes toward the water. An instant later, the car hit the ground, jerking my head so hard I thought my neck would snap. A bottle of Eric's beer from the six-pack in the backseat sailed over and smashed into the windshield. A piece of broken glass sliced my cheek.

Stunned, I hung upside down, suspended by the seat belt, my shoulder aching from the pressure—my whole body aching—and adrenaline pushing furiously. Blood ran into my eye from the gash.

Rosanne Cash finished singing "Take These Chains from My Heart" and swung into "I'm Movin' On." The engine was still whining and the headlights cut a swath through the brush. Did I smell gas? Panicked, I pictured the car catching fire, me trapped inside an inferno. I managed to wrestle the keys from the ignition and switch off the lights. The engine ticked and darkness closed around me like a coffin.

I strained to listen for the person who'd forced me off the road. But it was hard to hear over the gurgling of the ocean mixing with the still-teeming rain outside the car. Had a car door slammed? Who was this? And why were they after me? If I stayed here, I could be picked off like the slowest goose in a winter's V.

I forced myself to move. Feeling for the soft convertible top, I used my left hand to wedge my weight away from the roof. With some pressure off the seat belt, I was able to release the latch with my right hand.

I crashed to the ground, my neck snapped forward, and pain shot down my spine. I rolled off my back into a crouch, whimpering, then felt around for Eric's window crank. Thank God this was an older-model car. Not even letting myself think how sick he would be that I had trashed the Mustang, I rolled the window down and scrambled out into the brush. Into the cold rain to face whoever had run me down.

22

"Love is most dependable when it's edible."

—Kim Adrian

Once I'd crawled into the shelter of the palmettos near the water, I lay curled into an aching ball for a few moments, trying to catch my breath. The rain pelted my face and I started to shiver, both from cold and fear. The long-sleeved T-shirt and jeans that had felt warm and comfortable when I put them on this afternoon were quickly soaked through. Up the embankment on the road, the halogen lights that had been following me for miles glared through the trees, the palmettos spiking like drawn swords in their path. Then I heard the sounds of someone crashing through the brush in my direction.

I desperately wished for my phone, but there was no time to return to the car and search. I pulled myself into a squat, wincing as pain sliced through my wrist and shoulder. Duck-walking toward the water, I pushed through the sharp leaves of the palmetto bushes that formed a thick hedge along the shore. One slingshotted back and slapped me across the cheek. I cried out before I could stop myself.

There was no place to go. Caught between Eric's car, the ocean, and the approaching footsteps, I kicked off my sneakers and waded into the frigid shallows of the Atlantic Ocean. I dropped into the water, my breath catching at the shock of cold, and pushed off with a frog kick, trying not to think about alligators, spiky lionfish, Portuguese men-of-war—whatever might be there. Not more than a week ago the *Citizen* had run an article about a stingray leaping up out of the water to pierce a woman's lung, breaking several of her ribs. She only lived because she was a trained paramedic. Or was it her boyfriend? Either way, I was cooked.

Something slimy brushed my leg and I squeaked and splashed furiously to get away. A loud crack hammered out from the shore and splashed in the water just feet from me. A gunshot? I pictured a hunter in camo lurking in the mangroves, me in his sights. I pushed off from the murky bottom, dove down into the water, and swam as hard and deep as I could, back toward the Saddle Bunch Bridge, years of forced swimming lessons as a kid finally paying off. Under the protective concrete overhang, I might have the best chance of survival, assuming I could outlast whoever was after me. Or stay alive until daybreak—many long hours away.

As I dogpaddled silently under the bridge, fighting against the current that pushed me toward the open water again, I heard several more shots, even closer now, as though the hunter was emptying all he had into the water sloshing under the highway. I frog-kicked closer to the sloping concrete, holding just my nose clear of the water to reduce the size of my target.

And then, in the distance, I heard the welcome *whoo-hoo* of an approaching siren. I paddled in place, listening as the man chasing me crashed back through the brush, got into his car, and screeched off down the highway, back over the bridge and away from Key West. The lights of an emergency vehicle strobed through the darkness, then two doors slammed. I swam over to the edge of the water and hoisted myself onto a stand of mangrove roots.

Flashlights probed into the bushes where Eric's car lay balanced on its roof. Two officers stomped down the embankment and peered into the vehicle.

"There's no one in it," called one man to the other, "but it sure smells like a brewery. And the engine is still warm."

"Hello?" hollered the second officer in a deep voice. "Anyone out here? It's the police. Come out and show yourself."

"Over here. Please don't shoot. It's Hayley Snow." Trembling uncontrollably, I stabbed my hands in the air without being asked and scrambled back through the bushes. Their flashlights raked my face. "I haven't been drinking, honest. Another car forced me off the road and a bottle of beer hit the windshield and exploded."

"Who was in the other car?" asked the cop with the deep voice.

"I have no idea. I've just come from a restaurant in

Miami and—" I couldn't help it; I started to shake even harder.

"She's shivering," said the other cop. "Soaking wet. Let's get her into the cruiser."

He patted me down, then took my elbow and helped me pick my way up the bank, then opened the back door of the cruiser, which idled at the side of the road. He popped the trunk and came back with a silver survival blanket and handed it to me. The baritone-voiced cop slid into the driver's seat, picked up the radio, and called for an ambulance.

"I don't need to go to the hospital," I said, teeth still chattering. "I swear I just need a ride home."

"It's standard procedure," said the first policeman. "Besides that, you're bleeding and you just came through a rollover."

While we waited for the paramedics, they grilled me for more details of what had happened. I told them how I'd been to dinner in Miami Beach and that I had no idea who was in the black car and explained again about the chase and the gunshots.

"It's a borrowed car," I moaned. "My friend is going to kill me. It's his vintage Mustang. Painted by Rick Worth. He's that artist in Key West. At no small expense." My head dropped to my hands and I swallowed a sob.

Fifteen minutes later, the ambulance arrived and two burly paramedics emerged. After a quick exam, they recommended a spinal X-ray.

"You could very well have a fractured vertebra. It's not worth the risk to ignore it."

They rolled a gurney out of the back of the van, fastened a padded support around my neck, and loaded me onboard. The van bumped back onto the highway. Finally beginning to feel warm and safe again, I tried to puzzle out who could have been in that car. When had I picked up the tail? In the parking lot of Hola or somewhere along the Keys? Given the doggedness of the driver, it seemed impossible that the chase was random. Someone had wanted me dead. I started to shake again.

Ten minutes later, we pulled up in front of the Lower Keys Medical Center and I was wheeled into the emergency room. I checked my watch, which had somehow managed to survive the ocean dunk. It felt late, but it was barely ten. An orderly parked my stretcher in a hallway and I dozed off for a half hour, exhausted by the drive and the chase.

By midnight, the police had taken a complete report on the car incident and I signed off on it. A tired-looking physician checked me over, read the spinal X-ray, and diagnosed a sprained wrist and wrenched shoulder. He determined that the cut on my cheek could be managed with a butterfly bandage, no stitches. All of which I could have told him without lingering three hours in the ER. A brisk nurse wrapped my wrist and instructed me to ice it the next day and take copious milligrams of ibuprofen.

I was dying to get home to bed. My muscles ached, my clothes were clammy and salty, and my head pounded. The towing company the police had phoned promised to tow Eric's damaged car to a body shop on White Street by morning and to deliver my purse to the police station. I didn't dare call Eric for a ride home. I knew Connie wouldn't be available—she and Ray were visiting friends in Marathon overnight. I had the definite feeling they'd made those plans because they needed some space. From me and my infinite drama.

But I had no money for a cab. That left Richard Kane, my underimpressive lawyer, or Chad's secretary, Deena, who had barely agreed to talk to me in broad daylight and certainly didn't owe me any late-night favors.

I approached the attractive black receptionist at the information desk and asked to use her phone. She pushed it across the desk and watched as I dialed Kane. He answered on the fourth ring, sounding sleepy and possibly a little drunk. I explained what had happened and where I was, already beginning to wish I hadn't called.

"I guess I'm wondering if you could help me out and maybe send someone over to pick me up."

There was a long pause. "Miss Snow, I would suggest that A, you call a cab. I'm certain the hospital can provide you with a list of phone numbers. And B, phone my office on Monday morning and schedule an appointment to come in. With this kind of behavior, you are not helping your case." And then he hung up.

Stunned and furious, I slammed the phone down. I was a fool to have thought he'd help. The receptionist, watching all this with great interest, pushed a list of taxicab companies across the surface of her desk.

"They'll all charge you about the same thing, but the West Sider will probably get here the quickest."

I thanked her and made the call. The dispatcher assured me that a cabbie would pick me up in a half hour.

I sank into the seat next to the receptionist's desk. "I don't even have any cash to pay for the ride."

"They'll wait while you run into your house. I heard you say your purse is MIA—these guys are used to having people pay them when they get home. You aren't the first passenger without a red cent," she said, smoothing a lock of hair back into its bun. She adjusted reading glasses with brightly colored rims on the bridge of her nose. "Your lawyer sounds like a piece of work. I couldn't help overhear. I'm Esmine." She reached over the desk to shake my hand. "I'd give you a ride home myself, but I'm not off work until seven."

"That would feel like a long wait." I thanked her for her kindness, suddenly thinking she might be able to help me locate Miss Gloria.

"Listen, Esmine, my neighbor was brought in here yesterday with a head injury," I told her. "I'm so worried about her. Would you happen to have any information on a Gloria Peterson?"

Esmine clattered a few lines into her computer and read off a room number on the second floor. "She's listed as stable. Of course, it's way too late for visiting hours now." She narrowed her eyes and looked at me over the top lip of her glasses.

"Of course," I said, with a bright smile. "And my cab will be here any minute. Can you tell me which way to the ladies' room?" I limped off in the direction she pointed and then ducked into the stairwell and up to the second floor. Miss Gloria's room was two down from the stairs. I'd poke my head in to make sure she was okay.

Tucked into her hospital bed, my neighbor looked

like a child, her face floating pale and delicate in the wide expanse of white sheets, bed rails hemming her in on both sides. Her thin wrist was tethered to an IV. A second old woman snored in the bed near the window. Miss Gloria's eyes flickered open and she recognized me right away.

"Hayley." She reached out with the free hand, her voice tremulous but clear. "I'm so glad to see you. Could I possibly trouble you to check on Sparky? I've been so worried about him. I couldn't remember your number or I would have called."

"He's fine," I said, squeezing her hand gently and perching on the chair beside her bed. "We brought him down to our boat after you were taken to the hospital. And he's settled in so well." I didn't mention how Evinrude had gone missing—I'd start weeping and she'd worry herself sicker. "Tell me how you're feeling. How long are they keeping you here?"

"I'm okay," she said, slipping her hand from mine and touching the bandage on the crown of her head. "They can't seem to believe an old lady could manage at home. They won't release me except to a relative. But the longer they make me lie here, the weaker I'll get. My son's flying in tomorrow. He's talking about a nursing home in Dearborn. Michigan in winter? I'll just die." Now she started to cry and I patted her birdlike forearm, thin and practically translucent. She seemed more fragile already.

"He's just worried about you," I said. "This incident probably scared him half to death. With any luck, this nursing home idea will blow over and we'll get you settled back at the marina."

She smiled weakly and dried her tears on the sheet.

"What in the world happened yesterday? Did you see the person who hit you?" I asked.

"I walked down to the end of the finger to stretch my legs before supper. It was dusk—don't you hate how early it gets dark this time of year?"

I nodded with encouragement. "And then?"

"I thought I saw someone on the dock near your houseboat. But it didn't look like you or Connie or Ray. So I called out, 'Hello, can I help you with something?'" She touched her head again and licked her lips. "I thought maybe someone was lost. Maybe one of the men looking for the soup kitchen or—"

Her eyes welled up and tears spilled over onto her papery cheeks for the second time since I'd arrived. We'd had this conversation just last week—she hated how the homeless folks in town were automatically greeted with suspicion. Since when did being rich make you a better person?

"And then what happened?"

"And then he rushed up and hit me and that's the last I remember until I woke up here." She waved her hand weakly at the bedside table with its plastic pitcher, a cup with a straw dangling from it, and a Bible.

"Did you get a good look at him?"

She shook her head. "That stern policeman with the nice chin came back twice to ask me those questions. He's so cute, isn't he? And very kind to me."

"He is cute," I admitted. "If you like that type. I hadn't noticed the kindness." I steered Miss Gloria away from the attributes of Detective Bransford and back to the attack. "What did he look like, the man who hit you?"

"He wasn't a big man." She looked me up and down. "Definitely taller than you. But he had a cap on and some kind of bandanna over his mouth—"

A nurse bustled in from the hall, then stopped still and frowned, hands reaching for her ample hips.

"Who are you? What are you doing here? There is no visiting allowed at this hour. I'm going to call security." She slid her cell phone from the holster at her waist.

"Not necessary. I won't make any trouble." I stood up and started past the nurse, stopping at the door to blow a kiss to Miss Gloria. "I'll see you soon. Don't waste one more minute worrying about Sparky."

I hurried back down the stairs and through the lobby to catch my cab, an enormous sadness swelling my chest so I had trouble breathing. Hard to imagine how that frail little person with a patchy memory could be allowed to fend for herself on a boat. But how long would she survive confined to an old folks' home in Michigan where it fell dark in winter by four p.m.?

23

"Pastry is like people. Some dough needs a lot of kneading; some requires much less."

—Kathleen Flinn

The next morning at seven, feeling like the Tin Man before he discovered oil, I forced myself up and fed Sparky, who wound between my legs and purred his appreciation. Aching from nose to toes, I threw on some sweats and went out into the cloudy, cool morning—the kind of day that brought out down coats and mittens on the natives. I hiked the length of our dock, calling softly for Evinrude—no answer. Pushing back a rush of grief, I returned to the boat and set to work in the galley.

I'd promised to bring back Eric's car before he went to church this morning. Since I had no car to return, I hoped that delivering warm coffee cake and two extra-large coffee *con leches* to Eric and Bill would soften the blow. Cursing Chad yet one more time for chucking my stuff, I scratched out what I remembered of the recipe for my grandmother Alvina's crumb cake on the back of an envelope—mostly flour, milk, sugar, eggs, and plenty of butter. And then cinnamon cut into more butter and sugar for the crumbly topping.

Once the two pans of cake had baked and then cooled enough to handle, I packed one of them in foil and secured it on the back of my scooter. Before heading down Southard Street, I stopped by the body shop on White and set off to search the car lot.

Eric's convertible had been dumped in a weedy space behind the cement block building. I sagged against the cement; he was going to kill me. The manatees that had been hand-painted on the hood were dented and scraped. The roof itself was torn open and the school of tropical fish on the driver's-side door was smashed into an unrecognizable mass. How had I emerged in one piece?

I fled back to the scooter and drove down to the Courthouse Deli on Southard and Whitehead for the coffees. I wished I had thought to purchase a box of designer dog bones for Toby the wonder dog. More rodent in size and appearance than dog, he growled and snarled at anyone other than his immediate family. But Eric and Bill adored him, and a friend of Toby's was a friend of the guys. And I needed all the help I could manage.

On the last few blocks to Eric's place, I practiced what to say.

Blunt but mournful? *I regret to say I wrecked your car.*

Understated but cheerful? *There's a tiny problem with the Mustang . . .*

Immediately defensive? *There's been an accident—it wasn't my fault.*

The last was clearly the worst, but nothing felt right. I pulled into their driveway, which gaped nakedly without Eric's car. Their small house radiated warmth, with a wide front porch holding two green rocking chairs and shelves of plants. Maybe this would turn out fine. Eric met me at the door, Bill right behind him. Eric grinned when his gaze fell on the three large cups of coffee. Then he sniffed the air.

"Oh, Hayley, is that coffee cake? You didn't have to . . ." He scanned the driveway, his face puzzled. "You came on your scooter? But where's the car?"

"It's an interesting story . . . Coffee first, before it gets cold."

They welcomed me in, the screen door banging shut behind us. I crossed the room to set the breakfast goodies on their glass coffee table and distribute the coffees. Then I collapsed on the upholstered bark cloth couch. From his perch on a flowered rocker, Toby growled at me like the steady rumble of distant thunder as I explained last night's disaster.

"Had you been drinking?" Eric asked after a long silence, his face stony.

I didn't like the question, but I couldn't blame him for asking, really. "Chef Doug poured me a half glass of the house merlot to drink with his *carnitas*, but that's it. You can believe it or not, but I was forced off the road by a lunatic who then tried to shoot me."

The two men exchanged glances—the unspoken language of a solid partnership.

"That sounds absolutely terrifying," said Bill. "Excuse me. I'm going to get some utensils for this fine peace offering."

Eric said nothing. The language of a friendship circling the drain.

Bill came back from the kitchen with forks and plates, carved large squares of coffee cake, and passed them around. He stood for a moment behind Eric, massaging his shoulders and smiling at me. "The car can be repaired. We're just glad you're okay. Did you say someone shot at you?"

I snuck a look at Eric. Not so clear that he felt the same way. But at least he had started to eat. So I repeated in more detail how I'd crawled out of the car, plunged into the ocean, and dogpaddled under the bridge until the cops arrived. And then I described my conversation with the chef and the visit with Miss Gloria.

Eric's fork clattered to his plate. "If this accident is somehow related to the murder, you're over your head trying to figure things out," he said. "Is that what you think?"

"I don't know what to think," I admitted. "Seems like there has to be a connection. Someone went to a lot of trouble to see me silenced."

"Here's the thing, Hayley," Eric said. "If you couldn't identify the driver or the car, and Miss Gloria wasn't able to tell you anything that the police don't already know about who attacked her, it's time to let the authorities do their job. At this point, I regret that I encouraged you to do otherwise because you've apparently put yourself in serious danger." He patted his lips with a napkin.

If I had been him, I'd have wanted to mention ruining the car and Connie's houseboat too. But he held back.

"Did you tell the cops what you found out from the chef?"

Feeling sheepish, I admitted that I'd said very little to the police about the reason for my trip to Miami. "I hated to implicate anyone unfairly. And besides, they haven't shown much interest in my opinions and observations so far. I feel like I have to look out for myself."

"You need to tell them everything." Eric glowered until I agreed.

After leaving Eric and Bill's home, I rode up Olivia Street, past the Key West cemetery, whose worn stones and dreary fence about matched my mood. The bright yellow conch tour train pulled out in front of me, every seat in every car jammed with tourists. The amplified voice of the conductor explained the legends of the city's dead as he drove—the 1907 murder-suicide, the Spanish-American heroes, and most visitors' favorite grave marker from the town hypochondriac that read: "I told you I was sick."

"Making crap up since 1958." Ray liked to joke that was the conch train's motto. Nothing, of course, was mentioned about Kristen, who was surely the most recent cemetery resident.

On impulse, I stashed my scooter on the sidewalk outside the metal fence and walked through the main gate. I guessed that Kristen's remains would have been interred on the east side of the cemetery nearest Olivia

Street, where the ashes of the newer residents were secured in a hulking brown granite tomb.

I skirted a sad little child-sized crypt bordered in white and blue tile, unable to bear reading the inscription. Then I noticed a figure in a pink and yellow shirt depositing a bouquet of pink roses by the edge of the large, stone crypt: Meredith, the woman I'd seen weeping at the funeral. I seemed to have a knack for intruding on her private moments.

But it was too late to pull back and pretend I was heading in a different direction. She held her hand up in greeting, the sleeve of her flowered blouse fluttering to her elbow. Her hair was pulled back into a French braid and she wore a blue sweater tied around her neck. She looked tired, dark half-moons below her eyes.

"I guess if you have to end up in a cemetery, this would be the one to choose," I said, and immediately wished I could snatch the words back. "I'm sorry. It's hard to know what to say. You were obviously close to her."

"And you were obviously not."

She was not pulling punches. "We weren't great friends, no," I admitted. "Did Kristen have any enemies that you knew of?"

"You mean besides *you*?"

Her eyes bugged and I didn't get the idea that she was joking.

"I didn't kill her, no matter what *you've* heard," I said in a breezy voice, as though there was no doubt. "Punishing the woman who stole my boyfriend is definitely not worth a lifetime in jail. And the whole infidelity incident was as much his fault as hers. They say it takes two and they're right. As it turns out, I'm better off without Chad anyway."

Meredith snorted out a bitter laugh. "Men are most times more trouble than they're worth. And he was definitely no exception." She forced a smile. "As Kristen's sister's eulogy showed. But to your question, Kristen's family has enemies," she added. "They've lived on the island for ages and they own a ton of property. They're always trying to take development further than a lot of residents here prefer. Besides Easter Island, they're pushing the plans for the waterfront at the Truman Annex. I'm sure you've read all about it in the paper. A lot of folks don't think we need a huge stadium or yet one more fancy marina."

Meredith flashed a smile, then went back to rubbing her arms, staring at the name carved in granite. Faulkner.

"How did you meet her?" I asked.

"Kristen hired me at her place in Miami when I was just starting out," she said, adding a heavy sigh. "I had a rather useless certificate in baking and pastry from a school in Oregon and absolutely no practical experience. She was super-supportive." She fixed her blue eyes on my face. "Whatever you've heard about her, she wasn't a bad person."

I rubbed my chin thoughtfully and said nothing.

"She had promised me the pastry chef position in the new restaurant," she explained through a fresh onslaught of tears. "That's why I moved down here. We'd already met with Robert to talk about menus. One of the specials was going to be pistachio baklava. Neither of us likes walnuts— too heavy and oily." She smacked her lips as though masticating a mouthful of spoiled nuts. "She encouraged experiments. Moving away from the recipes on the page was what she said separated great chefs from merely good ones."

Meredith and I had more in common than I would have thought—big ambitions that appeared to have been thwarted. "Maybe it'll happen without her," I offered. "The restaurant, I mean. Is Chef Robert still in town?"

"I don't know for how long," she said. "Or even how to get in touch with him. I don't have his phone number. Besides, I doubt that Robert could get a restaurant off the ground without her. He isn't that disciplined. And as you could probably tell from the eulogy at the funeral, Kristen's sister is not interested in taking over." She peered a little closer. "My goodness, what happened to your face?"

"A car accident," I said, palpating the butterfly bandage and the bruise that had bloomed around it. "I'm really fine, but the car, not so much. The worst thing is, I'd borrowed it from a friend."

"That's awful. Did another driver hit you?"

"I think I must have fallen asleep at the wheel," I said, reluctant to go into details with this woman I barely knew. "Me versus the palmettos. The palmettos ran away with it." I crooked a smile.

"Back to Robert," I added. "Is there any reason you can think of that he might have killed her? Like maybe he was distraught about her hooking up with Chad?"

"Honestly, I don't know Robert well enough to know

what he might be capable of." She tugged her sweater close around her neck.

Something about that gesture reminded me of Allison, my chemist stepmother, and I thought of one more question. "You're an experienced pastry chef. Any ideas about what could have been put in that pie to kill Kristen so quickly?"

"It sounds creepy, but I can't stop thinking about that," she said, her voice wobbling. "The filling for key lime pie is so delicate—made correctly, the entire dessert is delicate actually. I can't imagine why she wouldn't have figured out right away that something tasted off. My mind keeps sticking on that—if only she'd noticed a little sooner and spat out the whole nasty business." She wiped her eyes on her sleeve and tried to smile again. "But pies have never really been my thing. I'm mad about cakes. And flaky pastries."

"Like the new baklava."

She bobbed her head, looking sad.

I stuck my hand out and shook hers, my gaze drifting to the pink roses. "Anyway, sorry to disturb you. And awfully sorry about your friend."

I gestured toward the grave and suppressed the automatic "have a nice day" that tried to slither out.

24

"Cooks are dashing, improvisational, wayward, intuitive; bakers are measured, careful, rational, precise."

—Diana Abu-Jaber

I drove back to houseboat row and spent a half hour cleaning up the kitchen and playing with Sparky. Connie had left a note pinned to the refrigerator saying she'd gone fishing and would probably have dinner with her fishing buddies.

When I moved to this town, I started out with two good friends and a lover. Chad was gone, of course, and good riddance. But I had also worn down my friendships with both Eric and Connie. And why not? I was responsible for the destruction of his car and her business and home. Either I had to straighten out this snowballing mess, or move on.

First I called Doug Rodriguez's cell phone in Miami. I

wanted to hear more about Chef Robert. And it wouldn't hurt to get his read on Meredith, while I was at it.

"Hello?" he answered, sounding sleepy and annoyed.

I explained how I'd just run into Meredith in the cemetery, and that my conversation with her had raised more questions about Robert. "You mentioned how intense his relationship was with Kristen. Supposing she dumped him . . ."

Which she definitely had: She'd moved on to Chad. And what if her ambition about the new restaurant died with the change in relationship? I swallowed hard. "Supposing she dumped him and told him he was now out of a job, too. After he'd quit his position at Hola and had broken things off with Henri and moved down here. Would he be angry enough to kill her?"

"Losing her, he would be losing everything," Doug admitted. "How he would react to that, I couldn't say. He threw a few pots and pans in his day, but that's the only violence I actually saw him commit."

"And what about Meredith? Did she have anything against Kristen, as far as you know?"

"Ridiculous. Meredith would never have hurt Kristen," he snapped. "She was utterly grateful for the chance to work in a good kitchen. She adored Kristen. Is there anything else?"

"Just that your dinner was fabulous and thank you again."

I hung up and slumped across the love seat, Sparky warm on my chest. "None of this makes any sense," I told the cat. "Why would someone be trying to kill me? Unless they think I know too much. If I know too much,

I don't know that I know it. Do you know what I mean?" The cat stretched out one paw, nails extending and then retracting, and purred.

I finally decided Eric was right: I should call Detective Bransford and tell him every last thing. Let him figure out whether any of my ideas would bear on the case. I found the business card he'd given me on my first visit to the station and dialed his cell. He picked right up.

"Oh, Miss Snow. I understand you had another eventful night. I was planning to check in with you today—if you're willing to talk without your attorney, that is."

My hackles rose the instant he made the lawyer comment. And couldn't he at least have asked how I was? But I had no choice but to ignore his sarcasm. "I was wondering if anyone had turned in my purse—it went missing in the accident last night."

"It's right here on my desk," he said. "I could bring it over."

I felt that possibility like a blow to the solar plexus. The neighbors had seen quite enough of me interacting with the police over the past week. "I'd rather swing by and pick it up."

I retreated to the bathroom to wash my face and examine the ravages of the night in the mirror. Nothing was going to help the deep shadows under my eyes or the oozing bandage on my cheek. I zipped on a layer of mascara and some lip gloss and shut off the light.

Minutes later, I called the detective from the intercom phone outside the main door of the police station. "I'll come down and meet you," he said in a voice that would melt butter, and then buzzed me into the hallway.

I heard footsteps slapping on the tile floor and then he turned the corner, hair still damp, wearing black jeans and a crisp striped Oxford shirt. Undeniably cute, as Miss Gloria had pointed out. He motioned me to follow him and I tried not to notice the way he filled out those jeans. We filed up the stairs to his office. Inside, he sat at his desk chair and leaned back. I spotted my purse on the bookcase behind him.

"Are you feeling all right?" he asked, teeth flashing white against his tan. "That was quite an acrobatic spill you took in your friend's car."

His solicitousness felt good. If odd. Reminding myself that he wasn't on my side right now, I lowered gingerly onto the chair beside his desk. After the adrenaline of telling Eric the bad news had subsided, everything had started to hurt. "I'm okay; a little rattled, as you might imagine. Do you have any leads about the car that was following me?"

"Good question," he said, snapping his seat forward and tapping a pen on the calendar blotter in front of him. "We had a team combing the site all morning. I have to be honest, there wasn't any compelling evidence regarding a chase."

I straightened, my fists balled. "What more do you need than my freaking car upside down in the bushes?"

Another impish smile. "Oh, it was clear enough that you'd lost control on the bridge—your tracks were all over the place and you left half of your friend's car paint on the Jersey barrier. Of course, lots of folks stop in that area to fish and so on. So there were multiple sets of tire tracks in the sand alongside the road." He paused and squinted his eyes a little. "You didn't happen to catch a license number? Make and model of the car? Even a few numbers or letters could help us narrow things down."

Okay, big misread, he didn't care about how I was feeling—he wanted the case solved and off his desk. "You don't believe it happened the way I told you." I stood up and would have stalked out if my purse had been in reach. But I couldn't leave without my phone and wallet.

"Easy does it, Miss Snow," he said. "I didn't say I didn't believe you."

"What about the shooting?" I demanded.

"I believe you *thought* someone was shooting at you," he said with a graceful shrug. "Fear does funny things to the brain. It's dark; it's raining; maybe someone is following too closely. You're blinded by the lights in the rearview mirror. You panic. Your car loses traction. You yank the steering wheel a little too hard and spin out of control—you flip over. Bushes are crushed; branches crackle; your senses go on highest alert." He picked up the pen again and made a check mark on the blotter.

"But unfortunately—or maybe it's fortunately—my guys weren't able to find any evidence of gunshots at last night's scene. No bullets, no casings, no nicks in the concrete." He dropped the pen and cocked his head, which Miss Gloria might have found endearing. But I was too angry.

"On another matter, we did canvass the neighbors at your boyfriend's building again yesterday. Several folks mentioned the screaming match you had with Mr. Lutz only a couple weeks ago. Something about you standing on one side of the gate, while he and Ms. Faulkner were relaxing at the pool? Is this sounding familiar?"

My face flushed completely scarlet; the cut on my cheek throbbed with the rush of blood. That screaming match had been a low, low moment. I'd gone back over to Chad's condominium to ask him to return my missing items the same day I'd found him with Kristen. He didn't answer his door buzzer, so I'd walked around back to the water side of the building. And lost it when I saw him lounging by the pool. I shouldn't be surprised that one of my former neighbors had reported it to the cops, but it was totally humiliating. I'd hoped that day would stay buried in the annals of mistakes made in the name of love gone sour.

"I would like to leave now. I would appreciate it if you would return my purse."

He held my gaze for another moment, then got up, retrieved the bag, and handed it over. I stormed from the office.

Outside, I slid back on my scooter and waited until my hands stopped shaking to start it up. Obviously the detective was worried about me, but his concern had to do with the fact that he thought he was dealing with a fruitcake. A fruitcake who might possibly have lost control and committed murder. I motored over to the pier and stumped back down the finger to our houseboat.

Now I felt at serious loose ends. I paced from the bedroom out to the galley and back. For the first time, the small living space on the boat felt claustrophobic. The only thing that would really cheer me up was a call from Wally at *Key Zest*, announcing that I'd been hired for the food critic position. And what were the chances of that on a Sunday morning? Or even better, a call from my lawyer saying they'd found someone who could clearly substantiate my whereabouts the morning of the murder. But considering his brush-off the night before, I could grow old and senile waiting for Kane to come through. This reminded me that I'd forgotten to ask Ray about the lawyer, as Eric suggested several days earlier.

I punched his number into my phone. "Ray, it's Hayley." I told him that I was trying to decide what to do about Kane. The connection was crackly—I could hardly hear him.

"Oh gawd, Richard Kane. Is that who you hired? Connie never mentioned the name. My brother had him a couple years back. First of all, he coached him about how to lie in court. And then he took his money and did nothing. Bart spent six months in the pokey because of him. Dump him fast—that's my advice. Gotta go. Connie's landed something friggin' enormous and she can't reel it in. We'll see you later."

"You guys want to get some dinner tonight?" I asked.

"We're celebrating our anniversary," said Ray. "Another time, okay?"

Now I felt anxious and antsy. Not to mention like a major third wheel. I'd suspected that Kane was a dud all along, but still . . . a little part of me had hoped he'd really be on my side. In only the most honorable way. I went down to the dock to buy the Sunday paper, but paged through most of it in a half hour. My eye caught on an advertisement for the Key West Garden Club's sale at Martello Towers, an old brick fort on the ocean side of the island with astonishing tropical foliage and solicitous docents. It would be the perfect place to find a few replacements for some of the plants that had been trashed on Connie's deck the other night—a perfect going-away and thank-you gift.

Because even if she tried to forgive me for everything that had happened, I was convinced that she needed more space for her and Ray: Time for me to move on.

25

> *"It is illegal to give someone food in which has been found a dead mouse or weasel."*
>
> —Ancient Irish Law

In spite of the gray skies, the plant sale was bustling with both customers and volunteers. I wandered inside the brick walls of the old fort, browsing for specimens that Connie might like. Every plant vibrated with good health in this climate—I took photos to e-mail to my mother: bromeliads, orchids, and mother-in-law tongues, and a golf cart bursting with flowers in pots. She would enjoy seeing tropical-sized versions of the houseplants she tended back home.

The smell of grilling sausages and coffee drew me into the interior courtyard where two men in green aprons were cooking bratwurst on giant Weber grills. I'd been craving a sausage since I'd smelled Mr. Renhart's dinner the other night. Though it was only eleven, fatigue from the early morning and last night's fright had settled into my bones, leaving me ravenous. I ordered two sausages, one loaded with sauerkraut, onions, relish, and mustard, the other with mustard and chili. God help the food critic in me, I couldn't choose only one—I had to sample both. Settling onto a concrete bench with the wursts and a large coffee, I bit into the first sandwich, my teeth snapping through the crispy skin to the juice inside. Simply heaven.

As I stuffed in the final delicious bite, the sun broke through the clouds, warming my face. I sat a few more minutes, savoring my full belly, perfectly content—as long as I didn't think about anything. I concentrated on the clack and rattle of the palms along the water, trying to keep my mind from spinning into action. My cell phone rang—Dad.

"Hayley, I've been trying to reach you all morning."

"I'm here now," I said cheerfully. I got up to throw out my trash and moved away from the lunch crowd toward the side of the park that bordered the ocean. Better not to have the world overhearing my conversation.

"Allison said you have a problem with the lawyer. He came highly recommended from Sid, who attended Rutgers Law School with him. They've been in touch on and off since then." He cleared his throat and his voice dropped lower. "It would surprise me very much to hear he isn't doing the job. But we'll find someone else if it's absolutely necessary."

The thought of starting over made me sick to my

stomach. "I don't think I'll need another name, Dad. This morning, I had a chat with the detective in charge of my case. In my opinion, they don't have enough evidence to arrest me. Everything's hearsay and circumstance."

Which was not at all what the detective said, but I knew for certain that Bransford would arrest me the minute he thought the case would stand up in court. He was not holding off in order to be nice.

My father launched into a rant about letting the professionals do what they're hired to do and why was it that I thought I knew enough to make this kind of decision. The more he pushed, the more sure I was that I was ready to can Attorney Richard Kane and handle my problems myself.

I broke through. "Excuse me, Dad, but sooner or later, I will have to start making my own decisions. And some of them won't be so hot. But I'm ready to take responsibility for my own life. And Richard Kane is out. Even though I so appreciate your input and the trouble you took to find him."

"It's not a good idea—" He listed off more reasons that I should listen to Kane, and to him.

"Is Allison around?" I asked when he seemed to be finished scolding me.

My stepmother came on the line. "How's the weather down there? We've got this awful cold rain, but they're talking about it changing over to sleet and snow by nightfall. And it's only November!"

I silently blessed her for changing the subject.

"A little chilly. Whitecaps on the water," I said, not wanting to rub in the glorious day. People who've escaped to Key West tended to get a perverse pleasure out of lousy weather reports from up north. And the northerners get testy when unfavorable comparisons are made.

"I wondered if you'd had any more ideas about the chemicals in the poisoned pie?" I asked her. "I was talking to a pastry chef this morning who thought it would be hard to suspend something foreign in the body of the pie."

"Unless it was ground very finely and used in a small quantity, the particulates would change the consistency of the pie," she agreed. "I've done some reading. So many possible compounds could have been used. But almost all of them have a bitter aftertaste or a peculiar flavor," Allison said. "Now I'm wondering about something crunchy that would seem like it belonged in the crust."

"Maybe some kind of nut? That sounds exactly right." After a little more weather-related chitchat and a defensive parry about coming home for Thanksgiving, I hung up. Then I prowled the perimeter of the fort until I located the information desk that had been set back among some palmettos near the entrance.

A silver-haired man in a Key West Garden Club T-shirt and a bright green apron manned the desk. He listened to my question about poisonous nuts grown in tropical climates. "You're not planning to do anyone in, are you? Ha, ha, ha," he added.

I grinned. "No plans for that. Just plain old medical curiosity." Whatever that was.

"I'm not a particular expert," he said. "But let me think." He combed his fingers through his neat beard. "Angel Wings are grown as foliage plants in Florida—ingestion of any part of the plant causes blisters in the mouth." He looked at me and I shook my head.

"Then there's the Jerusalem cherry. All parts of the plant are toxic, but especially the berries."

"Would they leave a sour taste?" I asked.

"Never tried them, but I can't imagine they wouldn't."

"What I'm looking for would either taste good or have no taste at all."

"If you'd like to leave your phone number, I'll call if I think of something," he said.

I thanked him and looped through the plants one more time to decompress. How would it help me to know what agent might have poisoned Kristen? It didn't. I was still bubbling in the same stew.

I bought as many houseplants and flowers as would fit in the carton on the back of my scooter and started home. As I drove, I came to another conclusion: Time to bake my first key lime pie.

After arranging Connie's new plants on the houseboat deck, I drove back to Old Town and parked in front of Fausto's Market. I'd taken a moment to skim several recipes online and decided to start with a variation of Emeril's. The ingredients were fairly basic—graham cracker crumbs, condensed milk, eggs, sugar, key limes, and a layer of sugared sour cream over all. I also bought small containers of unsalted cashews and almonds to try in the crust. My mouth was watering just imagining it. The trick would be not eating it before the filling set.

Back on the houseboat, I whirred the nuts into finely ground pieces, and the graham crackers into crumbs, and mixed them separately with melted butter into three different sections of crust—one plain, one with almonds, one with cashews. I patted the crust into a pie pan and popped it into the oven. Twenty minutes later, I added the lime/condensed milk filling and put it back in the oven.

My phone rang—a 305 area code.

"Hello?"

"This is Jerry Touger, from the garden club sale. I thought of another possibility for your research: the *Jatropha curcas*. Its common name is the Physic or Barbados nut. The seeds are used to create biodiesel fuel in some countries, but the plant is dangerous because the seeds are delicious. And poisonous."

"Is it local?" I asked.

"It's found in the tropics, though we don't have one on site. For obvious reasons. Can you imagine the liability issues if one of our customers ingested something poisonous right here in this garden?"

I thanked him profusely and took the pie out of the oven. It was a lovely pale green—nothing like the horrid poisonous green glop that had done Kristen in. And it smelled delicious. I transferred it to the refrigerator and settled on my bed with Sparky to read my e-mail and troll for new recipes.

After a half hour, I couldn't take it any longer. I took the pie out of the fridge, frosted it with sweetened sour cream, and began to spoon it right out of the pan—sweet, sour, smooth, crunchy, rich. All three of the crust variations were delicious. I could imagine exactly how Kristen ate enough to do herself in.

26

"Never eat more than you can lift."
—Miss Piggy

A loud bang startled me awake early on Monday morning. The noise came into focus as our front door rattled under a rain of forceful knocking.

"Miss Hayley, Miss Hayley. Are you home?" More loud rapping. I pulled on my bathrobe and staggered out to the living area before the whole neighborhood called the cops.

Peering out through the stained-glass window, I was surprised to see Tony, the homeless cowboy. He looked dirtier and more rumpled than usual and staggered under the weight of a knapsack stuffed full of who-knows-what junk. I had to admit to a moment of ungraceful recoil.

"Miss Hayley!" he hollered. "Miss Hayley Snow! Are you home?"

I cracked open the door with my finger to my lips.

"Shhhh, you'll wake the dead. What's up?" I asked, clutching my robe around my waist and stepping onto the deck so I wouldn't have to invite him in and run the risk of waking Connie and Ray.

"Morning, ma'am." With a big grin, he swept his cowboy hat off his head and bowed, wafting a wave of stale cigarettes and fermented booze at me. "Got any java brewin'?"

I hesitated. First of all, I wasn't decent. And second, Connie would not be thrilled to come down for breakfast and find him at the table waiting for coffee. And third, why was he here?

He watched me struggle to decide, and then settled the hat back on his greasy hair. "No worries. Came by to tell y'all that Turtle—you remember him?—red-haired guy who wears shorts on top of his jeans?"

I nodded. "I know who Turtle is."

Tony pulled a crumpled pack of cigarettes from his shirt pocket and lit one up, then leaned back against the railing. Settling in.

"Anyway, he's new this year. Came down from the north somewhere—Connecticut, I think, or Massachusetts. Anyway, he was staying out at the shelter on Stock Island, but he hated it. Too many people all jammed into one space. And some of them—pardon my French—are just crazy as crap."

He blew out a stream of smoke, scratched his head, and shifted the battered backpack from one shoulder to the other. "I figgered out the same thing when I got here. Better to take my chances on the beach or a car somewhere than to sleep with all those restless souls. You just never know when someone might rise up in the night with a knife." He thrust his head forward, slashed a finger across his neck, and then tossed the burning cigarette into the water.

I nodded, feeling awkward in my robe, and suddenly vulnerable. Wondering why he'd come. "So anyway, Turtle's one of the new guys . . ."

"Turns out he spent the night camped on a boat Monday night because it poured rain and he needed somewheres dry and he couldn't take one more freakin' night with those loony tunes at the shelter. Actually, he and his dog slept two nights on the *Danger*. Then the owner found him and routed him out."

"The *Danger*?"

"That party boat right outside the administration building. Remember you were askin' if any guys might have been fishin' last Tuesday mornin'?"

I nodded again, my brain cylinders finally starting to fire. If Turtle had seen someone besides me go into the complex with a pastry box, the detective might finally believe me. I pulled my robe tighter across my chest, as if that could contain the furious beating my heart had started up.

Tony pulled out another cigarette and rolled it between his fingers. "I couldn't get him to come with me because he's afraid he'll get in trouble. He don't trust any authorities—with plenty of reason if you believe his story. But he might talk to you if you came to him. Guaranteed he'll be at the gay church in the sandwich line. Guar-un-teed. He's always hungry. Ten or ten thirty," he said, a flash of gold in his smile. "I'll meetcha there and tell 'im it's important."

He wheeled around and shambled down the dock before I could ask any more questions. Or tell him I'd start some coffee. Or even give him a couple of bucks for a *con leche* at the Laundromat.

"Tony, wait!" I called out. I hurried inside to wrap up two pieces of Alvina's crumb cake and brought it back out to him. "Thanks so much for coming by."

He doffed his hat again and left. I watched him step off the dock and start up the road, feeling like a heel and wondering what twists in his life had led him to this moment. And where *he* had spent the night on that rainy Monday.

While the coffeepot burbled, I washed my face and brushed my teeth—even those actions would be a luxury for Tony and Turtle—and dressed quickly. Still feeling a little sick from all the pie I'd eaten yesterday, I gobbled a sliver of coffee cake and motored down Eaton toward Mallory Square. The party sailboat called the *Danger* was usually docked at the pier in front of Chad's apartment complex. If it looked like it had a good angle of vision, I'd try to track Turtle down and persuade him to tell me what he might have seen last Tuesday.

The monstrous cruise ship *Norwegian Queen* had just disgorged its passengers when I arrived at the red brick Customs House near the pier. I parked the scooter and wove upstream through the current of round-bellied cruisers eager for a dose of Duval Street and then turned left at the water. Most of the charter sailboats were still tied to the dock—the day was a little too chilly to appeal to adventure-seeking tourists.

The *Danger*, with its tall mast and deep blue hull, bobbed gently at its mooring. A pile of lime-green ocean-going kayaks roosted on its deck, providing lots of nooks and crannies where a person might tuck himself away to spend a night out of the wind and rain. I sat on the bench directly in front of the boat and looked over my shoulder at Chad's condominium. There was a perfect sight line from the boat to the main door of his building, assuming the person who delivered the pie had either entered through the water-side gate, or come in through the garage underneath the other apartments and passed by the pool to that main door. Either way, no one got through those gates without a key. Unless a resident buzzed them in or they slipped in on someone's draft. And there were enough workers and renters and people with unauthorized keys in their possession to make this quite possible.

Or had Kristen been expecting a food delivery? Seemed unlikely so early in the morning. And for sure the cops would have looked into that angle. It didn't seem fair to sic them on Turtle without first trying to find out what—if anything—he'd noticed on the morning of the murder.

27

"If you can't feed a hundred people, then just feed one."

—Mother Teresa

The Metropolitan Community Church squatted oblong and solid on a residential section of Petronia Street just a block from the major cross street, White. I stashed my scooter at the bike rack in front of the white two-story building and sat on the steps to wait, hoping that Tony would show. I felt certain that Turtle wouldn't talk to me without his friend as buffer.

Sandwich-seekers began to drift down the street in groups of twos and threes, entering the gate to follow the sidewalk along the building. Most were men that I'd seen at the beach or loitering outside the grocery store or, occasionally, causing a ruckus on Duval Street. I couldn't help wondering again what had led them here (not counting their current growling stomachs).

I glanced at my watch. Ten thirty. I decided to go in

and ask the folks working whether they'd seen Turtle or whether they expected him. A sign directed me around the side of the building to the basement entrance. A friendly older man in khaki shorts and a flowered shirt greeted me as I entered. On the table in front of him were stacks of sandwiches on white bread and piles of small paper sacks, plastic bags of peanuts and raisins, and others containing crackers or cookies.

"Good morning," he called out heartily. "Welcome to lunch at MCC. Today we have a choice of peanut butter and jelly or tuna salad." The men being served on either side of me turned to stare. The helpful man began to pack saltines and a sports drink into a paper bag and waited for me to make my choice.

"I'm not here for lunch," I stammered, keeping my gaze pinned on the jelly leaking through the top sandwich, staining the thin white bread purple. "I live out on houseboat row and I was talking to a guy, Tony, earlier this morning and he told me that his friend Turtle often visits here about now." I tapped my watch.

The men around me shrank back and I realized that I probably looked like pure hassle. They'd probably picked up the odor of cops, or something worse.

"He may have seen something that pertains to a case I'm involved with." Now the nice man looked worried, too. "He's not in trouble," I added quickly, "but I am."

The man pushed his aviator-shaped glasses up his nose and gave me a nod. "He's out on the back porch. Follow the walk around the corner. Can't promise he'll talk to you, though. He's always quiet, but today more than usual. I let him sit back there awhile because it seemed like he needed a quiet space." His voice dropped lower. "Possible that he ran out of his medication. Or decided he was through taking it." He rubbed a hand across his jaw. "Just be a little careful. Don't push."

I skirted around the walk to the back porch and found Turtle smoking at a plastic picnic table, a Styrofoam coffee cup in front of him, his dog at his feet. His dark red hair was long and tangled and his eyes seemed wild, like those of a trapped animal. I stopped still so as not to spook him. The dog uttered a low growl, his snout still resting on crossed paws.

"Turtle, I'm Hayley," I said gently. "We met a couple days ago at the beach when Henri Stentzel sent me over with a sack of burritos. She cooks awesome food, doesn't she? I never can make it taste the same at home in my kitchen." I took one step closer and kept talking. "Tony told me I might find you here. I swear I wouldn't bother you if it wasn't so important. It's possible that you might have seen something that could keep me out of jail."

Turtle hunched over his cigarette, sucking in air until it burned hot red down to the filter and then to his fingers. Then he dropped the glowing stub to the deck and ground it out. I swore I could smell the burned flesh.

"Listen," I said, my voice barely above a whisper. "Maybe you heard about the lady who was poisoned last week? They think I killed her and I can't find anyone who saw me at home, even though I swear I was right there on the boat the whole morning."

I inched a little closer and then stopped, trying to imagine I was approaching a feral cat. "I guess I did have reason to hate her, but really I should hate my boyfriend, right? He's the one who invited me down here and then cheated on me. I swear I've never been so embarrassed in my life. I always think I would never cheat on someone because I know what it would feel like and I wouldn't want to be the cause of that much hurt in someone else. But on the other hand, you fall in love or lust or whatever and it just seems like it's the only thing that matters in the world. So I guess I'm saying I didn't think I'd do that to someone else, but I proved I can get swept away with the best of them. After all, I'm here instead of home in New Jersey, right?"

Turtle didn't say anything, but how would he be expected to answer my nervous jabbering? I edged onto the bench across from him and the dog lifted his head and snarled.

"Easy," said Turtle, then glanced up and focused on something over my shoulder. His eyes were pale blue with a dark blue rim around the outside and wide dark pupils. In other days, when he maybe hadn't looked quite so crazy-fragile, those eyes would have stopped women cold on the streets. He mumbled something I couldn't understand.

"Excuse me?" I asked, leaning a little closer.

"Don't want no trouble," he barked, startling me backward on the bench.

"No trouble," I echoed, holding crossed fingers up. And thinking just how bad I'd feel if I did have to sic the police on him. If I had to throw him under the bus so I could shake the albatross off my own neck.

"Not too tall, not short either," he whispered. "Yellow slicker, with a white plastic bag. Squarish shape. Hung out behind the bushes next to the gate until a man came through walking his dog. That's how he got in. Big black and white Australian shepherd with a silly haircut."

A crop of goose bumps covered my arms. Sounded like Turtle had really seen Kristen's killer.

He made a sound like a low growl, then scrambled to his feet and bolted off the deck and down the path alongside the building, his dog loping behind. I followed him out, but they took off running down Petronia Street, crossing White, dodging a truck and a scooter, and heading toward the cemetery before I'd even reached the bike rack. I returned to the church basement.

"I'm so sorry. I'm afraid I spooked him," I told the sandwich man.

I drove back to Tarpon Pier and popped the scooter onto its kickstand, just dying to tell someone about what I'd learned. From the parking lot, I spotted Miss Gloria sunning herself on the little deck of her boat. A man in black was poised on the chair beside her, one arm out as if ready to hold her back in case she tried to leave. As I drew closer, I saw he looked hot and sweaty in jeans and a long-sleeved shirt. And grumpy, as though he'd been on the losing end of a serious conversation.

"Hooray! Miss Gloria's home!" I called.

"Oh, Hayley, it's so good to see you," she said, starting to push out of her chair. But her legs wobbled and she collapsed back down. I hurried over to hug her small frame. She still looked pale and delicate, but a hundred times better than she had in that hospital room.

"Have you met my son Freddy? Thank you for taking

care of Sparky. Could you bring him back over any time that's convenient? I really miss that little rascal. How did he and Evinrude make out?"

A lump rose in my throat. I couldn't see the sense in protecting her from my bad news, so I told her how Evinrude had been missing since the day she went into the hospital. Her hazel eyes watered and she reached a hand out to me. I took her fingers and squeezed gently.

"I'm so sorry, Hayley. You can keep my cat a little longer if you like, for company."

"I wouldn't dream of it," I said, trying to sound cheerful and not shaky like I felt inside. She'd had more pain than one old lady should have to bear over the last few days. And from the glower on her son's face, it looked like she was headed for more.

I trotted down the dock to Connie's boat to retrieve Sparky and his belongings. By the time I returned, Miss Gloria had gone inside, leaving only her son on the deck. I handed over the cat, but he scrambled out of Freddy's arms, ran mewing to the front door, and disappeared inside. Miss Gloria's sweet voice seeped through the screen, murmuring how much she'd missed her baby.

Freddy clapped his hands off and brushed an imaginary black hair from his black shirt. "My mother tells me you've been a good friend. We appreciate that. Thank you," he said, nodding his head briskly. "We'll be putting the boat up for sale and moving her to Dearborn by Christmas. Maybe we'll get lucky and find a nursing home that'll take a cat." His lips curled down, like he thought that was unlikely. Then he nodded a second time, as though I must surely agree with his sensible decision.

I was feeling awful about spooking Turtle. And losing Evinrude. And the whole nightmarish week. Month, really. But Miss Gloria's impending losses trumped all that.

"She's not my mother, so I hate to be nosy, but I think it'll just kill her to move away from here."

It would kill me, and I hadn't lived here for decades, the way Miss Gloria had. I hadn't fused my ways to the ways of the island, the turn of the tides, the way life was appreciated—each day on houseboat row cherished like a piece of polished sea glass.

"It'll be a shock for her to move to Michigan. We understand that. But for her own good, it has to be done. It's not responsible to leave an elderly woman alone down here. The health care on the islands is appalling. A million things could go wrong—that's already been proven. Thanks again for being a friend."

He cracked a mirthless smile and ducked into the boat.

28

"Most bereaved souls crave nourishment more tangible than prayers: they want a steak."

—M. F. K. Fisher

There were a lot of things lately I couldn't do a darned thing about—Miss Gloria's situation was only one of them. Turtle's hard-knocks life was another. My mind began to work over the bits of information he'd given me about what he might have seen the morning of the murder.

The deliverer of the pie was medium-sized and wore a yellow slicker. Both of which applied to me. At least on the days I borrowed Connie's extra raincoat, which was almost every time it rained, as my maroon jacket soaked right through in a downpour. And if you counted five foot four as medium-sized, which some people might not.

A picture flashed into my mind: Wally Beile slinging

his wet raincoat on the peg next to mine the other day in the *Key Zest* office. As my worthless lawyer might have said: A, he was not a big man. And B, his slicker was yellow. But what could I do about it? Stop by his office and ask if he hated Kristen enough to poison her? A ham-handed interrogation would not likely produce the information I needed. Nor would it help my job prospects.

I pushed myself to think harder. Someone tried to run me off the road last night and that driver had not meant to only scare me. I was convinced he intended to kill me. He'd emptied enough bullets into the water to turn me into Havarti cheese.

If Wally had been in that car, was it possible that he believed I had died? What if I showed up for a chat? Might his reactions to seeing me alive (though battered) confirm his identity? Of course, I wouldn't be dumb enough to say anything—I'd take my suspicions directly to the cops.

I trotted back down the finger to my scooter and fired her up, my stomach gurgling with anxiety and hunger. I glanced at my watch. Twelve thirty. With any luck, the *Key Zest* receptionist would be out to lunch and I could burst in unannounced and get a clear view into Wally's psyche.

I drove down Southard and parked in the back lot, fluffing my hair on the way to the magazine office. Then I shot up the stairs and paused in the hallway outside the office.

Keep it simple, I told myself. *Passing by—just wanted to shout out a big hello and see if you need anything else for my application.*

Then I'd flash a big smile and watch, like a pelican waiting for the shrimpers to dock. I sucked up a lungful of air and stepped into the waiting area. As I'd hoped, the receptionist's desk was empty, but the light bled through the blinds from Wally's office. My heart was beating so hard I thought the real estate agents on the first floor might be wondering about the banging.

"Helloooo?" I warbled weakly.

I heard a slight rustling in the back office and then Wally appeared at the door, glasses crooked on his nose and hair standing up as if he'd had a good fright. Annoyance and then confusion flushed his face. "Oh, Hayley. Adrienne didn't tell you to come over, did she? We're really not ready to make our decision. I've been bombarded with work since Kristen's funeral."

"Sorry. So sorry to bother you," I mumbled, hitching back a step. "I don't mean to be a pest, but I wondered if there's anything else I could do to help with my application. I know you said it was complete and all that, and you'd be in touch, but . . ."

But I felt like a fool. He was surprised to see me, yes, indeed. But it was the surprise of a harassed boss with too much on his plate, not the shock of a murderer who hadn't finished his job.

"I won't bother you again. I can wait with the rest of the supplicants."

I grinned and waved and stumbled out of the office as fast as I could. Rolling my shoulders to shake out the cricks of tension, my stomach rumblings ratcheted up to a howl. Next stop: Bad Boy Burrito, where I could kill two birds with one stone—get lunch and check out

Henri Stentzel's reactions to the living, breathing me. If she'd been the person hounding me down Route One in the driving rain last night, I thought I might be able to see it on her face.

I drove east on Simonton Street, trying not to think too hard about whether I'd torpedoed my chances for the critic job by irritating Wally. The sun emerged as I parked the scooter in front of the burrito shop. Two blocks down the street, whitecaps glinted cheerfully on the ocean. Hard to feel too down on a day like this.

I pulled open the heavy door to the shop, breathing in the scent of fried onions and chili peppers and maybe a pinch of cumin. As I waited in front of the counter, I spotted Henri at the back of the kitchen. She stood pressed against a tall man, one hand around his waist, the other reaching to caress the streak of silver at his temples. On tiptoes, she stretched up to kiss him. Over her head, he caught sight of me, murmured something to her as he pulled away, and took three quick steps out the back door.

With an audible sigh, Henri squared her shoulders and marched across the kitchen to greet the customers. Her face paled and her welcoming expression turned to a glare when she recognized me. I was too nervous to wait for her to speak.

"I'll have two fish tacos, all the way, double the verde sauce. And why not double the sour cream while you're at it. What's a few extra calories between friends? And let's see—what kind of smoothies are you serving today?"

She didn't pick up her order pad or make any move toward the stove.

"Doug Rodriguez called me late last night," she said, her voice grinding like tumbling stones in a fast current. "He mentioned that you happened to be in Miami Beach, and just happened to stop by Hola to interrogate him about my relationship with Robert." Her head dipped almost imperceptibly toward the rear of the restaurant.

And it clicked who the tall guy must have been: The mysterious and exquisitely talented Robert who'd cheated on her to be with Kristen and left her restaurant's helm for the so-far nonexistent restaurant on Easter Island. It didn't take a psychologist to diagnose the strong feelings still lingering between them. I hated to think it, but given all their history, probably hers were deeper than his. As Eric would say, nothing predicts the future better than the past.

I began to babble. "I know that must seem intrusive and appalling, but the thing is, the cops still believe I killed Kristen. So—"

"So you figure you'll shunt them off in my direction?" She planted her hands on her hips and scowled.

"Well, that's not—"

"I don't suppose I could expect you to imagine what the last six months have been like for me."

"I can certainly understand the cheating boyfriend part of it," I offered, baring my teeth with a girlfriend-to-girlfriend grin.

"I didn't just lose a man. I lost my livelihood," she said in a grim voice. "Do you know how long I saved up to buy that place? And how long it takes to build a staff that can work together? A staff that cares about the place even half as much as you do? And then build a clientele who are willing to come back over and over and spread the word to their friends?"

"I'm sorry it happened that way," I said. "I know it's a terribly hard business. My mom would say it's challenging enough to cook decent meals at home for your own family. And Doug told me the *Miami Herald* food critic was planning a major spread on your place right before Robert left."

She looked near tears.

"Robert was the linchpin in that kitchen. He was the spark that made the difference between good food and great. Maybe I would have stayed on if the review had been written, but when the critic canceled . . ." She shook her head. "That disappointment was a knife to my gut. I couldn't go on pretending everything would be fine. I'd find another chef. We'd rebuild our reputation. Never mind the excruciating personal embarrassment."

She wiped her face with the edge of her apron. "When things go really bad in my life, I stay sane by stripping life down to what I can literally control. In this case, I decided I could make burritos. One by one. Jalapeños, guacamole, shaved cabbage . . ."

She took off her apron, folded it in quarters, and slapped it on the counter. "I'm sorry about Miss Faulkner's death, but I had nothing to do with it."

Then she came around the cooler, marched past me to the front door, and flipped the OPEN sign to CLOSED. She held the door for me.

"We will not be serving lunch today."

29

"Cooking is like love. It should be entered into with abandon or not at all."

—Harriet van Horne

My stomach pitched and yawed, more from shame now than hunger. Everything I touched on this island seemed to turn sour. I dialed Detective Bransford's phone extension and a left a message telling him about what Turtle had seen from his perch on the *Danger* and my stepmother's suggestion about poisonous nuts in the pie crust. Let him do the police work—I was obviously a disaster.

I mounted the scooter and started it up, with no place to go and no one to talk to. I motored over to Higgs Beach and slouched at an empty picnic table, lowering my cheek to rest on the cool concrete and willing my mind to empty. A black and white gull hopped up on the bench beside me, pecked at some crumbs, and splattered the edge of the table with poop.

"You ingrate!" I yelped.

"You talkin' to me?"

Tony's drawl startled the bird away and me out of my daze. I shook my head and pointed to what the bird had left.

He shrugged and grinned. "When you gotta go . . . Did y'all find Turtle? I haven't seen his ugly mug anywhere today."

I sat up straight and smoothed my wrinkled cargo shorts. "We did have a chance to chat and he told me what he saw. But then I'm afraid I scared him half to death."

"Easy to do," said Tony, doffing his hat. "Y'all have a good day. The cake was awesome."

"Thanks." I mustered a smile and he sauntered away.

My phone rang and Deena's name came up on the screen. What in the world would she want with me? The way things were going, Chad had probably told her to call and ream me out. About something.

"Hayley," she said when I answered. "I feel silly about this after our last conversation, but I didn't know who else to talk to."

"What's up?"

"I can't find Chad."

I let loose a snort of laughter. "You're barking up the wrong banyan here, Deena. I'd be the last one to have any insight on that topic." I glanced at my watch. "Monday morning. If I remember correctly, he ought to be right there in the office harassing you about how you're not typing fast enough to keep up with his dictation."

"That's why I'm worried. He had an appointment in

court first thing this morning and two new clients back-to-back wanting to talk about filing for divorce. Litigious clients with deep pockets. He didn't show for either and now they're mad at me. And he isn't answering his cell. Or my text messages."

"That's weird," I agreed. "Silence from the man whose e-mail trigger finger is the fastest gun on the island. You tried his home phone?" Not that I'd ever seen him use it for an actual phone call—he only had it installed to buzz repairmen through the locked front door.

"I tried it," she said grimly.

"Has anyone else seen him?"

"He was here early this morning. His office light's on and he left a couple of files open on the desk." She sighed. "Oh, well, you were a long shot. I shouldn't have bothered you."

"No problem," I said. "Hope he turns up."

Deena's call left me with an uneasy feeling. Chad may have been lousy at texting or calling me, especially as our relationship nose-dived, but he was always in touch with Deena. I walked over to the water and sat by the sand, doodling with a stick, letting the events of the last week flit through my mind. I'd talked with a number of people who disliked Kristen, but none of them seemed angry enough to kill her. Wouldn't committing a murder have to be fueled by toxic rage? The kind that Deena heard often through the closed doors of Chad's conference room. I threw my doodling stick in the water, watched it wash away, and settled on one disturbing question.

What if the pie had actually been meant for Chad, not

Kristen? And the murderer didn't know him well enough to recognize his aversion to sweets in general but especially the key lime flavor? If that were all true, Kristen ingested the poison accidentally. And all the ideas I'd had about who wanted to kill Kristen meant nothing, because nobody did.

The next question followed logically: Who would actually want Chad dead? Because of his divorce practice, I imagined there might be a number of possibilities. He was ruthless when it came to protecting his clients' assets. I remembered the nasty memo I'd found in his apartment when I'd gone over to clean. With Chad's killer lawyer instinct, surely there were more like this in his office clipped to the files of other clients. Many more. I pulled out my phone and redialed Deena.

"You've heard something?" she asked.

"Sorry, no. I was wondering about those files Chad left on his desk this morning. Whose were they?"

"You know I can't tell you that."

I could imagine her pursed lips, painted, glossy, and disapproving. "You called me for help, not the other way around."

"Sorry," said Deena. "After ten years' working for him, client confidentiality is so ingrained—at this point it's almost a genetic trait. Chad would fire me in an instant if I said anything about anything. Even if his life was in danger."

"And it might be," I said, and explained my idea that Chad might have been the murderer's target. "After all, the poisoned pie was delivered to his home, not Kristen's. She wasn't actually living there, was she?"

"Oh my God," she said. "But what do the files have to do with any of that?"

"They might be related; they might not. But, if I were in your position, I'd go through all of them and make a list of the people he's represented in horrendous divorces. Especially the cases that dragged on awhile—and maybe focus on the ones that he won. And then, if it were me, and he doesn't show up in good time, I'd call the cops. Detective Bransford is the guy I've been talking to." I read off his cell number. "He's overbearing, and takes himself awfully seriously. But he's kind of cute," I added with a strained laugh.

She thanked me and signed off.

I leaned on my elbows back in the sand, the weak sun warming my face. Wishing for a sandwich. Or a couple of those amazing crabmeat choux pastries that had been served at Kristen's funeral. Made by Chef Robert, I now knew.

Deena called again.

"Hayley, I listened to his office voice mail." She paused and I could imagine her thinking through how much to say. "One of his clients, who shall of course remain nameless, called to report that his black Audi sedan was stolen on Saturday. The client keeps it garaged a few blocks away, so he didn't notice until yesterday evening that it was missing. They found it abandoned in the golf course parking lot out on Stock Island. This case fits the description you mentioned—it was ugly and he won big."

The puzzle pieces slid into place and I jerked up to sitting, visualizing the grille of the car that had tried to run me off the road. Had it been an Audi?

"Who was the client?" I demanded.

"I can't say the name," she said. "But I'm worried."

"Oh, for crying out loud—then call the cops," I said.

I hung up, reviewing the names I could remember from the weeks I'd lived with Chad. Not that he talked to me about his clients—he was more close-mouthed than Deena. But I couldn't help sometimes seeing bits and snatches of the work he brought home. If Chad had been the murderer's target, wouldn't he or she be highly distressed about killing Kristen?

My brain worked itself back around to Meredith, the pastry chef who insisted to Eric at the funeral that Kristen didn't deserve to die. What if she hadn't known that Kristen was staying with Chad, and she killed her accidentally? I thought about her despair in the cemetery and her loyalty to Kristen. And how she'd come so close to landing a dream job in a fancy restaurant. I couldn't remember if she'd said she was divorced, but she certainly had no kind words for men. And I imagined that she was quite capable of constructing a sophisticated piecrust containing ground, poisonous nuts, so delicious that the person eating the pie would never notice the addition. In fact, the nibbler would only notice the unusual and delectable sweetness. Possibly even gobble a second piece, just as I had, before the poison infused her system and began to shut it down.

And Meredith had the same initial as the woman mentioned in the memo I'd seen on Chad's desk when I was cleaning. The woman who'd been fleeced in her divorce settlement, losing her home, her car, and worst of all, her dog. If Meredith accidentally murdered her friend instead of doing in her ex-husband's divorce lawyer, her hysteria made perfect sense. And it might even make sense that she'd tried to kill me, because she knew that I was asking way too many questions about the murder: I'd interrogated her twice in some detail. I hoped I was dead wrong, because I liked Meredith. She was struggling with the same kind of career angst as me.

But if I wasn't wrong, Chad was still a moving target. I called Deena back but was shunted to her voice mail. "It's Hayley again. This is urgent. Go to his desk and check on the files. If there's a file open on someone named Meredith who lost everything to Chad's client, he could be in big trouble. Call me."

Next I considered calling Eric, but we hadn't spoken since that awkward conversation about his ruined Mustang. Would he even care? Hopefully, a long friendship would trump painted sheet metal. I left a message on his voice mail, explaining my new theory.

This was the problem I'd been grappling with all week: Who really cared about my theories? The answer should be the man I was paying to defend me. I held my nose and dialed my lawyer. If he didn't react reasonably, I would fire him on the spot. Luckily his beleaguered secretary answered and offered me the choice of getting transferred to his cell phone or put through to voice mail.

"Voice mail would be fine," I told her quickly and waited for his pompous introduction. When the beep sounded, I considered telling him about Turtle's observations. And mentioning my new theory that the pie hadn't been meant for Kristen at all. That someone had wanted Chad dead, not Kristen. But what came out of my mouth was: "Mr. Kane, this is Hayley Snow. I will no longer need your services."

Then I dialed Detective Bransford, feeling unaccountably nervous when his voice mail beep sounded.

"So, I had this idea that Chad Lutz was the target of the poison, not Kristen Faulkner. Uh, I should say this is Hayley Snow, but you've probably figured that out, being a detective and all. What I'm suggesting is that the killer didn't realize that Chad despised key lime pie. He wasn't a big fan of desserts in general because, let's face it, he's very vain and can't bear the idea of a potbelly. But I'm not talking about that. This is probably too much information, but he puked his guts out a couple of years ago after eating a piece of KLP. You know how you develop an aversion to a certain food once it's hurled back up the wrong way?"

I sounded like an absolute idiot. "What I'm trying to say is . . ." What was I trying to say? I continued to blather to his voice mail. "There's a pastry chef in town who's a big fan of Kristen's. You may have seen her at the funeral—she was devastated to the point of becoming publicly hysterical. And what if that makes all the sense in the world because *she's* the one who killed Kristen? By accident?"

His voice mail cut off. If he was at all interested, he could call me back. I considered phoning Meredith. But if she were the killer, she'd figure out I was onto her and bolt. Maybe better still, I would drop by Cole's Peace Bakery. If Meredith were there, I'd buy a loaf of bread, chat innocently as if I knew nothing, and then call Bransford the second I left the shop. If she wasn't, I could try to wrangle her address out of one of the other workers.

It was almost four p.m. by the time I got across town. The bakery was closed. I was swamped with a mixture of disappointment and relief. In the window of the Restaurant Store attached to the bakery, a small red fifteen-percent-off sale sign had been taped to the door. This was too tempting to ignore. I went directly to the cutlery department and perused the knives. Finally, I chose a Japanese paring knife and a plastic protector and carried them to the counter. While the clerk rang my items up, I said: "I was hoping to talk with Meredith who works next door about a catering gig. She does desserts, right?"

The clerk nodded. "Pastries are her specialty."

I clapped my hands. "My boss is looking for someone who can bake amazing pastries—she mentioned pies, éclairs, and maybe baklava. She's throwing a big party weekend after next. She'd pay really well because of the short notice. But she's going to hire someone today and Meredith's voice mail doesn't seem to be working."

"Wow, that sounds perfect for Meredith," said the clerk. "Bummer that you can't reach her."

"Do you happen to know where she lives? Maybe I could swing by her house and tell her in person."

The clerk studied me for a moment, eyes narrowed and lips pressed together. Then she pulled a piece of scrap paper from the drawer beside the cash register and scribbled an address on it. "She shares a house on Grinnell Street. I'm sure she'd want to hear about your catering gig. She likes working at the bakery and all, but it's not a dream job, you know? Half the time she's slapping sandwiches together or working the cash register. And the hours are wicked early."

I thanked her profusely and she handed over the knife, packed in its plastic sheath, which I stashed in the long pocket of my cargo shorts. Did I have the nerve to go to her house? Did I have any business getting more involved? But if not me, who else would even care?

I felt frightened and frozen. Then I thought of Lorenzo, my tarot reader, who was probably setting up for the usual crush of Sunset tourists. Even if he didn't have an answer, talking things through over the cards should help me decide what to do.

I drove down Eaton Street and scored a parking spot right in front of the Waterfront Playhouse. Sprinting past the sculpture garden and the man dressed as a soldier but sprayed from head to toe with gold paint, I found Lorenzo preparing to open shop near the water. His cloak was draped over the back of his chair and he was spreading a blue cloth over the card table.

"Lorenzo! I'm in kind of a hurry. Do you have time for a three-card reading?" My mother started every morning by reading her own cards while her coffee was brewing. I'd rather have it done by an expert. Why would I believe my own magic?

"Absolutely. And this one's on me." He grinned and retrieved his deck from a canvas bag under the table. I waited nervously while he straightened the corners of his tablecloth and donned his cape. To my left, the Cat Man unloaded carriers of hungry felines. To my right, the fire-eater and his assistant laid out thick ropes on the concrete to define his space. Finally Lorenzo handed me the deck.

"Is your name really Lorenzo?" I asked while shuffling the cards.

Even under the thick layer of pancake makeup, I could see him blush all the way up to his black turban.

"I was Marvin until I moved down here from Georgia," he admitted. "Marvie to my mother. But who's going to believe a tarot card reader called Marvin?"

"Point taken." I handed him the deck.

"Think about the question you bring to the table today," he said, eyes closed and fingers to his temples.

Was Chad safe? Who ran me off the road? Will I get the job? Will I ever have another boyfriend? The questions tumbled through my brain, but there was only so much three cards could tell me. I focused on Chad and nodded at Marvin. Lorenzo.

He dealt out the cards—the three of swords, the moon, and then the eight of swords. My stomach seized. The only card I hated more than the tower was the first one he'd laid on the table: three swords piercing a heart, with rain falling in the background.

"I see there has been deep sorrow," Lorenzo said quietly, staring at me, his hand on the first card. "A divorce. Maybe an affair? A great fear of rejection and loneliness."

He focused back on the table. "The moon. Hmm. Things are not as they seem. Are you fooling yourself? Denial brings chaos."

"Fooling myself how?" I asked.

"You're the only one who can answer that." He shrugged and pointed to the third card.

"You have been floundering," he said, tapping the card. "Feeling vulnerable. And trapped." He looked up from the table and into my eyes again. "No one can save you from yourself, Hayley. You must take action, not wait to be rescued."

I whooshed out a breath. "Thanks. I think." I smiled weakly, got up from Lorenzo's table, and left the pier, head spinning. Since meeting Chad, nothing had turned out to be what it seemed. Of course I had to depend on myself, but what exactly did that mean?

I wove back through the crowds gathering for the sunset celebration, slid onto my scooter, and tried calling the detective again. Still no answer. I decided to run by Meredith's rental house and take a look. If something seemed awry—like suppose she had Chad tied to a tree in the backyard with three swords piercing his chest—then I could drive down to the police station and round up a couple of officers. I snickered at my own joke, revved up the engine, and veered into the traffic to cross town.

30

"A hungry man can't see right or wrong.
He just sees food."

—Pearl S. Buck

I parked my scooter two blocks from the cemetery and approached Meredith's house on foot. If she was home and Chad was in trouble, I'd be making a dangerous mistake to let her catch me snooping. An enormous banyan tree with multiple curved roots reaching skyward obscured the front of the white conch house. It must be wicked dark inside, especially with dusk falling. I waited a few minutes by the neighbor's fence, breathing more heavily than the short walk would explain, trying to figure out a reasonable plan.

I crept down the side of Meredith's house that was shaded by the big tree. Edging up to the building, I peered through the first window. I could barely make out the shapes of the living room furniture: a denim futon, a large-screen TV, and several pillows scattered on the beige tile floor. This had the feel of a student crash pad, or, more likely for Key West, the home of several minimum-wage workers forced to share quarters.

I inched farther down the alley between the fence and the house. The next window was covered by an off-white shade, the bottom grimy with fingerprints, one rip patched with duct tape. The bathroom?

I heard a scratching noise behind me and whirled around to face it. In a great explosion of flapping wings, a rooster sprang from the bushes crowing at the top of his poultry lungs. I clutched my hand to my chest, my heart lunging, and crouched down to wait and see if I'd been exposed by the rooster's racket. But nothing happened.

I crept a little farther along the side of the house and peered into a window with jalousie blinds. The flap nearest the bottom was slanted open. Inside, Chad was seated on a battered wooden chair, his hands tied behind his back, his mouth taped with the same silver tape I'd seen on the shade, and his feet bound to the bottom chair rung. The tape lapped over one nostril and it looked like he was having trouble breathing. His body language vibrated with outrage and fear.

Then a hand clapped over my mouth and I felt something poke me in the small of the back. I shrieked through the grabbing fingers.

"One more syllable and I shoot," a woman's voice hissed, poking me again with what I now realized had to be the barrel of a gun. "Hands on your head."

Meredith. Rigid with fear, I raised my hands and planted them, as instructed.

"Move." She gave me a rough shove and I wobbled around the back of the house, finally getting a glimpse of her as we turned the corner. Wearing a pink flowered sweater and white pedal pushers, she looked like a Palm Beach housewife, not a kidnapper. We filed through the back door into a small vestibule crammed with shoes, fishing equipment, and bags of empty beer bottles and cans. She slammed the door shut and locked it behind us and then grabbed a handful of bungee cords from a hook on the wall and pointed to a room on the right with the gun. As I stumbled in, Chad's eyes bugged wide and he rocked in his chair, making muffled noises that sounded like mmmrffff, mmmrff, and mmrrrff.

"I think he wants to know what you're doing here," said Meredith with a dry laugh. She pushed me toward another chair. "Sit. Hands behind you."

I sat. She dropped the gun on the faded quilt that covered the metal daybed and wound one cord around my wrists and another around my ankles. Then she backed away and retrieved the gun from the bed, her hands shaking visibly. She was as frightened as I was. How had she managed to capture Chad? He rumbled again underneath his tape.

"Just for kicks, let's see what your boyfriend has to say." She strode across the room, grabbed a loose corner of the tape on Chad's face, and ripped it off.

He howled from the pain, both his upper and lower lips now bleeding. He tapped them together gingerly, feeling for damage, and then frowned at me.

"What in the name of God are you doing here?" he finally asked.

Any sympathy I had been feeling drained away. "Deena was worried because you didn't show up for court. Or your new customers."

"Big bad lawyer was going to fleece some more women?" asked Meredith in a voice that would have soured milk.

"You should have hired a more competent attorney," Chad told her.

"There was no need to include the dog in the settlement," she spat.

"I work for my clients, not their exes," said Chad. "My job is to protect their interests in the biggest possible settlement. My job is to win."

Meredith looked angry enough to blow into a million pieces, but instead began to weep.

I turned to glare at Chad. "Could you possibly shut up?"

I closed my eyes for a moment to steady my breathing, and then glanced around the room to assess my options. Which looked, quite honestly, lousy. Meredith's hand was still shaking. Even before Chad's needling, she had begun to take on a shell-shocked glaze, like she was assessing the situation too—and coming up empty. A poisoning was one thing—death at a distance. Two face-to-face shootings were something else altogether. Could we use her distress to our advantage?

"Meredith," I said softly. "I realize you didn't mean to poison Kristen. She was your friend, your ally."

She nodded, so I kept talking.

"But that means you delivered the pie to Chad. Did you hate him that much?"

Chad started to protest, but I shushed him quiet.

Meredith blinked furiously and jabbed the gun at him. "Not only did he clean me out, but then he lured Kristen away from Robert. He totally screwed up the plans for the new restaurant."

"I don't understand," I said. "Why would it matter whether she slept around and with whom?" That crack was aimed at Chad.

"You think Robert would continue to work for Kristen if she was sleeping with this cretin? All of us needed to pull together for the project to get off the ground. Superstud here ruined everything."

She was gasping for breath now—waving the gun in loopy figure eights. Even Chad looked terrified. Superstud. I needed to calm her down if we had any chance of escaping alive.

"Listen, Meredith," I said in a soothing voice. "The courts will understand that poisoning Kristen was an error, that you only intended to make Chad good and sick. But if you shoot two of us in utterly cold blood, you'll spend your life in prison. If you're lucky."

The blood drained suddenly from Meredith's face and she clutched at her stomach and ran from the room.

"She's had the trots all afternoon," Chad hissed. "Do something!"

"You are such a horse's arse." If I could have managed getting out of the house alone, I would have happily left him there. "Maybe later you can explain to me how one small woman managed to incapacitate a bruiser like you using only duct tape," I needled.

He muttered a string of curses.

I tried to stretch the cords binding my ankles and

wrists. She had wrapped the hands tightly, but there was give around my legs. I managed to scrape my sneakers off and wiggle one foot out of the cord and then the other. I leaped up and hurried over to the back of Chad's chair.

"There's a knife in my pocket," I whispered, squatting down and leaning one hip against his hand so he could work his fingers into the opening. Once he'd wiggled it out, and worked open the plastic shield, I held my wrists away from my back so he could saw at the cord. "Try not to cut me."

For several minutes, he fumbled the knife against the cord. "Go!" he said finally.

I snapped the fraying bungee, ripped my hands free, and grabbed the knife from Chad. "I had to buy this to replace the one you refused to return. You owe me fifty bucks."

"Hayley, please! Can you save the recriminations until later?"

I heard the toilet flush down the hall and then the scuffling noises of Meredith's shoes on the tile. I bolted across the room and ducked behind the door. As Meredith turned the corner into the room, I sprang out, brandishing the knife, and screaming like a modern-day banshee.

Chad howled along with me. I knocked Meredith to her knees; the gun skittered across the tile. She butted her head into my shoulder and the knife arced through the air and clattered into a far corner. I struggled to grip her wrists, but she flattened me to the floor, her strong hands circling my neck, slippery with sweat. Hardly able to breathe, I flailed my arms and twisted my hips trying to knock her off. Then Chad launched himself across the room, chair attached. He knocked into Meredith's body and smashed her away. I rolled over, groaning and clutching my bruised windpipe.

"For God's sake, Hayley! Get the gun!"

I scrambled to my feet, found the gun, and trained it on her. She sank down to the floor. Then I eased the iPhone out of my pocket and hit redial on Detective Bransford's number.

"This is Hayley Snow. I'm on Grinnell Street, holding a gun on Meredith the pastry chef. I would appreciate it if you could get here as soon as possible and take over. I would hate to have to shoot her."

Two beeps announced another call coming in. KEY ZEST the screen read.

I steadied the gun on Meredith. "You make one move while I take this call and I swear I will shoot out both of your knees."

31

"The scent of baking will untie knots of misunderstanding."

—Barbara O'Neal

"It's Wally. Wally Beile. About the food critic job. Did I catch you at a bad time? We loved, loved, loved your latest piece and would like to offer you the position. Can you come in tomorrow for a staff meeting? Say nine o'clock?"

"Oh, fantastic! I'm thrilled! Oh, thank you so much."

"One concern, though. All of the pieces you submitted focused on more down-market restaurants. Places our readers would feel comfortable taking their kids or their dog. With the exception of Seven Fish, of course. Which is great, but I want to be certain you don't have anything against the higher-end eateries. We'd want them covered, too."

"Only my wallet had a problem with those," I assured him and clicked off the call, grinning like a fool.

"Oh my gosh, you'll never guess what just happened." I whooped with excitement. "Maybe you thought I was on the way out of town, but looks like you'll be seeing me around, like it or not," I told Chad, my gun wavering.

"Could you keep your focus, please?" he answered, tipping his head at Meredith.

A trio of policemen burst in through the door, their guns pointed at me. Detective Bransford followed behind them, also holding his weapon drawn. On me.

"Miss Snow," he said sharply, "put your weapon on the ground and your hands on your head."

"Fine," I said, and bent down to place the gun on the tile. "It doesn't belong to me anyway. Here's the situation." I pointed to Meredith, feeling ever so slightly melodramatic.

"Stay!" yelled one of the cops. "Hands over your head."

I raised them slowly. Another policeman approached me and patted me down. "All clear," he said.

"Now tell us what's going on," said Bransford.

"This woman killed Kristen Faulkner. But she did so by accident. She was trying to poison him." Keeping my hands up, I bent my pointer finger at Chad, sprawled sideways on the floor, still taped to the chair. "Apparently he represented her husband in a nasty divorce."

"He stole my dog!" Meredith curled into a ball and began to weep again. "Gerald doesn't even like animals. Ask him if he ever, once, took that dog out for a walk." Her shoulders shook with sobs. "And who's caring for Chuckles now? There was no need to take it that far."

"You don't call poison in your pie crust taking something too far?" I muttered. "Sheesh!"

"Get her cuffed and down to the station," said Bransford to the nearest officer.

For one frightening moment, I thought he meant me. But two of the officers approached Meredith, forced her hands behind her back, and snapped handcuffs on her wrists. They pulled her upright, knees rubbery and face wet, and marched her out of the room.

"Now," said the detective, "I can't *wait* to hear how all this unfolded." He extracted a Swiss Army Knife from one of his pockets, cut the tape from Chad's wrists and ankles, and helped him to his feet. Chad pushed away from the detective, rubbed his hands together, and stamped his feet.

"Thanks," he said, without much grace. "What the hell did that crazy witch do with my phone?" He knelt down to look under the bed and swept his BlackBerry out along with several tumbleweed-sized dust bunnies. He began to thumb through his messages and dialed a number—probably Deena.

The detective waved a hand in front of Chad's face. "If it's not too much trouble, Mr. Lutz, I'd like the two of you to come down to the station now and give your statements."

Chad frowned. "Right now?"

"Now."

He rolled his eyes and spoke into the phone. "Deena, it's me. I'm on my way to the police station, but I'm going to need you to work late tonight and help me untangle today's mess. Put a call in to the two clients who had appointments this morning and let them know I'll get in touch shortly. And Judge Tabor too."

As he finished barking orders at Deena, I explained to Bransford that Chad had been able to cut me loose with my brand-new knife. "Okay if I collect it?" I asked. "You're welcome to hold on to it until we get to the station. But it set me back almost fifty bucks."

Fifteen minutes later, we were settled in chairs in front of Detective Bransford's desk. He offered us cups of bad coffee and bars of stale chocolate from the vending machine down the hall. Chad took one bite, made a face, and pushed his away. So I ate them both. It was past dinnertime and I'd never gotten lunch and the terror of being held at gunpoint had left me ravenous. Three uniformed cops leaned against the wall and a tape recorder had been set to run on the desk. Chad was asked to tell his part of the story first.

"I got to work early this morning because I had a lot of appointments. Then Meredith phoned me—Ms. Warner. She said she was leaving the island today. Permanently. She had decided to accept all the terms of the divorce. Frankly, I was a little surprised that she rolled over that easily—she's been a litigious nightmare for months. And why call me, rather than having her lawyer tie up the loose ends? But fine, she must have finally figured out I was the alpha."

I bit my lip to keep from laughing. Eight hours' duct-taped to a chair and he was still a puffed-up dope.

"And I was happy to close the case," he added.

"Then why did you go to her home?" the detective asked.

Chad sank lower in his seat. "She said she had Kristen's iPhone and Kristen wanted her to be sure it got to me. She was willing to hand it over if I'd come by to pick it up. Or she'd turn it over to the cops on her way up to Miami. My choice." He knocked the side of his head with his fist, looking embarrassed. "I can't believe I fell for that. But I knew they were close and it seemed plausible that she had the phone."

My eyes widened. Why was it plausible that Meredith had her dead friend's phone? And why wouldn't he want her to drop it off at the station or to Kristen's family?

Chad looked down at his shoes. "Anyway, she sounded like she meant business and so I agreed to run over and pick it up. Only she met me at the front door with a gun."

"Excuse me for being dense, but I don't get it," I said. "Why in the world would Meredith have Kristen's phone? And why would you care enough to go pick it up?"

"I can answer that," said Bransford. "We examined Ms. Faulkner's phone in the course of our investigation and found some unusual photographs."

Chad turned scarlet. "Is it necessary to go into the details? I don't see that they have any bearing on this discussion."

"Photos of what?" I asked.

Chad refused to answer.

Bransford tapped on his desk to get our attention. "What happened when you arrived at her home?" he asked Chad.

"As I said, she had a gun. You saw how it played out." Chad grimaced and ran his fingers through his hair, already looking disheveled and a little greasy. "She taped me to that blasted chair where I stayed all day, while she tried to work up the nerve to finish the job. Then Hayley turned up and you know the rest."

"But how does a hundred-twenty-pound woman tape a big man to a chair? Did she have an accomplice?" the detective asked.

"More like a hundred and fifteen," I said.

Chad scowled. "No, she didn't have a damn accomplice. She said she'd shoot me if I didn't cooperate and I believed her."

"You believed her." It looked like the detective was trying not to laugh.

"She wanted to kill me," said Chad. "And she knew Hayley had been snooping around all week asking questions about the murder. She was certain that Hayley had figured out who was responsible for the pie. In fact, she panicked on Saturday, followed Hayley all the way to Miami, and tried to kill her by running her off the road. In the end, she had us both tied up, but she didn't have the guts to follow through."

"And you believe her motivation was the divorce settlement you negotiated for her husband?" asked Bransford.

"The settlement was very favorable to my client," said Chad, with a smug little smile. "Very."

"Taking her dog was purely mean," I couldn't help saying.

He rolled his eyes. "You're so naive, Hayley."

Before I could think of a shriveling retort, the detective signaled for another timeout and turned his attention to me. "So you came to Miss Warner's house because . . ."

"Because Chad's secretary, Deena, called to say she was worried. He'd missed three important appointments and the day wasn't over. And then I started thinking about my tarot readings over the last week and I got the strong feeling he was in danger."

Chad began to snicker, and then laugh so hard that he choked on his own saliva. The detective got up from his desk and came around to pound him on the back.

"The next time," I said, glaring at Chad with as much dignity as I could summon, "I will leave your sorry butt taped to the chair."

I turned back to the detective. "Anyway, as I was saying, I started thinking more about the pie and how much Chad hates desserts and how everyone I talked to commented that Kristen loved them. Especially key lime pie. What if the killer didn't know that Kristen had been staying with him?" I cleared my throat. "After all, I had just moved out.

"And then Deena called back again and said one of Chad's clients had reported his Audi stolen and he suspected his ex. The more I thought about it, the more I could almost picture those overlapping Audi circles in my rearview mirror the other night. And then I thought of the notes I'd seen about the divorce case of someone he called 'M' when I was cleaning his apartment"—I pointed at Chad without looking at him—"and it all fell into place. So I asked around and found out where she lived. I did leave you a message," I told the detective. "And I was going to call you again if something looked out of whack. You haven't exactly been taking my word as gospel this week."

It was Detective Bransford's turn to blush. "You're both free to go now, though we may need to contact you again later."

"Of course," I said, and followed Chad from the room. By the time I caught up with him outside the building, he was already on the phone arranging for Deena to pick him up and order his dinner.

Watching him bark his orders, I remembered the conversation with my stepmother about my desperation. And Lorenzo's latest reading, when he mentioned my fears of rejection and loneliness. It wouldn't be fair to blame all our problems on Chad, tempting as that might be.

"I understand you a lot better than I did a week ago," I told him once he'd slid his phone into his pocket. "And me too. I was leaning on you too hard to get things moving in my own life—you weren't really looking for that much intimacy. Kristen would have been a better match. Maybe."

He rolled his eyes. "Thanks for the free analysis."

"I have a little free advice, too," I said. "In the future, maybe you'd be better off thinking less about winning and more about what's fair. At least then your clients' spouses won't wish you dead."

I turned around and started home, hoping he was watching me go. But even more than that, wishing it had been Bransford.

32

"Yes! Live! Life's a banquet and most poor suckers are starving to death!"

—Auntie Mame

The tension of the day had twisted the muscles in my lower back to throbbing knots. I stretched out on the houseboat's tiny living room floor, drawing in my knees alternately to my stomach, while I described Meredith's capture to Connie. I had just gotten to the part where the rooster burst out of the bushes, when someone knocked on the door.

"Hold that thought," said Connie, getting up to answer. She gave a little whoop of delight and moved out of the way so I could see who was there. Miss Gloria with a huge armload of gray tiger cat.

I leaped to my feet and crossed the room in two big steps. "Evinrude!"

Miss Gloria loaded him into my arms and I buried my

face in his fur—which smelled a little like gasoline. He purred like the engine that had given him his name.

"Honest to gosh, I'd almost given up on him. Where did you find him?"

"I had to think like a cat," Miss Gloria said with a mysterious smile. "You know the boat two doors down with all the junk in the windows?" She gestured down the walk. "He must have slipped in there the day I was knocked out and your houseboat was wrecked. And then he couldn't get out. I saw his tail in the window and the dockmaster came over and let me in so I could get him."

"Thank you, thank you, thank you," I said. "You are a true friend."

The cat scrambled out of my arms and stalked over to the mat where his water and food bowls sat, empty. I filled them both and added a tiny Pyrex bowl of organic milk as a welcome home treat. Then I noticed Miss Gloria's son hovering outside our boat. He was talking on his cell phone, pacing, dressed in his usual black, but with the addition of a black blazer that looked too warm for the weather. I realized she was dressed up too, wearing a navy housedress, not her regular turquoise sweat suit with the shape of Florida traced in glitter on her chest. Traveling clothes. My heart gave a downward flip—was he moving his mother today?

"If you have a minute, my son has something to ask you," Miss Gloria said, smiling widely—not at all like a person whose Michigan winter prison sentence was about to begin. I came out onto the porch.

Freddy snapped his phone shut and stepped onto our deck. "I've been discussing our mother's situation with my brother back home. We'd like to propose a deal. If you'll consider living in the spare bedroom on Mother's houseboat and looking after her a little, the room is yours rent free. We know it's asking a lot and we'll understand if you say no. But it would sure be a load off our minds."

I thought it over for about forty-five seconds. I didn't know Miss Gloria all that well, but what I knew, I loved. Her boat wasn't very big, though the second bedroom was larger than my current digs. And I'd be near Connie, not on top of her and Ray. And I'd get to stay on houseboat row, rent free.

"Are you kidding?" I yelped. "Absolutely!" I clamped Miss Gloria into a big hug and kissed the top of her head.

I motored down Southard Street and parked in front of the Green Parrot, where Bill Blue was playing another sound check. At the bar, I bought a Key West Sunset Ale and told the bartender that I'd be running a tab for my friends. Then I waded through the crowd to claim the windowsill, where I'd sat with Eric just a few days ago. It seemed like months—so much had changed. Deena called as I was settling in.

"Good gravy, Hayley! Chad told me about what happened with Meredith. You could have been killed!"

"I'm okay. It turned out all right," I said.

"Chad probably didn't say it, but I know he's grateful. In fact, he asked me to call and tell you to pick up a box of your things. Looks like recipes and cookbooks. He said he brought it to the office by mistake."

"Fat chance of that," I said. "Thanks, Deena. I'll come by tomorrow. Tonight I'm celebrating."

After she hung up, Eric appeared in the doorway across the bar. He stood there for a moment, scanning the crowd. I waved him over, motioning that he should pick up a beer on the way.

I squinted as he got closer. "Have you done something to your hair?"

He smiled sheepishly. "Sun-In. It comes in a spray bottle."

"You're joking! I used that product when I was fourteen."

"So I'm immature." He put his arm around my shoulders and squeezed. "I can't believe what you've been through today. I got your text message too late. One of my patients had an emergency. I feel terrible that you had to handle this alone."

I smiled. "It was probably good for my character. Lorenzo told me I was going to have to start relying on myself. But honestly, I never would have gone in the house if Meredith hadn't forced me at gunpoint. I'm not that brave. Or dumb." I smiled up at Eric, feeling a rush of affection.

"By the way, I talked to the artist who painted your car. He said he'd be happy to do a retouch whenever the body shop finishes tapping out those dents. No problem. And now that I have a job, I can certainly pay."

"Sorry I was hard on you," said Eric. "I shouldn't own things that mean more to me than my friends." He held up his bottle. "To the new food critic. To my old friend."

"And mine." Connie materialized out of the crowd

and clinked her bottle against mine and then Eric's. "You'll never believe what just happened! The ring-leader of the mah-jongg table at the Truman Annex just called me. Three of them want to switch to Paradise Cleaning. Which will more than make up for losing Chad's business—and be much less annoying." She clinked my bottle again. "She said you talked her into it. So thank you."

A familiar head of wavy hair appeared at the Southard Street door to the bar. Then I saw Detective Bransford's gaze searching the room. His eyes locked on mine and he came over to our group. "Can I buy you a drink?" he asked me.

My heart gave a little sick-puppy lurch.

"Got that taken care of," I said, a little more snippily than I'd intended, and raised my beer. "Congratulations on getting your murder case wrapped up, Detective."

"The pastry chef with a key lime pie in the hallway," Eric muttered.

I held my breath, not daring to look at him for fear we'd start laughing and embarrass the heck out of the detective. Everyone was entitled a whopper mistake once in a while, weren't they? He'd only been doing his job.

"Nate, call me Nate. Your theory was right," he said, ignoring the suppressed snickers from Connie and Eric. "The pastry chef intended for Chad Lutz to eat the poisoned pie—she'd filled the crust with ground Barbados nuts. She hung around outside the gate until a neighbor walked in with his dog. He came forward this evening and identified her. Miss Warner knew that you had moved out of the apartment, but not that Miss Faulkner had moved in. She claims she only wanted to make him good and sick—the courts will decide whether they believe her."

I nodded. "Thanks for telling me."

"And by the way, she was also responsible for the break-in on Miss Arp's boat. As you suspected, she was worried about your figuring things out and came looking for any evidence that you might have collected. Unfortunately, your little neighbor was in the wrong place at the wrong time."

He shifted from one foot to the other. "Well. I'll let you and your friends get back to celebrating." He disappeared into the crowd.

"He's cute," Connie said, staring right at me. "I like the chin."

"He's a cop." I shrugged, sure the blush gave me away.

I leaned against the window, looking around the bar at my friends and all the other characters—the leftover hippies, the parrotheads, the folks sick of forcing their square peg selves into round holes. People who didn't quite fit in with the rest of the world had somehow blended into a wonderful, colorful family in Key West. I hoped to fit in too, because I was neither the Hayley Mills "girl next door" that my mother dreamed of, nor the hard-driven career woman that my father envisioned. But I had the strong feeling I would find a life I loved here.

"If you guys don't have any plans, I'd like to make Thanksgiving dinner for you. I know Miss Gloria would love to host a party," I told Eric and Connie. "I called my folks earlier—both sets—and told them not to expect me."

"Count us in," Connie said.

My cell phone rang—a blocked number. I answered, struggling to recognize the voice over the din in the Parrot. It was Detective Bransford—or Nate, as he insisted I call him.

"I know this is sort of a coals to Newcastle situation, but I was wondering if I might take you to dinner. Sometime. Anytime. You could name the place. I'd offer to cook, but I don't. Cook, that is."

"Make him wait," Eric whispered.

"I'll have to check my calendar," I said primly. Oh heck, wasn't I finished trying to act like I was someone other than me? I broke into a major grin. "Scratch that. I'd be delighted."

Hayley Snow's Leaning Tower of Eggplant

2 medium eggplants, sliced lengthwise
2 large tomatoes, sliced (Don't bother with this dish if they aren't in season.)
1 ball fresh mozzarella, sliced
Vinaigrette (see note)
Greens, washed and torn, and arugula for the top

Slice the eggplant and salt it, leaving it to rest for 20–30 minutes.

Once the liquid beads on the salted slices, wash and dry them; then dip them in beaten egg, followed by flour, and fry in hot peanut oil. (Keep fried eggplant in a warm toaster oven while you continue frying.)

When your eggplant slices are nicely browned and still warm, layer them alternately with fresh mozzarella slices (fresh is crucial—the rubbery white stuff won't do) and the garden tomatoes on a bed of greens. Sprinkle shredded arugula over the top and drizzle with vinaigrette. Serve while the eggplant is warm.

Note: For vinaigrette, whisk 1 tsp good quality mustard with 1 tsp sugar and 1–2 tsp water and whisk until smooth. Whisk in a half cup good quality olive oil until oil mixture is emulsified. Add balsamic vinegar to taste (usually 1/4 to 1/3 cup) along with salt and pepper, and whisk again.

Molasses Sugar Cookies

3/4 cup butter
1 cup sugar
1/4 cup molasses
1 egg
2 tsp baking soda
2 cups flour
1/2 tsp ground cloves
1/2 tsp ground ginger
1 tsp cinnamon
1/2 tsp salt

Sugar for rolling

Melt butter over low heat. Cool, add sugar, molasses, and egg. Beat well. Sift together flour, soda, cloves, ginger, cinnamon, and salt, add to first mixture. Mix well and chill. Form the dough into 1-inch balls and roll them in sugar. Place on a greased cookie sheet 2 inches apart and bake at 375 for 8–10 minutes. Cool on a wire rack.

Alvina's Crumb Cake

2 cups granulated sugar
1/2 lb (2 sticks) butter, softened
4 cups flour
1 tsp cinnamon, optional
4 tsp baking powder
3 beaten eggs
Milk

Rub or pulse the sugar, butter, and flour together like pie crust. Reserve one cup pea-sized crumbs for topping and add 1 tsp cinnamon, if desired. Set that aside.

To the same bowl with the remaining mixture, add 4 tsp (heaping) baking powder and 3 beaten eggs. Stir.

Mix in milk slowly until the dough runs off the spoon.

Pour into 3 buttered layer cake pans and sprinkle crumbs over top. Bake in a hot oven (around 425) about 20 minutes, or until a toothpick stuck in the middle comes out dry.

This is also delicious with a handful of fresh blueberries folded in before baking.

Note from the author: This recipe was passed down from my grandmother to my father. It was pretty much the only thing he cooked. We have not been able to identify Alvina.

Read on for a sneak peek at the next

Key West Food Critic mystery.

Coming in September 2012 from Obsidian

My new boss, Wally, slid his glasses down his nose and squinted over the top of the black frames. "Don't even think about coming back with a piece telling us offal is the next big foodie trend," he said. "I don't care what's in style in New York and LA. We eat grouper and key lime pie in Key West, not entrails." He leaned back in his weathered wicker chair, fronds of faux tropical foliage tickling his hair. "Clear?"

"Aye, aye, Captain." I snapped my heels together and saluted, though it wasn't easy to be serious with a man wearing a yellow silk shirt dotted with palm trees. Our company uniform. Which made my complexion look a little sallow, but I would have worn the houseplant and the straw lampshade that matched the other furniture were those required for the job.

Right before Thanksgiving, I was astonished and grateful to be hired as the food critic for *Key Zest*, the new Key West style magazine. They sure hadn't planned on shelling out big bucks so I could attend the "Key West Loves

Literature" seminar barely two months later. But after I explained how most of the top food writers and food critics in the country would be there and we'd look like foodie fools if we missed it, Wally finally caved. With the caveat that I keep up my schedule of local restaurant reviews and write a couple of snappy, stylish feature articles about the seminar as well.

At the time, that had all sounded doable. But right now, I had big-time jitters about meeting my writing idols and trying to sound smart. And I wished that my Christmas present brainstorm for my mother had been something other than tuition to this seminar. She was completely thrilled to be visiting here from New Jersey, and who wouldn't feel good about making her mother happy? But for my first major (and paid!) journalistic assignment, having my mom tethered to my side felt a little like looking through the oven door at a falling soufflé.

A block down from the white stucco San Carlos Institute building with its fancy Spanish railings, the usual suspects geared up for a night of Duval Street decadence. A gaggle of college students in flip-flops and shorts taunted one another in front of the adjoining empty storefront, looking as though they'd started drinking well before happy hour. Two fried-to-a-crisp couples giggled at the gross quotations featuring personal body parts on the T-shirts in the shop on the other side of the storefront. And the homeless man with his poorly tuned guitar and singing pit bull draped in Mardi Gras beads had set up on a blue blanket on his regular corner, ready to serenade the passersby. A handwritten sign explained that tourists could have their pictures taken with the dog—for five bucks.

Everything was for sale in Key West—for the right price.

I trudged the last hundred feet to the Institute, one half of me thrilled and the other half terrified. Three white arches funneled a bejeweled crowd buzzing with excitement into an enormous anteroom tiled in dizzying black and white. At the entrance to the auditorium, I flashed my press ID badge to a seminar volunteer and hurried down the right aisle to grab two seats as close to the stage as I could manage. Sinking into an upholstered seat, I studied the stage, draped in red velvet like a faded drag queen at the Aqua Nightclub. I would have killed to be up there, one of the foodie experts expounding on the latest trends and how to write about them. But right now I felt more like I belonged on that ratty street corner blanket with the howling dog.

I flipped through the program and found the write-up about the keynote speaker, Jonah Barrows. Could he possibly look as good in person as he had in the *New York Times* style magazine photo shoot last fall? For a guy who'd survived a stint as a food critic for the snooty *Guide Bouchée* and then moved on to take first Los Angeles and then New York City by storm—a tsunami of foodie controversy—he looked thin, young, and unscathed. On the printed page, anyway.

I waved my mother down the aisle to the spot beside me. She slid into her seat and reached over to pinch closed the V-neckline of my white shirt, and then smooth the drape of the pink polka-dotted sweater I'd layered over it. Her gaze slid down my khaki stretch pants to the Libby Edelman jeweled sandals she had presented as a thank-you gift for the weekend.

"Aren't they pretty?" she asked, and then tried to tuck some curls behind my ear.

I grinned and shook my head. She was always dressed for success—in this case in a brown suede jacket and narrow tweed trousers, with her own auburn curls gathered into a gold barrette—and ever hopeful that I'd pick up her sense of style in more than the kitchen. She whipped out a camera from her handbag and snapped three blinding photos in succession.

She was about to tap another patron's shoulder to ask that she take a picture of the two of us when the heavy-set director of the seminar bustled onto the stage and threw his arms open.

"I'm Dustin Fredericks! Welcome to the greatest literary house party of the year!"

The crowd roared with enthusiasm, including a loud and embarrassing "Hip-hip-hooray!" from my mother. Once the noise died down, Dustin went on to thank the program committee, the volunteers, and the many others who'd worked so hard on organizing the conference.

"The mayor regrets she can't be here tonight to award the seminar the honorary five-parrot seal of approval." More polite clapping. And then he began to read a lengthy proclamation from the honorary mayor of Key West, Mayor Gonzo Mays, chock-full of *whereas*es and *here-to-fore*s.

"Is he ever going to introduce Jonah?" asked the lady in front of us whose silver pompadour partly obscured my view of the podium. "I'm absolutely starving. We should have eaten before we came."

"It'll be worth the wait," said her companion. "When you're trying to impress four hundred foodies and food writers, you can't serve anything that isn't fabulous." She kissed the tips of her fingers and blew that imaginary kiss toward the stage. "I just know they'll have shrimp, piles and piles of Key West pinks. . . ."

My mother leaned forward, one hand on the velvet seat back in front of her, the other gently gripping the first woman's shoulder. "Shhhhh," she said.

I sank lower into my upholstered seat. But it wasn't just those ladies rustling and whispering—the audience was whirring with anticipation, as if they couldn't wait for the real show to start; as if they expected pyrotechnics and hoped to blow past Dustin's preliminaries to get there. Would Mom try to shush them all?

"I know you didn't come here to listen to me," Dustin was saying from the stage. "So I am thrilled to introduce our keynote speaker, a man who truly needs no introduction."

"But you'll give one anyway," I muttered.

My mother took my hand and pulled it onto her lap. "Oh, sweetie. Let him have his moment."

I rolled my eyes and squeezed her fingers back a little harder than I meant to.

"Jonah Barrows has had four major culinary careers in the time most of us have only managed one. His mother once reported that he had a highly sensitive palate right out of the womb—he would only suckle organic goat's milk."

The audience tittered. How completely embarrassing, the kind of thing a mother might say. Mine, in fact, was chuckling loudly. "Remember when you'd only eat strained carrots and your skin turned yellow from too much carotene?"

"Mom, stop," I hissed.

"Mr. Barrows was a restaurant critic for the highly esteemed *Guide Bouchée* for his first four years out of Columbia. No one—I repeat, no one—lands that job as a twenty-two-year-old. At twenty-six, he co-owned and managed the three-star restaurant *Ménager Bien* in Los Angeles before he was lured to the *New York Times* to write their food column for the young at heart, 'See and Be Scene.' And his memoir *You Must Try the Skate . . . and Other Utterly Foolish Things Foodies Say* has gone to its third printing, even though it went on sale only today! *People* named him a national culinary treasure, a wunderkind who will shape the way Americans eat for decades. The *Washington Post* called him the most frightening man to scorch the food scene since Michael Pollen. Without further ado, I ask you to welcome Jonah Barrows."

Then the stage curtains swept open, revealing a facsimile of an old diner—cracked red-and-black leather booths, Formica tabletops balanced on steel posts, fake carnations drooping from cheap cut-glass vases. All we needed was big floppy menus stained with tomato sauce and a worn-faced waitress asking, "What'll it be, hon?"

Jonah strode across the stage, waving a graceful hand at the crowd, grinning broadly, clad in tight black trousers, cowboy boots, and a gorgeous orange linen shirt. The other panelists for the weekend trickled along in his wake, taking seats at the booths and tables of the faux diner. When they were settled, Jonah clasped the director in a bear hug, and maneuvered him toward the wings in a fluid two-step. Then he blew a kiss to the audience, who clapped vigorously, finally working itself into a standing ovation.

Jonah waved us down. "I am honored to kick off this weekend. It's hard to know where to begin—it's customary, I believe, to be positive in a speech like this." He flashed a lopsided, regretful grin, teeth eggshell white against his tan. Then he turned to face the food writers seated behind him.

"But I have decided instead to opt for honesty. We have traveled so far from the basics of food and food writing where I feel we belong. We have competitive cooking shows featuring chefs oozing testosterone. We have food critics getting outed by disgruntled restaurateurs using a rush of Twitter posts and Facebook photos." He bounced across the stage to clasp the shoulder of an impish man and ruffle his dark hair.

"That's the food critic Frank Bruni," my mother said under her breath.

Jonah moved on to kiss the cheek of a heavyset woman in a flowered silk dress squeezed into the booth beside Bruni. Mom paged through the headshots in her program. "That has to be the novelist Sigrid Gustafson," Mom whispered, tapping the page. "She must have used an early photo. LOL."

"Mom, behave!" I whispered back.

Jonah continued to wind through the seated panelists, shaking hands with a petite Asian woman, massaging the shoulders of an elegant woman in black with a grand sweep of white-gold hair. Finally he returned to the lectern.

"We have message boards brimming with blustering

amateurs and unsuspecting diners following them like rats after Pied Pipers into the bowels of dreadful eateries. We have ridiculous modernism overtaking plain good food. Let's face facts." He pounded on the podium, his voice rising several decibels with each word. "This is one hell of a challenging time to write about food—or even to choose a restaurant meal! We can't afford a fluffy weekend seminar focused on extolling recipes and patting the backs of our illustrious guest writers. They must be held accountable for every word they write."

The audience lurched into a second ragged standing ovation. Dustin hovered in the wings, just off stage left, looking as though he might explode into the spotlight and drag Jonah off.

"Please sit," Jonah begged us. He strode to the center of the stage, his own golden hair glinting in the stage lights. Too perfect to be natural, I thought. "I promise, you'll be exhausted by the end of the night. And you must save some energy for the awesome opening party. And there's so much more coming this weekend."

As we took our seats again, he headed back to the podium and adjusted his notes.

"In my opinion, today's food writers are listing toward endorsing the esoteric and precious and superexpensive. Of course, if we wait long enough, the trends will circle back around. We'll be reading about mountains of creamy mashed potatoes and pot roast that melts into its gravy instead of musk ox sprinkled with elderberries and served on twigs. But while we wait, isn't it our job to call the emperor on his nakedness? Must we endure, or even encourage, the bizarre and the inedible?" He pivoted to the panelists behind him and opened his arms. The food writers rustled, their smiles frozen.

"He's absolutely right," said the woman in front of us.

Jonah clicked one leather-clad heel against the other and spun back to the audience. "I say no. Which is why I feel I must address the 'best of' restaurant lists. My God, what does it mean when a meal in the number one restaurant in the world costs in the neighborhood of six hundred dollars and is gathered from the woods nearby? *The woods*, people. And can someone spare us from Twitter-driven hyperbole in restaurants' popularity? Since when do untrained palates get to tell us what's good?"

He paused for what seemed like minutes, the auditorium deathly silent. He was asking for trouble—the hoi polloi loved to wax on about what they ate. And many of them were warming the seats of this auditorium. And the critics who wrote the reviews he was criticizing sat right on the stage with him.

"Here's what I think. Critics must push forward to take their territory back from the amateurs. We professionals cannot abandon this job to the Chowhounds and Yelp boarders. A, many of these people have no training. And B, they have all kinds of agendas aside from criticizing food. And we must be excruciatingly honest. If we shy away from criticizing bad or ridiculous food, if we only publish positive reviews, do our words not become worthless?"

"What the heck's a Yelp boarder?" asked the lady in front of us.

"It's a food Web site," Mom said. "Shhhh." The lady turned around and looked daggers at us as Jonah continued.

"From the restaurant perspective—and as Dustin mentioned, I've walked a mile in those moccasins, too—when an establishment chooses to open, they must take the chance of negative publicity. It's like publishing a book: Reviews ensue. When a meal leaves the kitchen, the chef leaves himself open for criticism.

"I can sum up the problem quickly: Honesty is lacking from public figures. I can't fix national politics." He clapped his hand to his heart and heaved a sigh.

"You can say that again," said the woman in front of Mom.

"But we can start right here in the food world. I've learned this as I've prepared to tour the country with my new book: Telling the truth and encouraging my colleagues to do the same has freed me up in ways I never imagined."

He ran a hand over his chin, the blond stubble of a new beard glinting in the spotlight. "You people—our public—deserve having the curtains pulled back, not only on the food you eat and the professionals who prepare it, but also on the people who criticize and write about it." He wheeled around again to face the faux diner. "Writers and critics—and you know who you are—you must step up to a higher standard. Food is not just about eating. Food is the very soul of our country."

His voice grew softer. "I am *so* looking forward to the panel discussions and to all my conversations over this fabulous weekend. Caveat emptor: My policy of utter transparency will be in full effect."

I finally took a breath.

Like all of the other four hundred plus attendees at the opening, I was dying for a drink by the time Jonah Barrows finished his lecture. I suspected some of them were thirsty for blood as well, and I hated to miss one second of the fireworks. But Mom had other ideas: a leisurely stroll down the busiest blocks of Duval Street with her camera in action on the way over to the reception at the Audubon House. She chattered nonstop the whole way.

Had I seen the woman with the mop of curly hair in the back row of the diner? That had to be Ruth Reichl. And the small adorable man with dimples and dark hair? Definitely Frank Bruni, another former restaurant critic for the *New York Times*. She'd recognize him anywhere—except he was smaller than she'd imagined for a man with such a grand writing voice. She loved him sight unseen for the way he loved his mother. And Billy Collins, former poet laureate—he looked, well, just like a real person. She could not wait to get books signed by each of them. And she could not wait to see how Jonah Barrows challenged each of those writers. From the grimacing and rustling on the stage behind him, it sure looked like it was going to be a lively weekend.

And she was thrilled with the weather—maybe seventy degrees with a breeze just strong enough to rattle the palms overhead.

"Did I tell you we're expecting our first snow in New Jersey this weekend?" she asked. "Not just a dusting either."

"You did, Mom," I said.

I listened to her with one ear while trying to formulate a pithy summary of Jonah Barrows's remarks and then a worthy journalistic response. Wally would expect something, if not tonight, certainly by tomorrow morning. Jonah had sacrificed a lot of sacred cows: amateurs on food boards and their Twitter-driven hysteria, endorsements of precious foodie trends, lack of transparency and fortitude from chefs and the writers following them. In forty-five minutes, he'd managed to spurn every cutting-edge trend in the food world. And some of them well deserved it. What could I possibly add to his brilliant dissection? And would I have a strong enough stomach to do so, anyway? And whom exactly did he plan to wrestle to the mud over the next two days?

"Hayley, wait! Isn't this the bar Hemingway used to drink in after he finished writing for the day?"

My mom stopped in front of Sloppy Joe's, where the noise roared out onto the street. Sunburned customers clustered around the tables covered with plastic tankards of beer and baskets of French fries and burgers. More people spilled out onto the sidewalk to smoke and drink beer. A trio of ponytailed men in tropical shirts played aggressive, pulse-pounding rock music on electric guitars at the far end of the bar. I'd never set foot in this place and I doubted that Hemingway would have enjoyed it, either.

"Let me get your picture here," Mom said, pushing me toward the painted sign that read ESTABLISHED IN 1933 and sighting through her viewfinder. "Now, smile!" She snapped four photos in succession.

"Hey, what's that?" She pointed to a camera fastened to the underside of the roof overhanging the sidewalk.

"It's the Duval Street webcam, Mom," I said. "They have it mounted on their Web site so people who aren't in town can see what they're missing. Remember when I first moved here last fall, I tried to get you to watch it and you couldn't get it to load on your computer? Let's get going. I have a lot people I'd like to meet. And wouldn't it be awful if they ran out of wine?"

"Or food," said my mother, tucking her camera into her handbag and trotting ahead of me up the street.

By the time we reached the Audubon House, a long line of hungry people snaked out of the gated white picket fence onto the Whitehead Street sidewalk. The ladies Mom had chastised in the auditorium—twice—were just ahead of us.

"What is this a line for anyway?" asked the woman with the helmet of silver hair.

"The bar," answered the other. "You would think they could plan better. This is not relaxing."

A waiter in a white shirt passed by with a platter of shrimp toast and I managed to snag two pieces just before the plate was snatched clean by the unhappy woman in front of us. Mom nibbled at hers and pronounced it delicious.

"I think they used fresh tarragon. And the mayo is definitely homemade. Oh, Hayley"—she learned over to kiss my cheek, her hazel eyes bright with sudden tears—"I'm having so much fun already."

I looked up from the notes on my smart phone and smiled. "I'm glad." I felt a needle of regret that I wasn't enjoying having her as much as she was enjoying being here. I swore to myself that I'd try harder not to allow my nerves or my reactions to her well-intentioned motherly ministrations ruin the visit. As we inched forward toward the bar, the pressure on my bladder grew intense.

"Mom," I said. "I'm going to run to the ladies' room. Will you hold my stuff?"

I handed her the canvas bag containing my phone, notebook, wallet, program, and the copy of Jonah's book I'd brought in case I ran into him, and dashed down a long brick walkway, passing groups of people chatting at tall cocktail tables with plates of nibbles and glasses of wine. Twenty yards to the right, one serving station was dishing up tiny lamb chops. The smell of roasted meat and garlic called to me like metal filings to magnet but I decided it would be rude not to wait for my mother. At the next station, more waiters were setting up coffee, tea, and enormous trays of chocolate-covered strawberries. Those I could not resist. I veered over and popped one into my mouth, savoring the bright burst of berry coated in a crisp shell of dark chocolate with the smallest hint of orange—no resemblance to the greasy, grainy, overly sweet chocolate I'd had from wedding fountains. I'd pick up one for Mom on the way back.

At the far corner of the property, at the end of another long brick walkway, I located the restrooms in a small white clapboard building shaded by dense green foliage—palms, ferns, and bougainvillea vines covered in hot pink blossoms. As a woman climbed the steps ahead of me, I recognized the white-blond hair and slim, black-draped figure of Olivia Nethercut, one of my food-writing heroines. Jonah was spectacular and controversial and brilliant, but I could picture myself having a career like Olivia's—food critic, philanthropist, and cookbook writer. My psychologist friend, Eric, had told me more than once that people who wrote down their goals achieved them more often than those who didn't. So on page one of my notebook, I'd dashed off a list for this weekend. Number one: an exclusive interview with Olivia.

"Ms. Nethercut," I said, panting a little as I caught up with her. "I'm Hayley Snow and I just wanted to say how thrilled we are to have you in town. Speaking at the conference."

She nodded blankly. My face flushed, suddenly realizing that accosting her in the ladies' room would probably be considered a journalistic faux pas. On the other hand, it was way too late to pretend I hadn't seen her. I started to hold my hand out, then realized my fingers were covered with melted brown goo.

I began to stammer like a waitress with her first table. "Isn't it a gorgeous night? They're so lucky that squall blew by to the south. I don't think they had any rain plan at all."

She ducked into a stall and I took the one next to her.

"I loved your book *A Marrow Escape*," I chattered. "And I sent a check off to your foundation at Christmas." So what if it was ten bucks? That was all I could swing working only part-time at my friend Connie's cleaning service before starting at *Key Zest*.

"Thanks," she said in a muffled voice. "You're very kind."

Feeling disappointed and slightly brushed off—she hadn't shown one smidgen of curiosity about who I was or what my connection might be to the seminar—I told myself that once we came out and were busy with the less personal task of hand-washing, I'd announce my credentials and request an interview. But by the time I'd exited the stall, she was gone.

I stumbled back down the stairs, mentally pinching myself for acting like a groupie instead of the professional critic and writer I was supposed to be. Though I *was* a foodie groupie, like my mother before me. What was wrong with that?

Maybe I'd annoyed her with my gushing. Maybe I'd broken some unwritten rule of courtesy by even speaking to her, even if it was to admire her cutting-edge criticism, gorgeous writing, and generosity. Maybe I'd crave the same kind of distance from scruffy fans in the unlikely event I ever got famous. In that case, why the heck attend a food-writing conference?

I wandered off to collect myself on one of the black metal benches by the reflecting pool in the corner of the property before rejoining the party. Lush staghorn ferns and mother-in-law tongues shielded the seating area from the restrooms. Two large metal birds—more egret in shape than flamingo—were posed gracefully in the water, and clusters of water lilies floated over most of the surface. I took a seat and tried to slow my whirling thoughts: This weekend could be fun if I would only relax.

A trickle of water burbled out from a pipe in the pool's wall, and I noticed that something was pushing the lily pads up, something surfacing from the dark recesses of the water. The wind gusted, causing the palm fronds overhead to clack like castanets and bringing a whiff of roasted meat that now smelled more rancid than enticing.

I edged a step closer, my heart ratcheting up to uneven thumps like a KitchenAid mixer loaded with dough. A third bird statue appeared to have been broken off at the shins and was lying on the bricks next to the pool, the sharp metal beak pointing to a sodden mass of—something.